The World Is a
Narrow Bridge

BLOOMSBURY PUBLISHING
Bloomsbury Publishing Inc.
1385 Broadway, New York, NY 10018, USA

BLOOMSBURY, BLOOMSBURY PUBLISHING, and the Diana logo are
trademarks of Bloomsbury Publishing Plc

First published in the United States, 2018

ISBN: HB: 978-1-63557-141-7; eBook: 978-1-63557-142-4

LIBRARY OF CONGRESS CATALOGING-IN-PUBLICATION DATA

Names: Thier, Aaron, author.
Title: The world is a narrow bridge / Aaron Thier.
Description: New York: Bloomsbury USA, 2018.
Identifiers: LCCN 2017036872 | ISBN 9781635571417 (hardcover) |
ISBN 9781635571424 (ebook)
Classification: LCC PS3620.H54 W67 2018 | DDC 813/.6—dc23
LC record available at https://lccn.loc.gov/2017036872

2 4 6 8 10 9 7 5 3 1

Typeset by Westchester Publishing Services
Printed and bound in the U.S.A. by Berryville Graphics Inc., Berryville, Virginia

To find out more about our authors and books visit www.bloomsbury.com and
sign up for our newsletters.

Bloomsbury books may be purchased for business or promotional use. For
information on bulk purchases please contact Macmillan Corporate and Premium
Sales Department at specialmarkets@macmillan.com.

For Sarah and Sid

Part I

ON THIS QUIET tropical night, while Murphy drools at her side like a man beaten unconscious, Eva lies awake reviewing the small traumas and embarrassments of the day. It's a routine moment of contemplation in the instant before sleep. She curses herself for buying the French vanilla yogurt instead of plain. She wishes she hadn't said that thing to that person. She wonders if the pain in her ear is the first symptom of a devastating illness that will culminate in her death. She is certainly not thinking about the Judeo-Christian god, nor of any other god, because she is a secular humanist who believes in goodness for its own sake, and in reason, and in fermented foods and renewable energy and a single-payer health care system. So imagine her surprise when she sighs and adjusts her pillow and there at the foot of the bed is Yahweh, god of the Israelites and troubled protagonist of the Hebrew Bible.

. . .

For context, if you're a lover of context, it's eleven o'clock on a late-April night in Miami. Nighttime lows have risen into the seventies, the convective outlook is general, and the black vultures have gone north for the summer. Gunfire can be heard, but only faintly. A reality-television personality has just been elevated to the presidency. Murphy and Eva are living in a temporary furnished apartment, just the latest in a sequence of temporary furnished apartments, and there is no prospect of a permanent residence, nor any prospect of real jobs beyond the freelance adjunct part-time work they've been doing for years. Eva is a poet, but she also teaches ESL classes. Murphy writes occasional restaurant and movie reviews for the local free paper, but he has yet to conceive of a more meaningful professional ambition. Those are the facts.

How does she know it's Yahweh? If this is a dream and not an authentic encounter with the divine, and it's reasonable to assume that it's a dream, then it's one of those dream moments when you're talking to a stranger but you also know that the stranger is your aunt Patricia. Yahweh is wearing sunglasses and an elegant linen shirt and he's attended by a deputy angel of some kind. The deputy looks more or less like Yahweh himself, minus the sunglasses. Both have a Levantine cast of feature. In fact they resemble Murphy, whose mother is a Lebanese Jew.

"This is her?" Yahweh asks.

"That's what I was told."

He gazes searchingly at Eva and scratches his chin. Eva is not afraid. She knows that gods enjoy doing depraved things to human women, but it looks as if these two are here on business.

"Can she talk?" says Yahweh.

"She's said to have an attractive throaty voice."

"Ask her to say something."

The angel nods. "You," he says. "Can you speak?"

Eva finds that she cannot.

"She can't speak," says the angel.

"She can speak. She's malingering. They always do."

"You," says the angel. "Repeat after me. 'From the sole of the foot even unto the head there is no soundness in it; but wounds, and bruises, and putrefying sores.'"

Eva says, "From a soul and a foot and even into the head, there are no sounds in it, but . . ."

"She does have a nice voice," says Yahweh.

"You," says the angel. "You will go where you're told to go, and speak as you're told to speak. You will ask the people you meet, 'Have you heard the name of the Lord, which is Yahweh?' And then they'll know that he is the Lord. Do you agree?"

"No."

Yahweh crosses his arms. The angel leans forward and glares at her.

"Do you agree?"

Eva says, "I'm innocent! You've got the wrong woman!"

"This is how she behaves in the presence of the Lord," says Yahweh. "The Lord of Hosts! Slow to anger and always merciful. It never fails to amaze me."

But it's a dream, it's just a dream, it must be a dream, because that's all there is. Next thing she knows, it's morning and the dust is dancing in a thick bar of sunlight.

As THE POET James Schuyler writes: "Now it's tomorrow, as usual." The sun rises, a bird begins to scream in the yard, and it's time once again to undertake the complex business of daily life. Murphy and Eva assess the day's likely meteorological scenarios and select clothing on that basis. They each prepare a breakfast that satisfies their unique dietary preferences without transgressing the rigid boundaries of nutritional requirement. They read the news with terror and incomprehension, like pedestrians witnessing a violent crime.

Today is a day like any other. Eva teaches her classes and doesn't think of Yahweh at all. Murphy reads a novel and takes a long walk. In the evening, when the world heaves a big sigh and the warm air turns to glass, they visit the Whole Foods downtown. It's important to do these things together sometimes—that's the foundation on which a solid relationship is built. But because they go together, they approach their task in an unfocused manner and forget both the plain yogurt and the olive oil. They manage to buy milk, a few passion fruits, bio-degradable trash bags, some toothpaste, and a bar of unscented soap.

Their conversation is less trivial than their errand. They are trying to decide whether to have a baby right away, i.e. as soon as possible, or later, i.e. in a year or two. They have been exploring this question for weeks and they flatter themselves by imagining that they have approached it "rationally," as if that were a virtue and as if the matter of hauling a new soul out of the cosmic ether were susceptible to reason in the first place. Tonight Eva argues that having a child under "these circumstances," by which she probably means America's toxic political situation as well as the temporary nature of their domestic and professional arrangements, is an "insane and hubristic thing to do," but she goes on to say that having a baby is always an insane and hubristic thing to do, since it means introducing an innocent person to the perils and sorrows of the universe, which is all to say, she says, shaking her head, that now is as good a time as any.

Whether they remember the yogurt or not, whether they chart a new course for their lives or not, the trip home should be a quick one. If all goes well, they should be able to get back to their apartment in fifteen minutes. But all does not often go well on the lawless highways of greater Miami. Tonight there's an accident at the very end of I-95, at the spot where you have to descend to US 1. It involves three cars and a tractor-trailer. There are no fatalities, thank heavens, but they're stuck here while the municipal authorities clear a path. At least the waiting isn't as psychologically taxing as it might be. The spectacle of the ruined vehicles fills them both with a sense of life's fragility, and although they use this time to check their iPhones and make tart observations about Miami's lack of public transportation and over-stressed highway system, they also count their blessings. Meanwhile, their Prius shuts off with a sigh.

"I just remembered," says Eva. "I had a dream last night about Yahweh."

"About who?"

"He had an angel with him. Like a bagman."

"Did you remember this because of the car accident?"

"Yes."

Murphy nods sadly. "Because you were thinking about death."

"They asked me to go around saying the Lord's name. I don't think I agreed, but I was having a dream problem where I couldn't really talk. At first I couldn't open my mouth at all."

Murphy is rocking back and forth and tugging at his seat belt. He has expressive hair and staring eyes. He's the kind of person who enters the elevator and rushes to press the door-close button before the doors close. Eva doesn't often press the door-close button, but she has staring eyes too, and her spirit is less placid than her languorous demeanor suggests. The two of them are almost exactly the same height, but because human women tend to be smaller than human men, Eva is considered very tall and Murphy is able to wear a medium right off the rack. This phenomenon is called sexual size dimorphism and it occurs throughout the animal kingdom. Sometimes it runs in the other direction. Ceratioid anglerfish males are tiny. They cling parasitically to the bellies of the much larger females.

Now Murphy is looking out the window at the thick slice of moon in the powdery blue sky. He tends to think of the moon as a cold place, he says, but he knows that's not right. During the day it must be very hot. It's no farther from the sun than the earth is, and there's no atmosphere to protect you.

Eva says, "You could get a moontan."

"Does the moon spin? I can't remember if it spins."

"I remember from somewhere that they did their manned lunar explorations at dawn, because of the sun."

"I guess it's probably like a desert. It's hot in the day and cold at night."

Eva nods. A moment later she says, "They used to think that sleeping outside under the moon would make you insane. But maybe only the full moon."

Murphy opens his window and pokes his head out, trying to see what's happening up ahead and meanwhile exposing his face to the dangerous glare of the rising moon. He's surprised to find that he can see the ocean from here. On this April evening, in the low sunlight, in the steady breeze, the water of the bay is a pale sandy blue, like Cool Mint flavor Listerine Zero Antiseptic Mouthwash. There are a great many islands floating around out there as well. Some of them are man-made. Some are private. Some are still uninhabited and some have been overwhelmed by Australian pine, which is not a pine tree at all but a flowering plant, an angiosperm, called casuarina in the Pacific because of its resemblance to cassowary plumes. We know this because we've just looked it up. It's easy to look things up. That's the world we live in.

Murphy gazes meditatively at the islands, the Australian pines, the Listerine-colored water, the iconic skyline. He counts ten construction cranes downtown—so much enterprise, and all despite the inevitable inundation of this low-lying coastal metropolis. Eva watches a few pelicans fly past with what the poet Elizabeth Bishop once called "humorous elbowings," a phrase she knows without having to look it up, although she could do so very easily, as we've just said.

When Murphy slides back into his seat, Eva says, "That's where we get the word *lunatic*. A lunatic is someone afflicted with moonsanity."

It doesn't spin, to answer Murphy's question. The moon is tidally locked, which means that it presents the same face to the earth at all times. The length of a lunar day is equal to the period of time required to complete its orbit of the earth. "With respect to the stars," this takes 27 Earth days, 7 Earth hours, 43 Earth minutes, and 11.5 Earth seconds, except it actually takes longer, or appears to, God knows why. Its "actual" average orbital period is 29 Earth days, 12 Earth hours, 44 Earth minutes, and 3 Earth seconds. We're just reporting the facts, or the putative facts. It's one thing to know and quite another thing to understand. In any case, lunar dawn is a couple of days long—plenty of time for some manned exploration. And as for the conditions up there: Surface temperatures in the equatorial and midlatitude regions vary from 224 degrees Fahrenheit during the day to about minus 300 degrees at night, although there are permanently shadowed polar craters where temperatures are as low as minus 397 degrees. We might have hoped for a less changeable moon, but no doubt you get the moon you deserve.

Now Eva declares that she's going to eat a passion fruit. Murphy seems distressed by this decision and observes that passion fruits are "so messy," but never mind about Murphy—it's not always possible to indulge him. Eva saws the fruit in half with her house key and eats it with a plastic spoon from the glove box. Meanwhile, she looks out at the tossing heads of the palm trees in the low light. It's a beautiful sight, but she experiences the beauty of this moment as a kind of longing. We might imagine that what she longs for is an alternative present in which she is not marooned on I-95, but that isn't true. In a sense, she longs for the very moment in which she's living, marooned or not. She longs to experience it completely, as she thinks a younger and more innocent Eva would have been able to do. An eighteen-year-old Eva, just escaped from the dank Pennsylvania woods. Then she has a cascade of troubling thoughts—that life is ephemeral, that beauty is ephemeral, that beauty is inseparable from the ephemeralness of life, that beauty *is* the perception of life's ephemeralness—and then she closes her eyes and tries to stop thinking about these things, which are nothing more, after all, than thoughts of death. She tries to savor her passion fruit, which is so delicious that she can barely taste it.

Murphy says, "I read once about somebody who set up a ton of mirrors to focus the moon's light. I want to say it was Galileo. He said he could feel the warmth of the moonlight."

"That's a recipe for a serious moonburn. Moonsanity would be the least of your troubles."

They're stuck here for slightly less than half an hour. It's a long time, but not when you consider the vast labor involved in clearing away the ruined vehicles. Maybe the most remarkable thing is not this magical human ability to move thousands of pounds of metal in short order but our unexamined conviction that the job can and should be accomplished so swiftly. It doesn't matter, because when they do begin to move, it's a short reprieve. Down here on US 1, which is also called the Dixie Highway, commuters from downtown are joining the aggravated motorists from I-95, and now a teenager in a champagne-colored Honda comes roaring down the ramp, darts in and out of traffic for a luminous high-spirited moment, and slams into a lavender Chevy Blazer. This causes a sequence of other traffic incidents and soon every lane is blocked and they're trapped once again, and trapped at the very worst point, where there's no place to exit.

. . .

This time there is to be no discussion of the moon, nor any wistful reflection on the impermanence of an individual life on this blue sun-dazzled pebble of a world. They have seen the accident, they know that it's the result of carelessness or drunkenness or texting-while-driving, and both of them are angry and frustrated. Murphy exits the vehicle immediately. Eva shuts the car off but stays where she is. It is no longer possible for her to apprehend the beauty of the light in the palm trees, or else, if beauty is nothing more than an aspect of sub-jective experience, and what reason does she have for thinking it's not, then beauty itself fades from the palm trees. They are no more than two miles from home.

Now Murphy is the one thinking about death. Even the sunniest of people must think about death now and then, and no one could justly accuse Murphy of being a sunny person. He squints and frowns into the breeze. All he knows for certain is that he and everyone he loves will die. The only way to avoid witnessing the deaths of his loved ones is to die a tragic and premature death himself, and in that case his loved ones will have to witness it. What kind of demented and malevolent deity would make such a world?

Eva watches him stamping back and forth on the median. She sees him stoop to pick some Surinam cherries, which he eats with every appearance of relish, morbid reflections notwithstanding. Above the incessant honking and the rush of the wind, she can hear the sounds of lawn care. In Florida, there is never a moment when you can't hear the sounds of lawn care. The aerial fig roots have to be cut before they reach the ground. Coconuts have to be removed and carted away so they don't fall and cause property damage or personal injury. The grass needs mowing even in the dry season because people like to water their lawns. Leaf blowers run all the time. Miami is the only major city in the contiguous United States with a tropical monsoon climate (Köppen climate classification *Am*), and the struggle to subdue wild nature is never-ending. Native flora encroaches upon the man-maintained tropical lawnscape; exotic plants escape from the lawnscape and invade untended spaces. Eva wonders why it's necessary to subdue nature in the first place. Whence the convention of the green lawn? Is it because the United States derives many of its preoccupations from Mother England, and England is a country of lawns? Or is it that we instinctively prefer a savanna-like environment similar to the one in which our species was born?

Two screaming parakeets flap by above Murphy's head, and he turns to shout at them as they go. Then he, too, thinks of his younger self—that morose little boy, so oppressed by the suffocating snows and obscene purple darkness of the northern winter—and wonders what he'd have thought if he'd known that the cries of parakeets would one day become a routine irritation.

Eva is still sitting in the car. She's looking at a box of latex gloves on the side of the road. It gives her a funny feeling. The integrity of it. The wholeness and singleness. The way that glove protrudes in just that way from the perforated opening. The whole thing seems like one fiber in a vast and inscrutable web of intentionality, and she finds herself thinking: a clue.

Eva, wistful Eva, feels a great weariness. She likes living in Miami, but she knows that Murphy, who has been having a difficult time these last months, will have been thinking of the traffic jam as evidence that nothing functions as well here as it does in his native New England. As if there were no traffic in New England! As if Boston drivers were not savages, with murder in their hearts and flecks of blood on their glasses.

A spray of flowers comes sailing out of the blue sky.

A mynah bird watches her from the guardrail.

Shadows, as Emily Dickinson wrote, hold their breath.

And then, gazing through the windshield at her fellow motorists, who are busy pounding their horns in the maddening and ineffectual manner of city people everywhere, she sees Yahweh again. He's sitting behind the wheel of an orange Lamborghini. He's in the right lane, a few car lengths in front of her, and he doesn't appear to have seen her. His posture is relaxed. Maybe he delights in the spectacle of destruction. And yet Eva knows intuitively, as she'd know in a dream, that he's here for her.

Once again, she is not afraid. Her only thought is to put some distance between herself and that orange car. This is why she decides to flee—for this reason and no other—and yet when she thinks of this evening much later, out there on the great American road, under the pale sky of the high plains or the sugar pines of the Sierra or the mists and fog of the Pacific Northwest, she won't remember the moment of decision or the sounds of lawn care or the light in the palm trees. What she'll remember is the box of latex gloves.

Eva rolls the window down and commands Murphy to return to the car. Then she eases the Prius up onto the median, reaches out to fold the side-view mirror back, and passes with an inch of clearance between two young mahogany trees. Murphy, to his credit, says nothing, and moments later they're back on I-95, northbound this time, the city disappearing behind them, the sun setting like a piece of pink candy over the Everglades.

PIECES OF A travel poem by Weldon Kees tumble through Eva's mind as she drives. *My hair fell out in Santa Barbara. Summer light and dust. And possibly the towns one never sees are best.*

She chooses to say nothing about Yahweh. It's a lot to explain, and it's outrageous, and already she wonders if she imagined it. Instead she says that she's had enough of the traffic and has decided, in a moment of inspiration, that they will take a diverting weekend trip. Why not visit St. Augustine, where Murphy frequently says he wants to go ("We could move there. It's much cheaper."), or Savannah, where Murphy frequently says he wants to go ("We could move there. It's much cheaper."), or even distant Charleston, where Murphy frequently says he wants to go ("I guess we could move there. It must be cheaper.")? Murphy, for his part, has accepted Eva's decision without question and almost without remark, which is remarkable in itself, and he seems amenable to any and all of these destinations. He reads out a few road signs: "Educational Schools/Institutes. Who do you call for your bail bonds?"

There was a landmark, I remember, that was closed. And sometimes, shivering in St. Paul or baking in Atlanta, the sudden sense that you have seen it all before . . .

She slides into the high-occupancy vehicle lane and accelerates to eighty-five miles an hour. She tells herself that it could not have been Yahweh in the orange Lamborghini. Why should an ancient Near Eastern storm god be sitting in traffic on the Dixie Highway in Miami? Why should he require that she, Eva, a secular humanist and poet, function as a prophet of Israel? It's an absurd and laughable conceit, and in short order she has convinced herself, or she believes that she has convinced herself. It could not have been Yahweh. It was only some crass banker or fruit company executive.

"But what'll we do about our library books?" Murphy says.

"We'll return them when we get home."

"But what if we don't return home?"

"Why would you say that? I guess we'd have to pay the replacement fees."

"We don't have our checkbooks or anything."

Eva turns to look at him. He's slumped in the passenger seat. He's all teeth and sinew in the flickering light.

"Why are you worried about your library books?"

"It's a social contract. Everyone has to behave responsibly or the library system doesn't work."

"I guess you can use your banking app to send a check, and you can have them include your library card number on the memo. You could also send cash."

"I don't like to send cash through the mail."

"Have the bank send a check, then."

"I'll send a check."

"Okay?"

He nods. Once again he says, "It's a social contract."

They drive north—the only direction available. They pass out of the tropical monsoon climate zone and into the humid subtropical climate zone (Köppen climate classification *Cfa*). They learn about the existence of an organization called the Robert E. Lee Junior Varsity Cheerleaders. They see billboards declaring that "Christ Is Lord" and other billboards advertising strip clubs and gun clubs and senior living communities. They see one that says "Mermaids . . . Wow!" The coconut palms and sea grape give way to palmetto and longleaf pine, and the live oaks get bigger. They decline to purchase ceremonial fireworks ("mortars, rockets, and mega-boomers"), but they do stop at a Walmart, hated place, where low prices come at such a high moral cost. Here they each buy a package of underwear and a toothbrush. They already have soap and some purportedly "natural" toothpaste from the trip to Whole Foods. They buy a cooler to keep the milk cold.

"And another thing," Murphy says. "I think I left my computer on."

"It's fine sleeping like that for a few days."

"But if it's on, can hackers infiltrate it?"

"Maybe. Did you read that thing about how they track UPS drivers?"

"I didn't read it," he says with apprehension. "I was *afraid* to read it."

"They know how long it takes them to deliver each package, and how fast they drive, and whether they're wearing their seat belts. The seat belts slow them down and they get penalized, but if they don't wear their seat belts, they get penalized for that too. There's no way for them not to get penalized."

"Who tracks them? The NSA? The Russians?"

"UPS tracks them. That's what I'm saying. It's all to maximize shareholder value."

Murphy considers this. "So of course someone can hack my computer while it's asleep."

"Luckily you haven't got anything anyone would want."

He nods. "Just drafts of restaurant reviews. 'The server put his whole thumb in my goulash.'"

They stop for the night at a Super 8 in Lantana Shores, Florida. They pay cash for the room and then Murphy tries to give the clerk a credit card for incidentals, but the man won't take it.

"You need it on file," Murphy says. "Don't you?"

"It's not necessary."

Is it madness to insist? The clerk sits under a pair of long fluorescent bulbs. He's like a person in a tanning bed, or a mirrored enclosure designed to focus the moon's ethereal glow. He's looking at Facebook on his phone. Eva, likewise, is sending someone a message. Murphy stands on the green carpet with his hands at his sides and it's as if he's all alone. He wants to check his own phone, but then UPS will know where he is.

They've got room 210, which has an excellent view of the parking lot and the highway beyond. It's stuffed with furnishings and devices manufactured all over the world, at who knows whose instructions. There's a king-size bed, a big Sharp Aquos TV, plastic cups in individual wrappers, an ecru ice bucket, and sturdy brown motel carpet. The towels are cobweb thin. There's a Magic Chef minifridge and microwave. There's also a tiny Cuisinart coffee maker with a pouch of Guest Choice Café Collection Regular coffee and a 4 Cup Filter Pouch of Select Decaffeinated 100% Arabican [*sic*] coffee (Cuisinart Private Collection). There are packets of NROOM nondairy creamer with red stirring straws. The heavy green curtains have white liners and Murphy has trouble tugging them open. Then he discovers that the window is jammed closed. Then he also discovers that the air conditioner turns on only when he turns on the lights in the bathroom. Eva is still fussing with her phone. Down there in the parking lot, the cars and trucks glow in the harsh white light, and the sound of traffic is like the sound of the ocean, and it's all very beautiful, very beautiful, and very peaceful too.

Now it's time to discuss their itinerary. Murphy is especially interested in St. Augustine, which, he says, is the oldest continuously occupied European city in the continental United States. This is a tantalizing claim, and Eva immediately contests it. She believes that the honor belongs to Santa Fe. They consult the Internet, but they are not able to resolve this question, and neither are we. In any case, they agree to go there, to St. Augustine, and then to Savannah as well. They'd like to go to Charleston if there's time, but Eva reminds him that they'll need to return home on Sunday so that she can teach on Monday morning. Murphy nods and repeats the word *home* in a neutral voice, thinking of their temporary furnished apartment.

Who makes NROOM nondairy creamer, and where, and by what alchemical process? The corporate world is a vast entangled ecosystem. Consider the motel itself. Super 8 is not a thing in its own right, but a subsidiary of Wyndham Worldwide, which also owns

Days Inn, Howard Johnson, Knights Inn, Microtel Inn and Suites, Ramada, Travelodge, and many other brands. The only motels here in Lantana Shores are the Super 8 and the Knights Inn, and they're just two aspects of the same hospitality group. That's how it is with so many things: You try to make a choice, but there's nothing to choose. Wyndham Worldwide has motels and hotels on every continent except Antarctica. They own ten billion dollars in total assets. "The roads end," wrote Weldon Kees, "At motels." But they don't. They end at the New York Stock Exchange.

Murphy says that St. Augustine will be great, but could they not also go anywhere else?

"We're adults. You said so yourself. We could do anything. We could eat candy for breakfast if we wanted."

"But we never would."

From St. Augustine to Anchorage is only eighty hours, which is less than four days if you're really committed, and at that point Fairbanks is just another six and a quarter hours, a brisk morning's drive. Eva wants to know how long it takes to drive from Fairbanks to Patagonia, but they discover that it can't be done. It isn't the canal, like you'd think. It's the Darién Gap, a famously treacherous part of the Panamanian rain forest. There are no roads through the Darién Gap.

"I think the Scots tried to found a colony there," says Murphy, "and everyone died of malaria or something."

There's a plastic sign on the bedside table that reads "This is a non-smoking room. When smoking occurs during your stay a $150 cleaning fee will be billed to your account." But the clerk doesn't have Murphy's credit card on file! Lucky for him, it's unlikely that smoking will occur.

If you think you'd like to become a motelier yourself, you should know right away that there are two basic options. First, you can purchase a franchise. This gives you a recognizable brand name and some financing options for your equipment and furnishings, although it also comes with some obligations, including an annual royalty. Alternatively, you can try to do it on your own, in which case there are plenty of Internet wholesalers from whom to buy supplies. National Hospitality Supply has everything you need. They sell a Trevira Quilted Polyester Bedspread Symphony ("The comfort of a 100% polyester front is joined with the strength of a 50% polyester/50% white cotton backing") for only $45.95 per king-size unit. Keep in mind that you have to buy at least forty-eight bedspreads to get this price. They come four to a carton.

Does the NSA know where Murphy and Eva are? Does UPS? Does Yahweh? Maybe not, that is to say not now, but anyone with access or expertise could locate them in short order. Like all of us, they leave a crackling data trail behind them wherever they go.

While Eva takes a shower, Murphy tries to watch a little basketball. It's the first round of the playoffs. The Eastern Conference game is ending; the Western Conference game is about to begin. An important player tells the courtside reporter, "We've got to stay aggressive." Another tells his teammates to think of every game as a game seven. Next there's a commercial for a small Audi SUV. It's a darker color than the cars the other moms are driving. If you buy it, therefore, what you're saying to the world is that you do things differently. This is followed by a beer commercial, but here the idea is not to do things differently but to do things with your friends. The implication is that if you have friends and you take time to drink beer with them, you might not be haunted later by the fear that you've wasted your life. Then the basketball game returns. The starting lineups are just what you'd expect. Thousands and thousands of fans in matching yellow T-shirts clap and shout. Murphy has tears in his eyes. The traffic sounds like the ocean. The shower sounds like rain. He hasn't been so happy in a long time.

YAHWEH DOESN'T RETURN in the night, nor does any dream of Yahweh, and Eva wakes the next morning to the pristine beauty of a godless world. Naturally her thoughts turn to the baby question, and although Murphy is barely conscious, she delivers a speech on this subject. First she discusses the theme of money, or rather their lack of money. Then she touches on the instability of their domestic situation, the devastations of climate change, and the incompetence and cruelty of the new presidential administration. But then, speaking in a rapid and expansive manner, she moves on to what she calls the "practical reality." She isn't getting any younger, and it's safer for both mother and child if the mother is young. In sum: The future is always uncertain, and it may be more conspicuously uncertain now than ever before, but one cannot argue with Mother Nature. If they have decided to have a baby *at some point*, and they have, then it makes sense to do it now. She doesn't mention her conviction that having a baby is an insane and hubristic thing to do. That concern is irrelevant as long as the decision to have a baby *at some point* has already been made, which it has.

And also, she adds, her voice easy and fluent, her posture casual, also, no big deal, but she doesn't have her birth control pills with her.

They get dressed, they toss their things in the car, and they confront the continental breakfast in the lobby. Breakfast on the road is a challenge for people like Murphy and Eva, whose political and ecological concerns limit their food choices so dramatically. They enjoy some passion fruit and milk from the cooler, and they've allowed themselves some Guest Choice Café Collection coffee, which Eva justifies as a "medical necessity," but they don't want to eat the poisoned fruit or synthetic egg. They pile into the car and drive ten miles up the road, where there's a Saturday market in the parking lot of a strip mall.

And here they are, drinking their coffee and luxuriating in the heavy damp air of the Florida morning, when it occurs to Murphy that they have just decided to have a baby. How could he have missed it? Shouldn't life's big moments ring like the blow of a hammer? He makes a self-conscious attempt to give this moment the gravity he feels it requires. He says to himself, "That was when we decided to have a baby." But it's as if the decision has simply overtaken them, and what he'll remember is this, right now: a quiet parking lot next to a six-lane state road—the moment when he realized that he didn't notice the moment when they decided to have a baby.

Certainly this is an inauspicious place to reflect upon so important a resolution. It's hardly even a place. There's a Jiffy Lube, a McDonald's, and a Laundromat, but it's as if these establishments simply appeared. As if they erupted like mushrooms from the salty soil. In the west, beyond the highway, beyond the unassuming stalk of another Super 8, a forest of slash pine and saw palm stretches away to the melting horizon. In the east, the forest gives way to sandy scrub and then, presumably, to the sea, because the trees in that direction are standing to their ankles in brackish water. An ominous sight.

There are only three vendors here so early in the morning. Two of them are selling jewelry, but the third is a real farmer. He isn't set up and he doesn't look like the kind of person you want to rush, so they wait as patiently as they can. For Murphy, who's had too much coffee and missed his morning run, this means a mobile, bug-eyed panto-mime of patience. Eva lets him be and takes a turn around the parking lot. They've left Lantana Shores behind, but there's some lantana growing here anyway. She admires the geometrical exactitude of its flowers. She breaks a leaf and sniffs it and rubs it on her arms. Murphy often says that lantana is a natural mosquito repellent, and there's no reason to imagine that he's lying outright, although he might be deceiving himself. As she strolls along, she becomes conscious of her gait and recalls a trio of models she saw walking on Miami Beach ear-lier in the week. She tries to imitate their distinctive strut. She takes long, bouncing strides, swings her arms extravagantly, and keeps her head and face absolutely still, chin lifted, eyes closed, lips pressed together in a rictus of neutral sensuality.

Meanwhile, Murphy is entangled in a discussion with a creased and weathered old woman in a blue parka and hospital slippers. She has been sleeping by the Dumpster at the eastern extremity of the park-ing lot, where he's gone to examine the flooded forest.

"It's because the moon is getting closer to the earth," she says, gesturing at the salty water, which has already killed much of the undergrowth.

"The moon again."

"It's pulling the seas close, like a blanket."

He turns to look at Eva, a tiny figure in the distance. She sees him and waves.

The woman says, "But it enables you to envision a real estate opportunity."

Murphy's legs and feet hurt. His heart is racing because of the Guest Choice Café Collection coffee. He wears a look of hunted alarm. He doesn't want to hear about a real estate opportunity.

"Just let me ask you one question," she says. "Just let me ask you this. Do you think the water's just going to *go away* somehow? Every day the moon gets closer. *Every day* it gets closer! Now let me ask you to answer this provocative question. What is the highest point in South Florida?"

"Forty-two feet. Near Jupiter or something."

"Very good!"

He knows the answer because he has spent many hours brooding on the problem of sea level rise. The highest natural point in Miami is only twenty-four feet. It's close to their apartment in Coconut Grove, which sits on a limestone outcropping called the Miami Rock Ridge, but that's an exceptional, almost alpine environment, relatively speaking. The average elevation of the Florida peninsula south of Lake Okeechobee is only six feet, and many areas are much lower. Miami Beach is just a mangrove spit enlarged with fill from the bay.

"Very good," she says again. "But incorrect." Her eyes are sparkling inside her hood. "I'll tell you what it is. It's garbage!" She laughs and tosses a Snickers wrapper on the ground. It blows into the flooded forest. Once more she says, "It's garbage! All the way up the coast!"

It takes Murphy a moment to understand what she means, and then he sighs and says, "The landfills. I never thought of that."

The landfills, yes indeed. The real highest point in South Florida is Mount Trashmore, formerly the Monarch Hill Renewable Energy

Park, formerly the North Broward County Resource Recovery and Central Disposal Sanitary Landfill. Mount Trashmore rises 225 feet above sea level. It towers above the surrounding landscape. Mount Trashmore will be a little island when the rest of South Florida has vanished beneath the waves.

Murphy sees that Eva is now interacting with the ill-tempered farmer, whose produce gleams on a gray folding table next to his truck. Murphy watches her gesture and laugh. A terrible anxiety grips him.

Here is the woman's idea: Acquire all the landfills in the lowland South and build on them. And it's a brilliant idea. Brilliant enough that Murphy is moved to ask her how she "ended up in that parka." She should be running General Electric.

"I'm in the process of repositioning myself for fresh success," she says enigmatically.

In any case, Murphy is welcome to the Mount Trashmore idea. It is an "open-source idea," she explains. Does he know the term? It's a computer term that he might or might not have heard. She is also an expert on computers. Only a fool would ignore them, she says, because it's the computers that are beaming all the instructions to us.

"Practically *all* the instructions come from computers nowadays."

She produces an orange prescription bottle from some recess in her parka. She removes two green tablets and then offers the bottle to Murphy, who politely declines.

"It's five o'clock somewhere," she says, swallowing her drugs. "Sláinte. Prosit. Cheers."

It's five o'clock in Karachi, but in Florida it's too early for revolutionary ideas, and Murphy makes for the car in a state of moral unrest.

Is it very bad to think about profiting from the inundation of an entire American state? Why should it be bad, as long as one does everything one can, in the meantime, to forestall that dreadful outcome? Not that it can be forestalled. He slips into the passenger seat and sits with his arms folded. The sky is chalk white and the heat is starting to hum. What about the guys who shorted the housing market? Are they scavengers or are they just smart people who took advantage of an opportunity? Eva appears a moment later. All she's managed to buy is a bunch of radishes, which neither of them want, but maybe this is for the best. There's a time to feast and a time to fast. Murphy turns the car on, and off they go.

Live oaks, wetlands, inlets, rivers, fast-food franchises, big-box stores, rehab clinics: Life on the American road. The Chitter Chatter Pallet Yard buys and sells pallets. If you pawn and redeem three times at Lending Bear, you become a VIP. The Vapor Station sells "E-Cigs and Juices." Bikers are welcome everywhere. The Huddle Hut has "The Best Food Yet."

An hour and a half later, they're at the famous old fort in St. Augustine, which was occupied at various times by Spain, Great Britain, and the United States, but never by France. They see the ancient graffiti in the guardroom—a drawing of a big ship under sail, writing with heavy serifs. They examine some old-time medical equipment. They learn that Osceola, the great Seminole warrior, was captured under a flag of truce, the white man's favorite deception, and held here for a time before being transferred to Fort Moultrie, in South Carolina, where he died. They stand in the sentry boxes on the limestone walls. The sentry boxes are tiny because people were shorter back then. Murphy looks out at the bay and tries to imagine the treasure fleet going by on its way back to Spain. Eva sees two pigeons fornicating on the roof. It reminds her of arm wrestling. Murphy doesn't notice the pigeons, not even when Eva tries to call his attention to them, and yet later, when he reads the poem she'll write about this moment, he won't be able to distinguish his memories from her inventions and he'll believe that he did see the pigeons after all. He'll decide that the failure of the Murphy-figure to notice them is just a literary contrivance, and he'll even feel a little hurt. He'll ask himself: Why doesn't she think I'd notice something as good as that?

They eat fish tacos for lunch. Nobody wants to live on passion fruit and radishes and milk. Then they walk through the old streets, but the old streets are not crowded medieval alleyways, as they hoped, and it's impossible to imagine what this city was like in the sixteenth century. The sublime essence of the place is imperceptible, or else it fails to accord with their expectations and they persist in believing that it's imperceptible. St. Augustine is a place for tourists. Murphy and Eva, who are tourists, are upset by this and lament that it's not a "real" city. But of course it is, and that's why there's so much pressure to monetize its history.

"I had a dream last night about a turtle that couldn't get comfortable," says Eva. "He was uncomfortable in his shell."

Murphy explains the Mount Trashmore plan in comical terms, perhaps attempting to minimize its beguiling appeal. He represents it as a kind of moonsanity. Then he amuses himself by identifying other kinds of moonsanity. There are people out there, for example, who believe that the moon landings were filmed on a soundstage in Hollywood. He speculates that you can see the junk and tracks up there with a good earth-based telescope, but the afflicted—the lunatics, so to speak—will tell you that the government put that stuff up there to fool us.

"Some people are so smart they can put a guy on the moon," he says, "and other people are so dumb or crazy that they can't be convinced it ever happened, and that's the problem of human society right there."

Eva waits a beat. Murphy frowns.

"We're assuming it did happen," he says anxiously.

"Yeah, we're assuming they didn't put all that stuff up there to fool us."

"Which somebody could easily have done."

But by now it's early afternoon. They've admired a fort; they've looked out over the hot still water toward the sparkling sea; they've dined on fish tacos; they've reflected on the time gone by, the years and centuries; they've discussed the moon; and they've each thought privately about American slavery, as one must when one travels in the old Confederacy. It is no longer the morning, the time of possibility, nor is it the evening, the time of sweet resignation. It is no time at all. It's the time of the shattering sun, and suddenly nothing is interesting any longer. The world seems emptied of possibility. This is a familiar kind of ennui that they call "Afternoon Sickness."

Eva grows morose and returns to her favorite theme. Having a baby, she says, means "forcing someone to do something they might not want to do," by which she means that the baby himself, or herself, is forced by his parents, or her parents, to be a human being and thus to confront the disasters of existence. Strep throat, heartbreak, aggravating holiday parades, standardized tests, embarrassing school presentations and/or performances, middle school dances, adulthood. And that's if she's lucky, or he, because there are any number of problems that can prevent a child from having a normal life in any sense of the term. The disasters of existence are what you experience if you're *fortunate.*

Murphy asks whether this means she has changed her mind.

"That's the cruelest part of this whole setup. I have the feeling that the worst catastrophe is what if I can't get pregnant at all?"

Murphy has been checking his weather app every few minutes. Knowing whether it's going to rain or not is not the same as knowing the future, but it's easy to make that mistake. At two o'clock, the app says that the UV index is "14 out of 12." Sweat is pouring into his new Walmart underwear, but he hasn't realized until now how uncomfortable he is. Why should he have needed to learn this, in essence, from his phone? More generally, what's he missing when he stands there staring at it, deaf and blind to the world? If it didn't exist, he wouldn't have to check it, and if he didn't know that it didn't exist, he wouldn't miss it. It's the phone that creates the need for the phone.

"Remember when you got that stomach infection?" says Eva. "Remember how unhappy you were?"

"I thought it was a dairy allergy."

"It wasn't."

"But the people at the doctor's office were so nice about it. I remember that too."

"You can't count on that. All you can count on is the infection."

This is the traditional siesta hour. It occurs to us that the siesta must be a cultural adaptation to combat Afternoon Sickness, but Murphy and Eva would never take a nap in the middle of the day. They are young vigorous Americans. When they're afflicted with Afternoon

Sickness in Miami, they take long walks, each of them alone, or they exercise. That isn't possible today, so here they are, marooned in time, and if they're not exactly at odds, they feel a kind of mutual exasperation. Eva pulls out her phone and cyberbullies a U.S. senator. Murphy tugs at his shorts and stares into shop windows. Shot glasses, margarita mix, key lime pie on a stick.

And yet now Eva has an insight that will prove important in the days and weeks to come. Although Afternoon Sickness can develop as the organic product of unusual circumstances, the fact that they're on the road means that they can simply drive away from each new set of circumstances. And so they do. They feel better immediately.

In Savannah, an old southern port town, one of the places from which the cotton set sail, they try not to think too obsessively about slavery. Sometimes you have to try to enjoy some pulled pork and cornbread, as they do now, despite the possibility that American barbecue traditions are partly rooted in the experience of slavery. Then they walk around in the last light, groaning and sickened by their meal, and admire the stately homes and the old squares and the wrought iron and the spreading oaks and the Spanish moss and the Venusian sunset. And obviously they think continuously about slavery, a hideous crime such as only a god like Yahweh would permit.

This place is a little haunted for them. Three years ago they were living in Gainesville, Florida, which is not far away, and they recognize the light, the Spanish moss, the smell of the air. This disposes them to reflections of a broad and general character. What have they learned in the last three years? What progress have they made? When will they be able to give up their itinerant bohemian lifestyle? They wonder if they could settle down right here in Savannah. Surely this is a place where they could live peaceful modest inexpensive lives, drinking tea on a wide porch, padding softly across creaking old southern floorboards, smoking their own pork, eating shrimp, and thinking continuously and in anguish of American slavery. Would their child be an Atlanta Hawks fan, or—unhappy thought—a Charlotte Hornets fan? What if their child doesn't love basketball?

The air is dusty and dry, and soon it begins to get cool. They make a quick stop at an outdoor clothing store and buy cheap wool sweaters and matching gray work pants. They look like they're in uniform.

Murphy reminds himself that their notional child can make his or her own choice about basketball, and he and Eva will respect that decision. Basketball is not for everyone.

There was a landmark, Eva thinks. There was a landmark. My hair fell out in Santa Barbara.

The evening passes like a sigh on the south wind, and before long they return to the car and motor out to the highway. There's nothing else to be done. They enjoy the powerful scent of Confederate jasmine in the dusty air. They believe they can detect the tang and sparkle of cellular data on the breeze. Eva wonders about those conjectural landfill islands. An apocalyptic Riviera. The new Florida Keys. Will civilization collapse entirely as a result of climate change, or will things just be pretty bad for a while? She thinks about Mount Trashmore, the jewel, rising high above the clear lifeless seas of the future. A future that their child will have to contend with *as long as nothing else goes wrong.*

Here's another Super 8, and once again they're in room 210. Here's the same king-size bed, the same big TV, the same plastic cups in the same individual wrappers, the same ice bucket, the same brown carpet. Here are the same thin towels, the same green curtains, the same jammed window. Murphy turns on the light in the bathroom and the air conditioner comes on.

"Cripey!" says Eva. "This gives me a funny feeling."

They listen to the rush of the traffic, which sounds like the sea. How do they know that this motel room is real, and not just a memory of the last one, or a vision of the next?

Murphy says that buying the landfill "poses no difficulty." The touchy part is "inspiring credence" and "changing the conversation about landfills." You need to 1) initiate, and, if necessary, fabricate scientific studies proving that living full-time on a landfill poses no health risks, 2) persuade the county or municipality to rezone the landfill so you can build condos and a hotel, 3) convince investors that people are going to want to live on a landfill, and 4) convince people that they're going to want to live on a landfill. Once these things are accomplished, he says, "there can be no obstacle to success." The attraction of high ground in a tropical setting will be irresistible, and there are other attractions as well. For example, landfills belch combustible gases— free energy.

"But I'm already convinced," says Eva. "How much money do we have?"

"Almost none. Very little."

She's trying to encourage him. Usually Murphy is an inveterate retailer of half-earnest schemes, but he's been so dejected the last few months that he hasn't had any ideas at all. His interest in Mount Trashmore is a good sign.

"How do we go about getting a loan?" she says.

"It's no problem at all. I'm sure there's some kind of system."

He waits a beat.

"But I'll tell you one thing," he says. "We're going to send that woman a good chunk of the proceeds. Let's say fifty percent. Open-source idea or not."

Eva takes a shower and Murphy tries to watch a little basketball. The Eastern Conference game is ending; the Western Conference game is about to begin. An important player exhorts his teammates to stay aggressive. Every game is a game seven—that's the spirit in which each player will approach tonight's contest. Tip-off is just a few moments away, but first here's an Audi commercial. If you buy this car, what you're essentially saying to the world is: I'm different, I go my own way. Next are some images of mountains and snow. A voice says, "It's what inspired us to cold-age our beer." Murphy thinks of all that ice and snow melting and running down to the sea.

IT LOOKS LIKE another godless morning in the American South, and Eva and Murphy are feeling pretty sharp. The milk has not spoiled, and there are some radishes and passion fruits remaining. They intend to visit Charleston, but first Eva takes a little walk and Murphy strolls across the vast damp parking lot to the Walmart, because there's always a Walmart, because Walmart, according to all the most recent data, is the world's largest company, with assets worth nearly $200 billion, a net income of about $14 billion, and annual revenue hovering around $485 billion, which is not much less than the GDP of Norway, a nation that has banned Walmart because of ethical concerns. Murphy has the same concerns, but there's nowhere else to buy a cheap pair of running shorts this morning. It's fortunate that he wore his running shoes to the Whole Foods the other night. Now he returns to the motel, changes his clothes, and heads out for a jog. It's just fast food and gasoline and parking lots out here, and it feels somehow unlawful to be on foot. This is another place that isn't a place.

Back in the room, he's able to spill some Guest Choice Café Collection coffee into the curtains. Then they check out and take the road north. But the pain in his legs and feet is more intense than usual, and the one thing you especially don't want to do, if you're having trouble with muscle and joint pain, is sit rigid and motionless in the car after your morning run. You might as well stretch out in a warm tub of lactic acid. Murphy feels like his connective tissues are dissolving inside the leathery envelope of his skin. He's in enough pain that he has to mention it to Eva, who has long since made her position clear—he must take a break from running or else cease complaining—and at the next gas station he purchases Advil and IcyHot Pain Relieving Balm, although the latter is not a product he has ever tried before. Meanwhile, Eva rebukes him. It's been months of pain, she says. He needs to take a break from running.

"Maybe I need to see a doctor."

"You need to stop running!"

"I've probably got a stress fracture."

"You don't have a stress fracture *yet*."

"It's probably some torn cartilage."

"It's inflammation or something. It's a craziness problem that makes you run and run."

But no, he says, that's where she's wrong. It's the running that alleviates the craziness. Sanity flows up from the feet, or actually it flows from gravity, because gravity provides the resistance. That's why astronauts have to be so psychologically tough, because otherwise the lack of gravity would immediately drive them insane.

IcyHot Pain Relieving Balm, like IcyHot Advanced Relief Pain Cream or IcyHot Power Gel, is a topical rubefacient heat rub intended to relieve minor pain associated with arthritis, backache, muscle strains, cramps, and sprains. IcyHot also makes a SmartRelief transcutaneous electrical nerve stimulation device, which is endorsed by a giant named Shaquille O'Neal. All of IcyHot's products are marketed by Chattem, originally the Chattanooga Medicine Company, which is a subsidiary of Sanofi, which is the product of a troubled merger between Aventis and Sanofi-Synthélabo, which are themselves the products of other mergers, just as nation-states are formed by the merging of city-states or tribal areas.

This is when Yahweh returns. You can't decide to have a child and then expect Yahweh to leave you alone. Having a child means contending with Yahweh, as everyone knows. Nor is there any way to pretend that it's a dream or a hallucination, because Murphy sees him too. He's across the road at the other gas station. He's wearing ostentatious Italian sunglasses and a black suit and he's staring off toward the highway as if he knows just what he's waiting for, although even a cursory reading of the Bible suggests that he never knows what he wants.

Murphy says, "It's Yahweh."

Eva ducks behind the car. "Did he see me?"

"He looks like he's waiting for something."

"He's probably waiting for me. I knew it! You see how it's unmistakable that it's him? Like in a dream. You just know."

"I knew it was him right away, yeah. You just kind of sense that it's him."

"I saw him again before we left Miami. I didn't tell you."

Murphy frowns. "You should have told me."

"What's he doing now? Does he have his Lamborghini?"

"There's a Lamborghini parked around by the bathrooms. What he's doing is saying something to some girls. He's laughing at them. Now he's following them back to their car. They seem scared."

"He wants to do something horrific and terrible to them. Like with Job."

"Now it looks like he's got some firecrackers or something. Those little ones. Do we call them cherry bombs? He's putting them into a mailbox."

There's a muffled concussion. Eva waits breathlessly, but Murphy doesn't say anything.

"Is the mailbox destroyed?" says Eva.

"No."

"Now what's he doing?"

"He's got something bigger. It's like a rocket or something. He's putting it in there . . ."

There's another concussion, louder this time, and Murphy sees charred envelopes spill out the bottom of the mailbox.

"That one got it. Now he's gone back to waiting."

Eva manages to open the back door and climb in without raising her head to the level of the window. Murphy backs the car out of the parking lot and drives away at a good speed, watching Yahweh in the rearview mirror as he goes.

"Just don't talk to me about Jonah," Eva says.

"I didn't say anything."

"Don't you even mention Jonah."

"I won't. I didn't."

They skip Charleston and veer west. Eva suddenly has the idea that they should seek refuge with her relatives in the mountains of North Carolina. That's where her father grew up, and her great uncle Orson still lives out there in the old family house. It's as good a place as any, she says. It's as "godforsaken as you could hope for."

She is badly shaken, and it falls to Murphy to offer comfort. First, his strategy is to point out that they are in no more danger now than ever. It has always been true, he says, that calamity waits just around the corner. At any moment, Yahweh could push them down the stairs and break their legs, or smash an asteroid into the earth, or kill everyone with disease. *Seeing* Yahweh changes nothing.

But this is hardly encouraging. Eva slides down in her seat and groans.

So now he tries a different approach. He reminds her of the secular humanist credo: They believe in what exists, or rather they believe "that what exists is what exists," and everything that exists is subject to scientific inquiry and explanation. If God exists, therefore, then God is simply another phenomenon to be explained, no different than a tornado, or a methane plume, or rising sea levels. What's true is true.

"But that's no consolation either," says Eva.

Murphy says, "True."

She has never taken him to visit her North Carolina relatives. She has stayed as far away as possible. But she's in the grip of an atavistic impulse this morning. When she was small, her father got into trouble with his gambling debts and they all spent two weeks hiding in North Carolina. For Eva, even now, the mountains are where you go when you have to run away.

"It's a godforsaken place," she says again, although Murphy has registered no objection and doesn't seem to require an explanation.

And so, by early afternoon, they've passed out of the lowland South, with its garbage hills and threatened seaside towns, and they are not far from Mount Mitchell, which at 6,684 feet is the highest point east of the Mississippi. The Appalachians are modest old mountains, and they can't compare with the wild volcanic peaks of the West, but at least they're high enough to shelter the Southeast from some of the colder Arctic air masses that sweep down across the plains in the wintertime. It's always nice to think of this effect. The Alps, for example, shelter Italy from the winter wind and account in part for that country's mild climate. It's easy to forget that Italy extends from the thirty-fifth parallel, or about the latitude of Charlotte, to the forty-seventh parallel, which is farther north than Montreal.

Murphy is still trying to distract her. Now he abandons reason and turns clownish. Consider, he says, the "worst-case scenario"—that God created humans and everything else.

"Big deal. Is it really so tough to make a human? Animals are just tubes. We're all just a tube of cells enclosing the GI tract. Like worms."

"A tube," says Eva, brightening a little, slipping a radish into her mouth, chewing briskly and efficiently. "Sure. And it's open on both ends."

Science and philosophy notwithstanding, sometimes our best course is to make light of Yahweh's existence, just as we learn to joke ruefully about the chilling fact of our inevitable death. Otherwise we have no chance of existing without going mad.

"The interior of the GI tract is *outside* the body," Murphy continues. "The tube is the body. Then you add some pincers, so the creature can stuff food into the upper opening of the tube. Then some tent pegs for it to stand on and a kazoo so it can bleat with joy or distress."

And don't forget some rudimentary sensors so that it can detect the presence of food and/or danger. The whole thing is then surmounted by an "electrical jelly" that coordinates all these functions.

"And voilà. You've created man."

Here they are in Appalachia, and if they were less distracted by their own extraordinary problem, there'd be a lot to discuss, like the fact that average life expectancy is dropping sharply in this part of the country, or the fact that everyone seems to be drinking a beverage called Cheerwine, or that sign over there that reads "Real Estate Store." All of this might contribute to the sense that they are not in America at all, but somewhere else, a new place. But they aren't thinking of these things. Murphy is thinking of nothing at all, and Eva is listening, so to speak, to the mixed-up chunks of Sylvia Plath that rattle around in her unsettled mind. If I've killed one man, I've killed two. A love of the rack and the screw.

"Does thinking in lines of poetry count as thinking," she says, "or is it something else?"

"Something else," says Murphy.

Over there is a man eating candy corn on a broken bench. His feet are horribly swollen and he's snuffing oxygen from a green tank. He waves as Murphy and Eva zoom past. Eva lifts her hand. Murphy looks right through him and sees nothing.

And yet somehow the mood in the Prius has grown less oppressive. Yahweh is in pursuit, sure, but he's always in pursuit. Why should they be any more fearful now? They admire the blue mountains. They think they see a bobcat. Eva looks up the difference between East Carolina barbecue and West Carolina barbecue. The difference is that they like to use the whole pig in the east, but up here in the mountainous western part of the state, they prefer the shoulder. Murphy tries to joke that the mountain people didn't go "whole hog" for secession either, but Eva doesn't react.

Meanwhile, her phone gives directions in an affectless female voice, and soon they've arrived. Here's Uncle Orson's street. Here's Uncle Orson's house. Eva experiences that flood of dreamlike images that always haunts us when we visit a place in adulthood that we haven't seen since childhood, but there's no time to think about these things, nor any time to think of Time itself—in the turbid river of which, alas, we plunge inexorably to our deaths, whether we succeed in making light of the fact or not—because a passage of high drama is playing itself out in the driveway. A pale sandy-haired young man with flushed cheeks and no shoes is rushing back and forth on the asphalt while a policeman stands nearby and speaks calmly into his radio. There's also a Hispanic woman in nurse's scrubs waiting in the grass. The young man keeps trying to open the rear hatch of an old Nissan Pathfinder. He isn't saying anything or making any sounds, but anyone can see that he's experiencing inner torments.

Eva parks a short distance away and rolls down the windows. The young man sees her and raises a hand in greeting, but he can't spare any more time because he has to attend to his business in the drive-way. Now they hear the policeman reading the Pathfinder's license plate number to someone on the other end of the radio. The young man pulls off his billowing white T-shirt and his pants fall down. Then he yanks them up again, rushes to the car, and bends the license plate double so that the number is obscured. Next he hops into the passenger seat and waits. The nurse gets in on the driver's side, buckles her seat belt, starts the engine, backs sedately down the driveway, and motors away. The policeman says, "Scratch that. License plate is bent. It's a Pathfinder with a bent license plate."

Eva frowns up at the house, which is stuck into the side of the mountain so that the leading edge hangs off into empty space.

"Too bad about Quaid," she says. "I wanted you to meet him."

"His name is Quaid?"

"He's my cousin. He's about three years younger."

It's a two story house, and the first-floor rooms in the back are below ground. Some of the window frames are covered in blue painter's tape and there are puffs of spray paint in various colors on the brown siding. It does look like a godforsaken place, although you could just as easily argue that it's a place *targeted* by God. In any case, Eva is feeling relaxed and easy. It's Murphy who's on edge. He wasn't prepared for this scene, he hasn't been paying attention, and now, for the first time, he appears to have realized where they are and he is asking himself the sad question of the age: Who did these people vote for?

They walk up the driveway and knock on the screen door. A woman answers—Great Aunt Jo, Orson's wife. She says, "Eva?"

"It's me!"

"I didn't recognize you because you look like a wire hanger. Don't poets eat food?"

"They do not," says Murphy. "I'm glad you bring this up."

It looks like Orson and Jo are in the middle of some renovations, but Eva knows that they'll never get past the demolition phase. Some of the wood paneling in the kitchen has been removed, for example, but now there's a horse-racing calendar pinned to the exposed insulation. The cupboards are missing their doors and all the food is out on the kitchen table, but the boxes and cans are gathering dust. Cream of Wheat, Skippy, Hamburger Helper, Libby's Vienna Sausages. There's black plastic over one of the windows.

"Quaid was in some kind of trouble out there," says Eva.

Aunt Jo rolls her eyes. "It's been a few days of ongoing trouble." Her accent is so thick that Murphy has trouble understanding her. "*Years.* The day that boy is out of trouble is the day I start at third for the Cincinnati Reds."

Uncle Orson calls out from the next room, "Which one is that? Who've we got now?"

Quaid is not the only cousin in residence, it seems. Cousins are constantly showing up. This is not only a refuge from God and fiscal responsibility, it's also where you come when your parents run off to Tallahassee to open an unaccredited dance school, as Quaid's mother did.

As for Uncle Orson, he sits in a broken recliner drinking a Krispy Kreme coffee. The vertical hold on the TV is screwed up, but they know from the audio that he's watching horse racing.

"It's all I do anymore," he says apologetically. "I'm hooked to this stuff."

Eva kisses him on the forehead—she loves her Uncle Orson. Everyone loves Uncle Orson.

Murphy is the child of academics, and his parents are the children of academics, and he grew up listening to them talk about things like the declining cost of solar energy, shape-note musical notation, and the delights of P. G. Wodehouse. He may not have noticed the sick man with the candy corn, but he knows how lucky he is. He was raised—we never tire of emphasizing this point—in the church of secular humanism, and such an upbringing is a tremendous privilege, the rarest kind of wealth. His life has been easier as a result. Given some of the dangerous habits to which he was inclined in his younger days, it's not unreasonable to think that if he were born to different parents in a different situation, he'd be barefoot in the driveway just like Quaid, his big white T-shirt the only thing holding his pants up.

Eva says, "Your chair is broken."

"He won't get a new one," says Jo.

Orson says, "This is my chair. You cain't get a new one. This is it. It's the one I've got."

Eva has not enjoyed the privileges that Murphy has, and Eva is okay, but that's because Eva is tougher than he is. She was the first member of her extended family to go to college. Murphy tends to forget this fact because she lives so entirely in his world now, but it's true. She was born in a house like this one, barely hanging on to the side of a mountain, and she had to *convert* to secular humanism. That's why he sometimes feels self-conscious around her, as if she—she who has had to fight for what she knows and believes—might someday realize that he, Murphy, doesn't know anything at all and is just repeating things he's heard grown-ups saying. But of course she has the complementary worry, which is that he'll realize one day that she doesn't know anything either, that she is just bluffing, that at heart she's the kind of person who might pin a racing calendar to an exposed strip of insulation.

Now she has a vivid memory of playing checkers with her grandfather on the floor of this very room. Grandpa—a man whom Yahweh has long since gathered back to his malevolent bosom. He had a canny smile and a persuasive way of talking, and once he built a machine that would suck bugs up from the porch and blast them back out into the yard. He sold drugs up and down the East Coast, and stole from all his wives, and got beaten up badly one time by one of his stepsons, but he would not hurt a fly.

She follows Aunt Jo back into the kitchen. There's nowhere to sit down, so Jo perches on the stove and Eva sits on the countertop.

"Is there something wrong with Uncle Orson?" Eva says.

"He won't eat anything. That man is living on Ensure and blood thinners."

"He seems unhappy."

"He's heartbroken over Quaid."

"What's going on with Quaid anyway?"

Aunt Jo slides off the stove and fusses with some dishes in the sink. She purses her lips. "All in all, it has been a bad spring for Quaid." Then she pauses to examine the sponge. Then she says, "One piece of housekeeping advice, darling. When you reckon you have to wash your hands after you use the sponge, that's the time to unwrap a new sponge. God bless America that sponges are so cheap."

Uncle Orson is a deeply weathered man with a round face and artificial teeth. Right now he's so much of a piece with the decrepitude around him that it's easy to mistake him for a heap of soiled laundry. His recliner slopes off toward the ground on the right side, where the leg and all the springs and other mechanisms have fallen apart. It's just the upholstery holding it together. On his TV tray there's an empty bottle of Ensure and a letter from Appalachian Debt Consolidation Solutions. He has written the names of horses in the margins: Mommy's Angel, Geronimo Rex.

"We've got a full house these days," he says. "There's Quaid, there's Ora, there's Fate, there's Imogene."

"Fate?" says Murphy.

"Fate, Ora, Quaid. Then there's Imogene. It might be there are some others."

"It must be nice to have your children and grandchildren around."

"I never see them! Ora works with the emergency squad. *She's* up at all hours. She comes home at five in the morning!"

"She drives an ambulance?"

"It's Imogene who's the wild one. Let me tell you what I found the other morning. Right there in that kitchen garbage I found a pregnancy test. It was negative."

"But that's good. You know she's not pregnant."

"I know that *someone* wasn't pregnant," says Uncle Orson, raising his crooked old index finger, "*at that time.*"

Here's Eva on the countertop, feeling unhappy and frustrated. She too is not pregnant, not at this time. She's looking at the Hamburger Helper and the trash can full of recyclable material and the Caloric Ultramatic stove and the strip of filthy brown carpet in front of the sink. The mismatched cutlery sits in an organizer on top of the fridge. Why have they taken everything out of the cupboards? Her own parents live like this too. It was just like this growing up. One house after another and all of them half-dismantled. One year she had to sleep behind a shower curtain in the front hall. One year a bear ripped the porch off the back of the house. If you wanted to go out the back door, you had to jump down five feet into the mud. Her father got a pool ladder to make it easier, but he never attached it. This kind of stuff is a boon to the poet, but first she must escape and work toward a new and different understanding of her place in the world. No mean feat.

Out in the living room, Murphy asks Uncle Orson if he's been watching the NBA playoffs.

"These players are happy to sit back and wait for their opponent to make the mistake," Orson says. "Is that playoff basketball? I'll tell you right now you have to come out aggressive. Set a screen. Penetrate. Move the ball. Don't wait for your opponent to give you the opportunities."

"You're talking about the Hawks, right? Are the Hawks your team? Or the Grizzlies?"

"I haven't even gotten to the Hawks yet. The Hawks! Oh boy."

"But there have been some amazing games. The Rockets scored fifty points in the first quarter the other night."

Uncle Orson looks up with wide eyes and says, "Honest?"

"They had something like eighteen assists in the quarter."

"Well—" and now he gives the impression of reconsidering everything he's held to be true "—you do not score fifty points in a quarter if your aggression is poor."

Jo returns to the living room and says to Murphy: "I hear you could be interested in my heart-attack peppers."

"Almost certainly yes," he says. "Did you say heart attack?"

"I use them to make my special muscle rub."

"Then definitely yes. I'm in a lot of pain. I need a radical intervention."

"Short of taking a break from running," says Eva.

"They're called heart-attack peppers because they get your heart going again if it stops," says Jo. "They don't *cause* heart attacks."

"Either way is fine," says Murphy.

"I cook them with some flour to make a paste."

"This is good," says Eva. "This is much better than IcyHot. Who knows what chemicals are in there? We need to return to a natural way of living."

"Did you read that on the raisins box?" says Murphy. "That's what it says on the raisins box. They've trademarked the phrase. I've been saying it to myself all day."

"It's what I believe."

"Return to a Natural Way of Living."

"We should."

The heart-attack peppers are in a Ziploc bag in the freezer. Jo won't even touch the bag with her bare hands. She puts on a pair of mittens. She also ties a towel around her nose and mouth. Then she puts on some old glasses to protect her eyes from any juices.

"It's so much better to avoid the IcyHot goo," Eva says.

"I agree completely," says Murphy. "Who knows what's in that stuff?"

"It's just some kind of toxic goo."

"The thing you have to remember is that these big pharmaceutical companies are only interested in the bottom line. It pays to remember that."

"For them it's all about the rack and the screw."

"We complain that we're so fucked-up," says Murphy, shaking his fist, "but what do we expect? You do not sell your well-being on the so-called *free* market and then complain when you're so fucked-up."

Jo opens the kitchen door so there's some ventilation. "I'm sure you all are right," she says.

"The market doesn't care about your health and well-being," says Eva.

"I'm sure that's true, darling."

"Does a corporation take the Hippocratic oath? It takes an oath to maximize shareholder value."

Jo tosses a pepper into a saucepan and begins to crush it with a wooden spoon. Then she stops and tells them to go outside because there might be some fumes when she turns on the heat.

"At least we'll know what kind of fumes they are," says Eva.

Murphy nods vigorously. "They'll be natural fumes."

"It'll be like pepper spray," says Jo.

Now here they are in the road with the blue ridgeline glowing in front of them. A blessedly godless place, or so it still seems, and Eva, thinking of Yahweh, reflects that she hasn't thought of Yahweh at all since they got here.

They turn around to consider the curious situation of the house, hanging there the way it does. Has the earth itself recoiled from this structure?

Eva says, "The way these guys live! And the worst is that this is what seems normal to me."

"I've been thinking about that. It breaks my heart to think of you as a little kid. At their mercy."

But now she frowns. "It wasn't so bad."

"Are you kidding?"

A misunderstanding has developed.

"You're always so hard on my family. But I turned out fine, didn't I? You love me. You *say* you do."

"I do love you, but that doesn't mean anything. You're exceptional. A lesser person wouldn't have been fine. Quaid is a case in point."

"You don't even know him and you call him a lesser person. It's not like I was abused or neglected."

"I was trying to agree with you! Remember when we found loose shotgun shells in your dad's bathtub? Jo is wearing hospital slippers."

"They're all doing their best. She's making you some muscle rub. And you make fun of her."

Family is tough. It's hard to decide on a position. Murphy feels bad when he thinks about Jo in there making him a thing he does indeed want and value. At the same time, he's a little angry. He knows who these people voted for and he doesn't forgive them.

He's about to offer an insincere apology when Eva says, "In the fridge, I found some mozzarella from 2002."

They subside into quiet contemplation. Eva looks out into the blue Appalachian afternoon. Murphy looks at Eva. He watches her tuck her hair behind her ear and frown, and he thinks of all the other beautiful girls he's known, all those beautiful girls tucking all those wisps of hair behind all those many ears and looking out meanwhile across all those bright fields or gray oceans or crowded cityscapes, and he knows that all those moments were just quantum pre-memories of this moment, this beautiful girl, this wisp of hair, this ear. That's how it works sometimes. The physicists have figured it out, or so we've heard, or read, or seen in a documentary, or somehow mis-construed, who knows. The way photons are going to behave in the future alters the way they do behave in the present; what Murphy admired about all those other girls were the things that pre-reminded him of Eva.

"I don't think they're actually hospital slippers," she says.

Murphy is certain they're hospital slippers, but he doesn't say anything.

"They don't have any information, that's all," Eva says. "They're just guessing. My grandfather wasn't like that. He had that con man's intelligence. Once he dropped off a black box and told us never to open it. Another time he dropped off a horse! He brought her in the bed of a tiny red pickup truck. He built the sides up a little with wooden slats."

They return to the house. Jo seems to feel that Murphy may be insufficiently robust for the pepper treatment, but it's too late now. Here she is with the saucepan in one hand and a rubber spatula in the other.

"Drop your shorts," she says.

"Drop my shorts?"

Eva says, "Drop your shorts, for God's sake. Do you want to be cured or not?"

He drops his shorts, exposing Walmart underwear and sharp Miami tan lines. Jo asks him to explain where he's having the pain. He tells her here and here, and also everywhere else. But mostly here and here. She uses a rubber spatula to spread some pepper paste on his quadriceps and asks him how it feels.

"It feels like cake frosting."

"Do you feel the pain relief yet?" says Eva.

He feels nothing. "It might be good," he says, "to abrade the skin with sandpaper, so the medicine really penetrates."

A few minutes later, Murphy is on his back with his legs in the air, saying, "I think it's helping" and also weeping and coughing because somehow he's gotten the pepper paste into his eyes and mouth. His shorts are still around his ankles. Eva and Jo hover close by. Orson remains in his chair.

"How long does the pain relief last?" says Eva.

Jo is remembering that she never did use a whole pepper before. She always just used a piece.

"Should we scrape it off?"

Murphy won't allow it. Once again he says, "It's good, it's helping."

Now Uncle Fate appears, but he's not really Eva's uncle. He's one of Jo and Orson's children.

"It's great to meet a man called Fate," says Murphy. He reaches up and they shake hands. But Murphy has pepper paste on his hands. Then Fate raises his hand to his face.

"Don't rub your eye!" say Eva and Jo.

He rubs his eye. Now he has to rush to the bathroom and flush it out, which is what Murphy should do as well, except the intensity of the pain relief is so great that he can't stand up.

When Fate returns a few minutes later—his eye red and watering, his hand scrubbed raw—he has had time to consider the situation and determine that it doesn't interest him. What really demands his attention right now is a horse in the fifth at Brookhill. He needs to discuss this with Orson. The horse is not Mother's Angel but Mother's Little Helper.

Orson says, "He has got a lot of speed, but I don't think he can go the distance."

"I *know* this horse," says Fate.

Orson shakes his head. "That horse has had a lot of problems."

Fate is holding his hand out, trying not to touch anything.

After consulting the Internet and dragging him into the bathroom, Eva pours a little milk into Murphy's eyes. The milk is supposed to have a detergent effect. Then she washes the muscle rub off his legs with liquid hand soap. Then she rinses his legs with gin. Then she sets him up on a folding chair by the television with a box fan to cool the affected areas. It's his eyes that look really bad, a fierce redness and a cascade of tears, but he says the pain relief is fading.

"I shouldn't have used that whole pepper," says Jo.

"It's okay," says Eva. "He isn't very resilient about these things. Another person might not have had a problem at all."

Murphy acknowledges the truth of this and tells them he's fine now, no big deal. He's in his underwear and he's feeling a little foolish, but the really important thing is that all the muscle soreness is gone.

Dinner is mixed vegetables boiled in the bag, Uncle Ben's Country Inn Rice Pilaf, and some white fish. There's no table and everyone has to sit where they can. They use paper plates and plastic silverware. Uncle Ben's rice is parboiled, which makes it resistant to weevils.

"Could I ask," says Murphy, still in his underwear, "how you got the name Fate?"

Eva says, "It's a family name, right?"

"It must be," says Fate. "People have been called Fate in our family for as long as anyone remembers."

The nice thing about spending time with a man named Fate is that anything you say acquires a deep aphoristic meaningfulness: Fate is not my real uncle. Fate sleeps on the couch in his parents' house. Fate told me about a horse. Fate is a gambler. Fate voted against American democracy.

"My granddaddy was called Fate," says Orson. "That man was five foot tall but don't let him hear you say so. Do you know Johnson City?"

"What?" says Murphy.

"Do you know Johnson City?"

"He's never been to Johnson City," says Eva.

"Do you know Texas Pete, who has the Cowboy Grill in Johnson City?"

"He doesn't know Johnson City," says Eva. "He's never been in this part of the country before."

"I'll tell you what Grandpa Fate would do. He would just disappear for a whole month. That's what he would do."

"And Texas Pete was involved somehow?" Murphy says.

Orson uncaps his Ensure and drinks half the bottle in one noisy swallow. When he's done coughing, he says, "How do you know Texas Pete?"

"Texas Pete is a kind of hot sauce," says Fate.

Now another family member appears: Cousin Imogene. All Murphy knows about her is that she may not have been pregnant a few days ago. She's tall and lightly built, like Eva, and she resembles Eva in other ways too—the air of abstraction, the quick wild grin. She nods at Murphy and Eva and says, "What are y'all doing?"

"Just on a trip," says Eva.

But nothing more is said about it. No questions are asked in this house because everyone knows that if you ask questions, you're likely to get answers that upset you. There's no mention of Quaid, for instance, which seems strange or even very strange, and although Ora is supposed to be asleep downstairs, that's really just the best-case scenario. She might be in lockup or she might be stoned at the fun fair. It's better to take things one step at a time and struggle only with the problem in front of you.

Orson says, "Fate is a good boy."

To Murphy, the fish tastes like a headache, and halfway through he feels the sweat start in the small of his back. That's not right. It's very cold in here and he's in his underwear anyway. Then the first wave of nausea sweeps over him. He rises, pats his mouth with his napkin, picks up his shorts, and says he'll just step away for a moment. Next he passes an unspeakable hour in the freezing bathroom. Jo and Orson are initially concerned to establish what it is that's happening, but they aren't surprised, not after the way he reacted to the muscle rub, and soon his illness becomes just another immutable fact about which nothing can be said or done. Murphy isn't very resilient, that's all. It's the way things are. No one else gets sick from the fish.

Eva is worried about Murphy, though it must be said that his reaction to the meal is nothing unusual and that many previous evenings have concluded in the same way. In any case, there's nothing she can do for him right now. She checks his status every fifteen minutes. The rest of the time she sits with Imogene and Jo and Orson in the living room. Imogene is drinking gin from a Dixie cup and smoking a cigarette.

"What have you been doing?" Eva asks her.

Imogene shrugs.

"Are you going to school?"

Imogene says, "Down at the Hennigans."

"What?"

She sips her gin. "Waitress."

There are only two books in the house. One is an anthology in which some of Eva's poems have just appeared. Her sister must have sent it here. The other is a Bible stolen from a motel. These are not reverent people and they've probably only stolen it out of a sense of duty or propriety. It's some kind of fast-food Bible, with a menu at the beginning from which you select items that will gratify your particular spiritual craving: "Help in Time of Need," "Guidance in Time of Decision," "Courage in Time of Fear," "Warning in Time of Indifference." There is no entry for "General Info About Yahweh" or "Why It's Forgivable to Have a Child."

Eva lets the book fall open at random and reads: "*Is* not this David, of whom they sang one to another in dances, saying, Saul slew his thousands, and David his ten thousands?" She closes the book and looks at the wall. It's the King James translation, which surprises her. Then she opens it again and reads: "And when the king of Moab saw that the battle was too sore for him, he took with him seven hundred men that drew swords, to break through *even* unto the king of Edom: but they could not. Then he took his eldest son that should have reigned in his stead, and offered him *for* a burnt offering upon the wall. And there was great indignation against Israel: and they departed from him, and returned to *their* own land."

She rereads this passage twice. What seems to have happened is that the Moabite king has sacrificed his eldest son to a Moabite god, a ghastly business, but somehow it's even more ghastly that the sacrifice is effectual. Of course, it's not surprising that the Bible is full of alternative gods, insistent as Yahweh is that he's the one true god. If it were true, he wouldn't have to make such a big thing about it.

"Have you read this?" Eva says.

At first Imogene doesn't seem to hear her. Then she says, "Of *course* I believe in the Lord Jesus Christ."

The television is on and the picture quality is better now. An athlete recently accused of making false statements is making another false statement, specifically that none of his previous statements have been false. Next up is a clip of the president making false statements of his own, and then some footage of a protest march in Chicago, and then coverage of a shooting in Oregon, where a lunatic has murdered nine people in a university auditorium. Then there's a story about a celebrity teen who has driven her sport-utility vehicle through a showroom window. She has been released from jail and she's in a good position to benefit from the publicity associated with her crime. She appears genuinely contrite, for all that it really matters. Eva feels contrite as well, but what does she have to feel contrite about? She hasn't done anything wrong. All she's done is carried on day to day and worked hard and ended up in a much better position than Imogene, who has been living here since she was in middle school, when her own mother ran off to Nevada to sell hearing aids.

Orson is snoring concussively in his chair. Jo gazes at him fondly and says, "My old valentine."

Here's a commercial that asks: "Have you been fouled by your wireless carrier?" And here's another in which good friends drink beer together on a rooftop, and you just know that these folks aren't going to wake up tomorrow with blood on their faces and remorse in their hearts.

Aunt Jo turns on a movie—a welcome distraction. It goes like this: Matthew McConaughey and Anne Hathaway have traveled to a distant galaxy only to discover Matt Damon. Unfortunately, Matt Damon has become demented in his cosmic isolation and he tries to kill them, a gambit that only results in his own death. After this, Matthew McConaughey performs the ultimate sacrifice, tricking Anne Hathaway into traveling home to safety while he himself descends into a black hole with his robot friend in order to gather the crucial data about gravity. What he and the robot could never have anticipated is that the black hole contains a fifth-dimensional machine sent from the future to enable them to send their data to Matthew McConaughey's daughter, Jessica Chastain. They achieve this by agitating the second hand of the watch that Matthew McConaughey gave her long ago, when she was still just a child actor, except that he also gives it to her now, because the fifth-dimensional machine contains a tesseract or even many tesseracts—a tesseract is the fourth-dimensional analog of a cube—in which, or through which, or by means of which, all time appears present and accessible. Jessica Chastain uses the data to solve gravity and save humanity.

Now sufficiently recovered, Murphy has taken a shower and retreated to the spare room off the kitchen, where he and Eva are supposed to sleep. He has retrieved the copy of *Moby-Dick* that he keeps in the Prius and he wants to read a little in order to remind himself who he is, but when Eva comes to bed a short time later, after the movie's thrilling resolution, he's sitting in the dark.

"Are you better?" she says. "We should try to have sex."

"I think I can manage it. I can try."

"We have to do it. It's where babies come from."

He shakes his head. "That doesn't sound right."

No one vomits during the ensuing attempt to conceive a child, thank heavens. Only afterward does Eva ask why he has been sitting in the dark. He says that he couldn't find the light switch, which is hardly a surprise, given that there's no light switch to be found. Instead there's a bare bulb protruding from the wall above the bed. Eva gives it a quarter-turn and the light comes on.

The decorative motif in this bedroom is alarming juxtaposition. When you remove the fishing hat from the stockpot and open the lid, for example, what you find is a Santa Claus figurine. And here on the empty bookcase is an electric shaver with no blade, and a bottle of Listerine from so long ago that it says "floor cleaner" on the label, and a hairless eyeless doll's head in a broken mug. An indigo ribbon that just says "Participant" has been nailed into the window frame.

"But who in this house," Murphy says, "could have been a participant in something?"

Eva rests her forehead on his shoulder. She has not been poisoned or covered in pepper paste, but she's feeling hollowed-out. She tells him that they'll leave tomorrow and they'll do something, and he agrees, and she says promise me we'll pull ourselves together and do something, and he promises, and she says she doesn't care if it's buying a trash mountain or what, it just has to be something, and he says yes, he promises.

"We're not just going to be participants," she says.

Then it's lights out. Murphy sleeps badly because of his various discomforts, although for once these do not include muscle pain. Eva wakes up at one point and says, "I was dreaming of a monkey named Heineken."

WHEN MURPHY RETURNS from his run the next morning, Eva is sitting with Uncle Orson in the living room. She rises to greet him and says that she needs to tell him something. She has done something impulsive and reckless, she says. Murphy waits for her to continue but she does not. He's sweating briskly in his Walmart shorts. His run was less painful than usual and he feels good.

"She couldn't help herself," Orson explains.

What she's done is acquire—accidentally, it would seem—a kind of pet. Murphy spots the creature behind the television. It's a small furry gray animal, whether dog or cat Murphy can't say, and neither can Eva, and neither can we. She presses her hands together and grins fiercely.

"Don't be mad!"

Murphy examines the animal. The snout is not so long that you can rule out cat, but not so short that you can rule out dog. Plenty of dogs have almost no snout to speak of.

"His name is Fluffy 2," she says.

"Is it a him?"

"I don't know. I looked down there but I couldn't tell. I've been saying *him* for convenience."

Fluffy 2 now makes for Uncle Orson with an air of determination. Orson says, "Get on up here, Bub," and gathers the animal into his arms.

The advent of Fluffy 2 has done nothing to alter Eva's plans. She is eager to get on the road as soon as possible. That's fine with Murphy. He's always happy to be in a hurry. He executes a single stretch—a forward bend, which he holds for three seconds—and then rushes away to shower and dress and drink a scalding cup of instant coffee. Eva steps outside with Fluffy 2. Orson continues to watch the news. There's no audio, but that's just as well, because the news is bad. A schizophrenic carpenter has gunned down a few of his colleagues and two bystanders at a job site in New Jersey.

Now Murphy joins Eva outside. She is holding Fluffy 2 in her arms and peering into his face, such as it is. He's so fluffy that it's hard to tell where he ends and the world begins. Murphy watches his ears and tail for hints. He extends his hand and Fluffy 2 licks it with his small pink tongue, which is rough, but not so rough that you'd feel confident saying cat. Eva says that she found him down there on the main road, near the Bojangles'.

"The guy was selling him. He was in a milk crate."

"There wasn't any specificity as to puppy or kitten?"

"There was a for sale sign, that's all. I paid ten dollars for him."

Murphy is taking this well. Why shouldn't he take it well? We misjudge him sometimes. Now he says that it doesn't matter what species Fluffy 2 belongs to, if in fact he belongs to any species at all. It would just be good to know because it would help them decide what to feed him. Dogs and cats have different nutritional requirements. Cats are obligate carnivores, but dogs can eat vegetables.

"Yeah," says Eva, nodding vigorously, "they like to eat carrots."

They look at Fluffy 2, who is staring vacantly into the woods. His tail seems to wag, but they can't be sure. It's possible that he is some third thing, neither dog nor cat.

"He looked so cute," Eva says, beaming and taking Murphy's hand. "He had his little paws up on the edge of the milk crate."

They say their goodbyes, they turn on the car, they back down the long driveway, and only when they reach the street do they remember that they have nowhere to go.

"Huh," says Eva.

So now they face a moment of decision. There's no particular reason to return to Miami, but there's no reason not to return, and there's no reason to go anywhere else. Yahweh could surprise them anywhere, but that's always true. They face the same trouble on the road as they do at home: a lack of direction.

Eva purses her lips. She taps the steering wheel. My hair fell out in Santa Barbara. Here one descends to shelvings of the pit.

"So let's just keep going," she says.

"Sure."

"You've been unhappy in Miami. And it's not like ESL classes are the endgame for me."

"I agree. I'm not arguing with you."

"Maybe we embrace the chaos and then some kind of structure or plan will emerge."

They stop at a gas station in town. Murphy buys a packet of Quaker Oats and eats it raw. Eva maintains that she is "still full from earlier," a suspicious claim. They get Fluffy 2 some dog food and cat food and mix it all together with bits of radish.

As if to clarify her position, Eva says, "It's not that I believe that life has any meaning, or that there's any order to the universe."

"There are pockets of order. That's my impression."

"Yahweh is probably just knocking around like we are, just reacting to things. Nothing means anything. It's not like I sought out Fluffy 2. He just sort of appeared. He became manifest somehow." She pauses to think of another image. "He crystallized, like rock candy."

They share the gas station parking lot with some motorcycle people in matching leather costumes. Their jackets say "Death Before Dishonor."

"You don't have to explain yourself to me," says Murphy. "I have a sort of belief in magic. I ate all the radish greens in the middle of the night. I was sure they would help."

"But that's not magic. That's just good nutrition."

"They were mostly rotten."

"Probiotic. Full of biotics."

He nods earnestly. "That's what I was thinking too."

In the end, Yahweh makes the decision for them, as he so often makes decisions for all of us. They're driving east, why not, and Murphy, who seems increasingly fixated on the shootings in Oregon and New Jersey, is discussing the possibility of a move to Denmark, or Canada, or "anywhere else in the civilized world." Eva has just left some insulting voice-mail messages for the members of a disgraced congressional committee, and now she listens to Murphy without interest or comprehension. Then, at a bend in the lonely road, they see a figure standing beside a smoking Honda Element. It doesn't occur to them that it might be an ancient Near Eastern storm god, and that's because devious Yahweh, so unmistakable at other times, has cloaked his divine being in everydayness. But when they stop—like the good citizens they try to be, like good secular humanist Americans who try to live charitable lives without subscribing to a preapproved religiously motivated moral credo—he reveals himself with a triumphant shout, and a magical light begins to shine from his dark hair. It looks just like the luminous gas cloud that sheathes the black hole into which Matthew McConaughey descends.

Yahweh is angry. He points at Eva and says, "You have done evil in the sight of the Lord."

"I didn't mean to."

"You ran away. You avoided out of my sight!"

She winces. "We didn't think you saw us."

"I see everything." He slams his fist into his palm and there's a little pip of thunder. "Nothing is obscure to me."

Murphy is aggravated. "Hold on," he says. "*We've* done evil? I saw that an elementary school in Oklahoma was destroyed by a tornado last week. Do you want to explain that one?"

Yahweh turns to Murphy with a look of surprise, but he must be used to this kind of thing. There's something about this god that inspires rebellion. After a moment he returns his attention to Eva.

"You will visit all the great cities, and the small cities, and the towns, and the county fairs, and harvest festivals, and sporting contests, and you will tell them the name of the Lord, which is Yahweh. And on the Internet."

"What about the Internet?"

"Tell it my name. That the Internet should know I am the Lord."

Murphy is getting angrier. Incredibly, or maybe not so incredibly, it seems as if he has chosen this moment to have an existential meltdown.

"This is the world you made? Are you kidding me? I'm supposed to hope for a painless natural death. If that's the way I die, I'm *fortunate*."

"Stop it!" says Eva. She grins at Yahweh. "I'm so sorry about this!"

Now Murphy ticks off some major crimes: the Rwandan genocide, Darfur, the Holocaust, the Armenian genocide. But these are all human crimes. Does he mean to say that he holds Yahweh accountable?

Eva is pleading with him to be quiet, but Yahweh doesn't seem particularly bothered. He asks her, "Are you able to subdue him, or shall I?"

She begins to push him back across the road. He returns illogically to the gun theme. "What if you happen to see a black child in your neighborhood?" he says. She gets him into the car and tries to close the door, but he holds it open for a second and shouts, "You wouldn't want to be unarmed, would you?"

Although Murphy's denunciation is unfocused, it's easy to see what he's getting at. He's been worrying about the arbitrary cruelty of the universe, but he's also worried about the cruel things that humans do, and in this moment he fears that all humans are fundamentally bad, that the struggle to do right is misguided and hopeless, that secular humanism is a fantasy. He is, in a sense, experiencing a crisis of faith. He's worried that Yahweh, god of rage and fear, is the one true god after all. And that might be why Yahweh isn't angry at him. Yahweh's principal goal, exclusive of any policy agenda, is to be regarded as the one true god.

And indeed, that's really the only message that Eva is supposed to bring to the people. She must drive around, Yahweh says, proclaiming the name of the Lord. His instructions are not specific, nor are his threats. If she doesn't obey him, an obscure evil will be visited upon her, that's all. We might wonder, as so many have wondered before us, why he is compelled to speak through prophetic intermediaries, but we'll never get an answer. That's one for the sages.

Murphy is now permitted to rejoin them—an indication that Yahweh intends to bring the meeting to a close. Eva presses this enigmatic deity for more information.

"I don't understand what I'm supposed to do on the Internet."

"I never said anything about the Internet."

She sighs. The whole thing seems cheap and tawdry. "You just mentioned it. You *just* said it."

"I never did."

Murphy interrupts them once again. He wants to know if Yahweh can do "some kind of trick" as a demonstration of his power. Eva apologizes and tells Yahweh to ignore him, but Yahweh doesn't mind. First, though, he asks Murphy to give him his phone.

"Why would you need my phone?"

"I'd like to check the weather."

"Don't you already know the weather?"

"I like to look at the radar sometimes. To admire my handiwork."

And when Murphy pulls his phone out of his pocket, he sees that it's now a phone-shaped piece of wood. He turns it around in his hand and tries to press the home button. He looks up at Yahweh, who, when Eva bends down to pick up Fluffy 2, gives him the finger.

Yahweh tells them to go to Winston-Salem. He doesn't say why. "The will of the Lord exceeds comprehension," he explains. Then it's time for him to leave, which he does like this: He leaps up into the sky, snatches for a moment at the air, and vanishes, leaving the ruined Honda behind.

Murphy stands in the sun with his wooden phone. A kind of understanding begins to dawn. Maybe Yahweh thought he was playing a trick on him, but the joke's on Yahweh. His phone has become a burden. It's like a crack in the broad plain of life. It's where bad news bubbles up. And now, because of an *act of God*, he's free.

Eva calls her supervisor and tells him he'll have to find someone else to cover her ESL classes. It pains her to abandon her students, but she is, by her own cheerful admission, not great at her job. There are plenty of energetic instructors ready to take over for her. Her students will be better off.

Murphy, on the other hand, has no obligations and hasn't spoken to his editor in weeks.

"I could fake a restaurant review from the road if I had to," he says. " 'This brassy bighearted nightspot offers gastro-fare with a postpunk Viet-Hungarian twist.' "

"Try the word salad."

Abandoning their apartment for an unspecified length of time causes no problem at all. A friend can be dispatched to retrieve their computers and other cherished and/or valuable items. None of the furniture is their own. Their things are rotting in a storage pod in Massachusetts.

Winston-Salem sits just below the mountains in the Carolina pied-
mont, and if Yahweh has chosen it at random, it's a felicitous accident
and Murphy and Eva are delighted to visit. There are dramatic swooping hills, inspiring vistas, handsome old brick buildings. Everything
is set off nicely against the pale windy blue of the spring sky. If only
they smoked, it would be like coming home: This is the birthplace of
the R.J. Reynolds Tobacco Company, which was founded in 1875 and
at various times made Camel, Winston, Salem, Doral, and Eclipse
cigarettes. It still makes Camel and Doral, and now it makes Pall Mall
and Misty and Capri and Newport as well, although it no longer makes
Winston or Salem. If cigarettes don't appeal to you, however, this is
also the birthplace of Hanes and Krispy Kreme.

"I think maybe one problem I was having in Miami," Murphy says,
"was that I couldn't *concentrate*. I couldn't find any time to sit down
and think about what I wanted to do with myself."

"It's very noisy. You feel like you're living in a construction site."

"It's more the light and the palm trees and the festival atmosphere.
Then you go to the beach, where you brine yourself in hot seawater
and bake your brains in the sun. No one can concentrate under those
circumstances."

"And then," says Eva, "next, here comes the parade of ladies in their
underwear."

"It's not congenial to concentration and focus."

The R.J. Reynolds Tobacco Company used to be part of RJR Nabisco,
just as Philip Morris used to be associated in some mysterious way with
Kraft Foods. Now it's part of Reynolds American Inc., whose other
subsidiaries include the American Snuff Company, the Santa Fe

Natural Tobacco Company, Niconovum USA Inc. and Niconovum AB, and the R.J. Reynolds Vapor Company. Reynolds American is itself a subsidiary of British American Tobacco, a corporation that has been implicated in some uninspiring crimes. Those are the facts. But it's possible that an understanding of these corporate relationships does not lead to an enriched understanding of the human experience.

"Plus," Murphy says, "it's always summer down there! It isn't that I like winter, but meat needs to rest after it's cooked."

Without specific instructions from Yahweh, they have no idea what they're supposed to do, so they visit Old Salem, a lovely and exquisitely well-preserved historic district, with many points of interest and notable buildings. There appear to be people from the past here as well. The fellow coming out of the Moravian bakery is wearing a frock coat, and here's a woman leading a horse to water and exhorting him to drink. It's peaceful to contemplate these visions of an older and quieter world. A pre-Internet world, needless to say. Fluffy 2 seems to like it as well. There are plenty of things to sniff, and plenty of things to stare at while standing rigid as a board and making no sound. A lovely place, yes indeed, and no reason to think too much about smoking—the leading cause of preventable death in the United States.

Could they settle here in Winston-Salem? Could they stand on street corners in the wind, learn to prune their crape myrtle, eat wafer-thin Moravian cookies, and raise children whose home NBA team—here's that problem again—is the Charlotte Hornets?

. . .

And what does "preventable death" mean anyway? Does it mean a death that is not attributable to the whims of Yahweh? Do such deaths occur? This is one aspect of the free-will question—another one for the sages.

Eva whispers Yahweh's name to a police horse, but she can't bring herself to say it to a human being. She is waiting, as prophets do, for a sign. She seems perfectly at ease, however, which is inexplicable and just goes to show you how unpredictable people are. Murphy is feeling good as well, although this is at least partly due to the fact that he is now unable to access the Internet or check his e-mail, which produces a holiday sensation. He feels as if he is at large in the world.

The number of cigarettes manufactured globally by all the different producers is around 5.6 trillion.

Murphy's legs and feet are giving him trouble again, and he's grateful when Eva suggests that they take a break and enjoy some espresso at a stylish coffee shop. Fluffy 2, who has had to be carried for the last hour, laps some water from a bowl and then subsides into a noiseless slumber, settling like a mop on the concrete floor. Words like *Reynolds* and *Camel* and sometimes also the iconic camel logo are half-visible on the faces of the brick mills. Ghostly outlines and echoes. And there are powerful echoes, too, of slavery. Disadvantaged black Americans wander past, abandoned by their government but not, alas, by their vengeful god.

Eva keeps thinking of the phrases "chemical afternoon" and "acid sunlight," which come from Wallace Stevens. It's a perfectly lovely afternoon, however. There's nothing chemical or acidic about it.

71

These phrases seem to bear no relation to the events and circumstances of the day.

It's when they gather up their slumbering animal and head back to the car that they get their sign, and the evening takes an extraordinary turn. What happens is this: A big round man hails them from the doorway of a hotel. He appears to recognize Murphy, whom he addresses as "Pierce."

"I didn't know if we'd get to see you!" he says. "Old Pierce. You're a sight for sore eyes."

Murphy bows.

To Eva, the man says, "And the lovely Mrs. Pierce. I'm P. F. Barnum Gaines. Barney. I don't need to tell you how valuable your husband has been during this trying time."

"I think you do," says Eva. "I know him in another context."

Barney grins and says, "They told me look out for that Mrs. Pierce wit. They told me she's quick as anything, that Mrs. Pierce."

Mr. and Mrs. Pierce—there's no telling who these people are. But Barney is satisfied that whoever they are, they are standing here before him. This is probably Yahweh's doing, although we can't be sure. Barney himself is a prosperous looking person in a creamy black jacket and dove-gray vest. The creases in his trousers are as sharp as the folds in a fresh newspaper. His hair is hard and silver and thick and his face is a tantalizingly pale pink. Murphy wonders who he voted for.

Now Barney apologizes for the small pouch that hangs from his shoulder.

"My gadget," he says. "What it is, they've put a chip in there."

"A chip?" says Murphy.

"What they've done is put a chip in my throat."

"I see."

"It measures the acid. Then it beams the data to this gadget here."

He opens the Velcro flap and shows them the device. The display says that his esophageal pH is 9.8, a dangerously alkaline value, but this could be because Barney is eating some Tums. Eva wonders aloud if these might prejudice the test, but Barney isn't concerned. What she has to understand is that the Tums have absolutely no effect. If they were any help, he wouldn't be in this mess with his acid. If anything they make it worse, which is why he keeps eating them. He wants to get a robust reading on his gadget.

Barney seems to expect them to follow him inside, but he's worried that Fluffy 2 won't be permitted in the main ballroom. He ponders this issue for a moment.

"I think we can leave him with my man in the kitchen. Ray will know where to stash this furry fellow. They'll bury Ray in his Cowboys jersey, but he's a good man."

There's no time to protest. He scoops Fluffy 2 up and walks through the doors. Mr. and Mrs. Pierce hurry after him.

Murphy is thinking about that chip. The data goes to the gadget, but does it also go to the Internet? His own phone has been transformed, and yet it's a mistake to imagine that he's safe. The Internet hums and pulses all around him. There's no escape. You might as well just write to UPS directly. Dear Friends, I thought I'd send along the day's itinerary in order to spare you the trouble. I'm cc'ing the NSA and the Kremlin. My esophageal pH is as follows.

.   .   .

Acid sunlight. Chemical afternoon. Eva can't stop thinking about Wallace Stevens, and there's no reason for it. Chemical afternoon. Chemical afternoon. It doesn't bother her, but it's inexplicable. The vivid, florid, turgid sky. The drenching thunder rolling by.

Despite the elegance of the hotel, the event is casual. No evening clothes. Still, most of the men are wearing coats and ties, and Murphy and Eva look badly out of place in their matching work pants and sweaters. Murphy looks particularly dissolute because he's got a five-day growth of beard as well, and not the tidy half beard that's so fashionable now but a dark growth, like mold, creeping up toward his eyes and down toward his chest. Eva, who has no facial hair and couldn't grow any if she wanted to—another example of sexual dimorphism—looks a little more tidy.

Murphy is excited to do some sleuthing and figure out who Mr. and Mrs. Pierce are. He also suggests that this might be a good place to find investors for the Mount Trashmore Apocalyptic Riviera Development Group. Eva, for her part, should be telling people that the name of the Lord is Yahweh, but she gets stuck wondering about coincidence. What if Yahweh has nothing to do with this? What if they simply happen to resemble this absent couple so strongly that all of these friends and acquaintances are fooled?

Now she outlines a hypothesis. Coincidence, she says, is a subjective thing. It's the *feeling* that an improbable conjunction has occurred. And that's because we subscribe to the idea that there's a pattern to this—and here she waves her hand, indicating the hotel, the street, the city, the sky, the solar system, the universe—this nonsense. We like coincidence because it seems like evidence of a plan or scheme, but couldn't you say that at every moment, because everything is just banging around all the time, the number of possible coincidences must be very large, and the chance of a coincidence occurring—or rather, an event that we perceive as a coincidence—is not really so tiny after all? It's only the probability of any *particular* coincidence that is, or seems, very small. Which is to say that coincidence, which feels like the evidence of order, is a manifestation of disorder.

"You don't think Yahweh is up to something here?" says Murphy. "You think what's happening is just chaos?"

"I'm saying it *might* be chaos. Just random action on an ordinary chemical afternoon."

But then she thinks: Maybe Yahweh himself is chaos.

Soon Mrs. Pierce is addressed by her first name, which is Jane. Then they learn that this is a party given in honor of a businessman or financier named Javier Mendez Menendez, who is either accepting a new position or retiring from an old one, or both. Two mysteries solved. Meanwhile, everyone recognizes them and greets them with terrific familiarity. Their shabby clothes are not the careless signature of two imposters but an eccentricity that is felt to be characteristic of this prominent couple.

"Maybe you could start a kind of investigative agency," says Murphy. "Mrs. Pierce's Metaphysical Detection Agency."

"Motto," says Eva. "We construe an explanation."

"You bring us one thread, we'll pull it until the whole sweater unravels."

Someone says to Murphy that he looks different. Has he lost weight? Has he gained weight? Murphy says that he's been taking better care of himself. Yes, the man says, someone mentioned something about that. Clean and sober. Wonderful news! Who would've guessed?

Murphy smiles sheepishly and says that enough was enough. Pierce's friend agrees.

"Do you remember that night at the Fonthill," the man says, "when you gave the speech about the coasters?"

"No."

A woman says to Eva, "I'm here three days now and I'm walking around and my clothes don't fit right, so I'm thinking to myself I'm thinking wow this weather the humidity or something I don't know. It's like my body is kind of swollen or something in all this humidity. I'm thinking am I sick? But this morning I realized I picked up the wrong suitcase at baggage claim and I've been going around in another person's clothes."

Eva sips her club soda and asks for clarification. It has been three whole days?

"I live in Phoenix is why the humidity is such a factor."

Maybe we'll be able to confirm that this existential mix-up is Yahweh's doing after all, but in a larger and grander sense, we can never be sure that the universe has any shape or order. It is undoubtedly true, however, that the universe is often characterized by the *appearance* of shape and order, just as Eva says. Isn't that what matters for a human, which is a creature that deals in appearances and illusions above all? We'll have to content ourselves with the illusion of order. Or else, as Murphy says, pockets of order. Or else dumplings of order formed by chance in the chaotic cooking-mash of space.

Now Murphy is chatting with a distinguished older woman in a dark blue dress. He tells her: "We're trying to buy a mountain of trash."

"Ah," she says. "A young man with a dream."

"We've got big plans for that mountain. But I've been mulling over a new project, which is that I want to destroy the Internet."

"Interesting. They'll say, 'Oh, Pierce has been helping with strategy for our support brands, he's been pursuing some interesting opportunities in Eastern Europe, and he's been working to destroy the Internet. Just a passion project of his.'"

"Right. Because my question is why does UPS need to know my esophageal pH?"

"It's absolutely gratuitous. I agree completely."

"And how do the phones know so much about traffic? And is the TV watching us when we watch it? Why does it care what we do?"

Eva spots Barney sitting in a club chair against the wall. He waves. He's fussing with a blood pressure cuff. She takes a step in his direction, but now a tiny mannequin of a man darts across her path and says, "I'm so glad to finally meet you. I'm so glad. Your husband has been a friend for a long time. And what is it that *you* do?"

"Oh," she says, "metaphysical detection, dream litigation, psychoactivism. I'm really a Jill-of-all-trades. Have you heard that the name of the Lord is Yahweh?"

The mannequin purses his lips and nods. "I've heard something about that, yes."

Here's Javier Mendez Menendez, the honoree himself, although Murphy has yet to determine what it is that he's being honored for. Menendez is wearing a red jacket, like a bellhop's. He grips Murphy's hand and thanks him for coming, and they engage in some amiable chatter. Fun is had at Murphy's expense: He is poorly dressed and unshaven. Murphy accepts this with a you-know-me smile and they pass on to other subjects. He finds that he has no trouble striking the proper note. He's making a good impression. While he and

Menendez chat, mute smiling people gather around them, just as celestial garbage accumulates around planetary bodies.

"Now let me tell you a story about our friend Menendez," Murphy says. "A few years ago I was at a shareholders' meeting and Menendez's name came up. Next time I saw him, I said, 'How'd you like to run a two-billion-dollar company?' He said to me, 'Pierce, I'm running a three-billion-dollar company now, but if I keep on like this I'll be running a two-billion-dollar company by the end of the week!'"

Riotous laughter. Menendez is laughing too. He appears to remember this moment, although it never happened.

"But seriously," says Murphy to Menendez, "so glad to be here with you. So happy for you. Here's to you, my friend."

He raises his water glass. Other people raise their glasses. Someone says, "Skål! Prosit!" Menendez beams. It's a moment of rich solemn heartfelt camaraderie.

Eva is impressed that Murphy has managed to appear so natural in this role. He plays the part well enough that we'd call it ruthless cunning if the performance were not characterized by such apparently genuine affability. He is not incapable of affability in the normal course of things, and in fact he's affable much of the time, but this is also a man who, just this morning, nearly wept with rage when he had trouble working the gas pump at the Kangaroo.

"You're doing a great job," says Eva, meeting him at the bar. "You're a natural."

"It's just my sense of noblesse oblige."

She raises a finger in admonishment. "But what have I told you about that? None of that talk."

A clinking of glasses. A hush. Menendez rises and thanks everyone for coming. He talks about arriving in the United States on a boat made from trash barrels and old lounge chairs, and now look at him: He's got a fur-lined bathtub and a chef who makes him hummingbird tongue whenever he wants, and he's got all the friends in the world.

When the evening begins to wind down, Barney takes them back to the kitchen to retrieve Fluffy 2. It does look like Fluffy 2 has had a good evening with Ray, and when he sees them he leaps around joyfully, a little like a dog, a little like a kitten, a little like a small goat.

"I hope we'll see you at the conference this summer?" says Barney.

"Oh yes," says Eva.

"The American Ideas Conference."

"Of course."

"There's nothing like Peach Valley in midsummer. If I can just make it there, I feel like I'll be cured."

"We wouldn't miss it for the world," says Eva.

And then it's home to another Super 8. That's how it works. You venture out into the great world and then, when the job is done and the hands are all shaken, you slip back to the peace and quiet of room 210. There are plastic cups in individual wrappers and an ice bucket and a brown carpet, and the window is jammed closed. Eva unplugs the air conditioner before she turns on the bathroom light. There's a coffee stain on the curtains. They smuggle Fluffy 2 in against regulations.

But they're too excited to go to sleep immediately, so they turn on a movie, and never mind whether the television is watching them watch it. In tonight's film, Matt Damon is not alone and mad in a remote galaxy, as he was last night, nor alone and sane on Mars, as he was in another recent blockbuster. Instead, he's on a space station in orbit around the earth. He's wearing an exoskeleton that gives him exceptional strength, but in effect this is his only asset. On the debit side of the ledger, he has sustained a heavy dose of radiation and the data he's loaded into his brain is, or are, if you like, giving him a headache. But it gets worse. The data is encrypted, which means that it will kill him if he tries to upload it to the space station servers. Thus he is faced with a decision: He can retreat and save himself, or he can make the ultimate sacrifice by choosing to upload the data anyway, killing himself but saving humanity, although in this case he will be saving humanity from problems of its own making—segregated housing and unequal access to health care—and not from the atmospheric nitrogen which was so inexplicably vexing to Michael Caine, Matthew McConaughey, and Jessica Chastain.

Eva grows tired of this and subsides into reverie. She knows she didn't do very well with her prophetic duties today. She only said Yahweh's name twice, once to a horse and once to a mannequin. She's also worried that Yahweh will exact retribution for the abuse that Murphy directed at him earlier in the day. And what kind of animal is Fluffy 2? And now she too is worried about the library books in their Miami apartment.

Then she says: "What if he makes me pregnant?"

"Who?"

"What if Yahweh makes me pregnant?" She unbuckles her pants. "I want *you* to do it. Before he does." She flops down on her stomach and says into the pillow, "Quick! Before he sees!"

We'll draw a stiff motel curtain over the scene that follows. Afterward, Eva watches the movie and Murphy stands before the bathroom mirror with a short length of dental floss and thinks about how to explain oral hygiene to a child. You can try for parsimony with your dental floss, he'd want to say, but if you tear off too short a piece, you can't get a good grip and you end up having to throw it out and tear off another. Then you actually use more floss than you'd have used if you ripped off a longer piece in the first place. There's a lesson here that's bigger than oral hygiene, although oral hygiene is important.

Now Matt Damon faces a new challenge. Before he can save humanity, he must defeat his well-equipped adversary, demented South African actor Sharlto Copley, who not only possesses a threatening accent and superior training but has been wired into an even more sophisticated exoskeleton. How will Matt Damon get out of this one? But Murphy and Eva can guess easily enough. Sharlto Copley's erratic behavior will probably be his downfall, and Matt Damon will indeed make the ultimate sacrifice, as all heroes must. So Eva takes a shower and Murphy switches to basketball. The Eastern Conference game has just ended; the Western Conference game is about to begin. One player tells the courtside reporter that the mentality you've got to have in this situation is you've got to treat every game like a game seven. He discusses the importance of being, and staying, aggressive. Tip-off will follow shortly, but first here's that Audi commercial. In a world where everything's the same, buying an Audi is a quick and effective way to distinguish yourself from your fellow suburbanites. Murphy hears himself muttering, "Innovation that *excites*," but what's that? That's Nissan, not Audi. Next there's a commercial in which a young woman rides a white horse down a tropical beach. The horse talks about what it's like to walk around on four feet instead of two.

THE NEXT MORNING, they buy some additional changes of clothes, large bags of dry dog and cat food, granola, more raisins, some cashews, and some vegetables. They buy a tent and sleeping bags. No more identical motel rooms for them. They buy a pair of collard plants at a nursery and put them in the back, under the hatch, so they'll have fresh greens wherever they go. Murphy notes that the milk they purchased in Miami is still good, but he feels certain that it must be on the point of going bad, so he drinks the rest of it, half a carton, with his breakfast.

At a rest stop, a willowy angel leaps out from behind a Dumpster and accosts them. Under different circumstances, this would be a remarkable encounter, but for Eva and Murphy it's already a matter of routine. The angel tells them to proceed up the road to Ludeyville, Virginia, and wait for Yahweh in the park. They know it's an angel because its feet don't touch the ground and its face glows with an interior light. It also lacks eyebrows.

So now here they are in Ludeyville. Fluffy 2 is eating grass, either because he is a dog or cat and seeks to alleviate some digestive complaint, or because he is a very small fluffy goat and requires the grass for nourishment. Eva is eating a carrot. Murphy is stretching his calves. The pain in his legs and feet has intensified once again. No doubt it was yesterday's morning run followed by rigid motionless sitting followed by walking for many hours followed by an evening of impersonating a prominent person well known for his eccentric behavior. No doubt that was the perfect storm of factors and pressures that combined to wake him up at three o'clock this morning, at which time he retreated to the hallway to stretch and apply IcyHot Pain Relieving Balm. But this is also why it was impossible to forgo his run this morning, when it was at last time to rise and greet the day. Running is the only cure for the ill humor to which sleepless nights dispose him, and therefore the need for his run only increases when the symptoms of running too much make it impossible to sleep. That need is especially urgent these days because he wants to be in top form in order to give Eva all the support she needs. In a sense, ignoring her demand that he take a break from running is the best thing he can do for her.

As he stretches, he finds himself thinking of Miami with a great rosy fondness. He remembers eating lychees in his blue cloth shorts, reading *Moby-Dick* at the picnic table with his bare feet in the Bermuda grass, discovering some allspice seedlings at the corner of Douglas and Loquat. All his irritation is gone. He can't bring the sound of a leaf blower to mind. He thinks of the iconic coconut palms against the dark sky. Guavas. Mangoes. Cotton candy clouds. A soft and insinuating tropical morning. He tries to remember the fierce heat of the sun, but in his memory the sun is mild and life-giving and the leaves unfurl languidly in a sweet breeze. His mind has scrubbed it all clean.

Coincidentally or not, Eva's thoughts run along a parallel track. She is recalling a moment last year when she was brushing her teeth and it occurred to her that she had just lived through a day on which nothing memorable had happened, a day that would probably vanish in its entirety from her memory. This realization was so striking and terrible that she remembers the moment with perfect fidelity. The tile under her feet, the green biodegradable handle of her toothbrush, the purple light in the window. She'll remember it all her life.

Now they discuss memory in general terms, and Murphy has a wild idea: Could you train yourself to experience daily life *as if it were a memory*? Could you learn to identify and fixate upon those features of the present that will be significant in retrospect, in the prismatic halo of nostalgia?

Eva considers this possibility. What will she remember of this moment? Maybe, she says, she'll only recall the impression of space and light, nothing more. Or maybe that very steep hill over there with the round top. Maybe the blueness of the mountains. She likes to think she'll remember how the air smells, but smells are hard. Sometimes you just remember that there *was* a distinctive smell. She wonders if that's why smells and tastes are so evocative. They get tangled up with other memories, but you can't recall them on their own, at least not voluntarily, and when you smell the smell again, or taste the taste, the whole tangle comes back.

"It's the Proust Principle," she says. "But will it be spoiled when our phones have the ability to take a picture of scents?"

All of this is related to what Murphy now calls "phenomenological relativity"—the feeling that travel alters one's perception of time.

Yesterday seems so long ago. This morning seems like last year. The faster you travel, he says, the faster life is transformed into a memory, so maybe if you go fast enough the present will shade and warp into a memory as well, or maybe not, probably not. No doubt there's a "memory horizon."

"Unless," Eva says, "you could travel faster than the speed of memory."

Murphy wonders if that's what heaven is—the place out there beyond the memory horizon.

"Where every moment is a sweet memory of itself," says Eva.

She fits her hand into his. It's a lovely day. It's cool even in the sun.

"I wish I could remember this," he says.

They hear the panicked honking and the squeal of tires before they see Yahweh himself. He's walking right up the middle of the road, causing wild agitation among passing motorists. He wears a red Adidas tracksuit over a T-shirt that says "Define Girlfriend," and he's serene and carefree. He shakes Murphy's hand. He says to Eva, "Pleasant afternoon."

He's in one of his less malevolent moods, go figure, and he wants Eva to know that he appreciates the difficulty of her new position. Today, he's happy to give her some specific instructions. Her task is to present herself at the University of Louisville, where there's going to be a public lecture on high-pressure physics. It isn't clear whether he cares at all about the practice of science, but he gives Eva to understand that he detests the *pretense* of science—the belief, cherished by so many, that scientific enterprise constitutes an existential threat to him, to Yahweh.

"Tell them," he says, "that the name of the Lord is Yahweh. That's all you need to do. Tell them that there shall be no more delay. Speak my words to them and then set your forehead against them, whether they listen or not."

Since Yahweh is in a receptive mood, Murphy tries to get some clarity on a few issues that have been bothering him. First, he asks about dark matter, i.e. matter that doesn't interact with electromagnetic radiation. Does it really exist, despite our failure to detect it?

"I think it's more complicated than that," says Yahweh. "But why would you care either way?"

"I'm curious. I'm only as God made me."

Yahweh slips a gold cigarette case from his pocket, withdraws a cigarette, and lights it with a snap of his fingers. It's a Camel, which begs the question: What is Yahweh's relationship to Reynolds American Inc.?

"I'd like to know how many dimensions you can see," says Eva.

"Seeing happens in three dimensions. That's what seeing is."

"What about a black hole?" says Murphy. "What happens in a black hole?"

"What do you mean, 'happens'?"

"What about neutrinos?" says Eva.

"The bellows puff. The lead is consumed by fire."

But that's all they're getting from Yahweh today. Other business requires his attention. He does a back handspring and vanishes, and they're left to themselves, two mortal creatures, two *things* sounding their kazoos and waving their pincers, at the mercy of time, God, the universe.

Eva extends a hand and says, "Shall we go to Louisville, Mr. Pierce?"

Now, at last, it's time to go west—the direction in which American lives and American history inevitably tend. By noon they're in the mountains of West Virginia, where the people speak with an incomprehensible accent but the ATM speaks BBC English. It asks, "How may I help you achieve your dreams?" And here's a sign that says "REAL GOLD TEETH. EASY LAYAWAY" and a billboard for a construction company called Cretin Homes. Here are two Maudlin

International Trucks. Murphy has driven on this highway before, years ago, on the way to California with some college friends, but does he remember this or does he in some sense remember that he should remember it?

It's true that today's encounter with the divine was less than ordinarily challenging, but there are other challenges on the American road. Out here in the mountains, there are vicious bumper stickers, gun racks, Confederate flags. There's a billboard celebrating the new president's purported love of coal. Eva won't even look up—she says that she's trying to "remain optimistic vis-à-vis mankind"—but Murphy is furious. He has venomous thoughts about his compatriots. He doesn't know that there are counties in southern West Virginia where life expectancy at birth is lower than it is in Guatemala, but he wouldn't care if he did know, not now. Scowling and gesturing in the acid sunlight, he now delivers an impressionistic speech. It begins with a denunciation of the electoral college and then spirals outward, comprehending all of American history in just a few swooping turns. He condemns Thomas Jefferson, who made pronouncements about liberty and yet never freed his slaves, and he condemns "the Indian murderer" Andrew Jackson, and he condemns the annexation of Hawaii, and the idea of manifest destiny, and "pirate capitalism," and even Brown University, which was founded or endowed by slave traders. He shifts to gerrymandering and voter suppression and then concludes by asking in fury why health insurance doesn't cover dental care. His speech is difficult to follow at the sentence or paragraph level, but the basic thrust is this: How can we accept that the world is the way it is?

"There's a hilarious story," he says, looking about as transported by hilarity as a dead pigeon in a game bag, "about Jefferson rebuking the students at UVA after they'd had some kind of gun riot."

Eva waits a beat, but Murphy is silent, his fists and jaw clenched.

"What's the story?" she says.

"What story?"

"About Jefferson and the UVA students."

"I don't know."

In Lexington, at a store that also sells stuffed bears, Eva buys a Bible. She pages through it as they take the road west out of town. Maybe God exists, maybe the world is a sorrowful place, but she's in an analytical frame of mind and she knows that knowledge is the path to understanding and compassion.

"Here's a part where Saul is trying to kill David," she says. "They're just chatting or something and then the evil spirit from Yahweh comes upon Saul and a javelin appears in his hand. He tries to pin David to the wall. David manages to run away. He avoids out of his sight. The problem is that Yahweh has abandoned Saul and he's with David now. I suppose it's hard to see why Yahweh *gives* him the javelin."

"But that's typical of Yahweh," Murphy says. "That's right in line with his other methods and strategies."

"And now listen to this: 'He hath, as it were, the strength of an unicorn.'"

"A unicorn?"

"*An* unicorn. Yahweh hath."

"As it were."

She studies the text in silence for a few more minutes. Then she frowns and says, "'She smote twice upon his neck with all her might, and she took away his head from him.'"

The clouds are tumultuously bright. The sky is vivid, florid, turgid. Or is it only that these phrases, once uttered, doggedly attach themselves to the world? Eva ponders this new problem. Does art distort perception? She mutters another phrase from Wallace Stevens, "The honey of common summer," but she can't remember the context, and so, in a sense, can't complete her thought, if it's right to call it a thought.

They arrive in Louisville with time to spare, but it takes the better part of an hour to find parking on campus. Eva has been able to stay positive and upbeat all this time, but Murphy can sense that her resolve is weakening.

"What do I do?" she says. "Do I just sort of interrupt?"

It's a sin to interrupt a lecture, unless the lecture is evil. She wishes Yahweh had given her some powers or some special knowledge that would make her more convincing.

"Do I look okay, at least?"

"You look beautiful."

She peers at herself in the side-view mirror.

"You don't think I should tart myself up a bit?"

The lecture takes place in the first-floor auditorium of a Stalinist laboratory complex. The setting reminds Murphy of his stormy younger days, during which he worked in laboratory complexes just like this one. He was not suited to the repetitive labor of scientific research and quickly lost his mind. Now, however, the anguish and loneliness of those days is sufficiently remote that he remembers that time with longing.

Eva is trying to work out her strategy. She has an obligation to tell these people that the name of the Lord is Yahweh, but there's no reason why she has to leave it at that. She also plans to explain why his existence is no cause for despair. In that sense, she'll still be an advocate for goodness.

"Because the chilling follow-up question," she says, "is how do you remain compassionate in a world where he exists? How do you live a good life, despite God?"

This is what Murphy was getting at earlier: How can we accept that the world is the way it is? For now, however, it looks like Eva is convinced that we *can* accept it. A confrontation with God, she says, is nothing more than a test of faith. Do they believe in kindness and generosity because an ancient Near Eastern storm god has mandated that belief? Of course not. Goodness in the service of a divine being is not goodness. It's a moral abdication. They believe in goodness for its own sake. That is their faith. And they need only remain true to it.

"So even though I'll be functioning as Yahweh's prophet," she says, "I'll actually be able to spread a hopeful message."

They sit halfway back on the left side, close to an exit. The house lights dim. The speaker and his handler mount the stage. Both men are clean-shaven, boyish, and severely bespectacled. They are distinguishable from one another only because the handler has not been able to button his shirt in the correct sequence.

Murphy turns to look at Eva, who grins and gives him a thumbs-up.

Alas, the lecture is incomprehensible, although it begins simply enough. As Yahweh has already mentioned, the topic is high-pressure physics, or maybe it's fusion, or maybe these are the same thing, who knows. The speaker begins by saying that he and his colleagues have been discovering all kinds of new phases of matter. He says that matter, as one might expect, behaves unexpectedly when you begin mashing it. First you mash the electron shells together, and then you mash nuclei into other nuclei. But it's at this point that Murphy and Eva lose the thread. How, for example, does this fellow create the extraordinary pressures necessary to crush nuclei into nuclei? They gather that a laser is required, but he keeps mentioning compression waves and something he calls a "gold can." Soon he's talking about an Easter egg filled with heavy hydrogen.

Eva waits for the question and answer period. It's not until she opens her mouth that she realizes she's not going to be able to say what she wants to say. She begins, "Have you heard the name of the Lord, which is Yahweh?"

The speaker is silent for a moment, and then he says, "Is that a question?"

"This city shall not be a pot for you," she continues. The words come to her naturally, in exactly the way that a line from Wallace Stevens might come. She doesn't understand them, but that's okay. Much of Stevens is also impossible to understand. She continues, "This city shall not be a pot, nor you the meat in it. The fulfillment of every vision draws near. And then you'll know that he is the Lord."

She might have hoped for kindness from this audience, which presumably consists of secular humanists like themselves, but she isn't going to get it. People stare. Contempt ripples through the crowd. She says nothing more.

The speaker adjusts his glasses and frowns. Then—and this is his unpleasant way of dismissing her and inviting more questions—then he says, "Has anyone else stopped taking their medication?"

It's a disappointing evening. Luckily, it's soon over. Murphy holds her hand during the time that remains, but he's been swilling coffee and soon he has to rush off and find a bathroom. Eva heads out to the parking lot, where Yahweh is standing by the Prius with Fluffy 2. The lecture has impressed her with a sense of all the incredible things we know, and all the things we don't know, and all the things we can't know, but even though Yahweh appears more considerable in this light—even though he is an embodiment of the great and terrifying mystery itself, the huge intractable Why of it all, and even though he looks taller today, more imperious, and somehow radiant with sexual menace—she has had a humiliating experience and she is hurt above all. Now it's her turn to have a meltdown.

"You set me up!"

He nods. "I hardened their hearts."

"You did what?"

"I hardened their hearts. And stiffened their necks."

She sits down on the curb and puts her head in her hands.

He continues, "I have my purposes, and it's not for you to wonder about them."

"What purpose could it serve to make everyone wonder about your purposes? You're supposed to be all-powerful."

"And you antagonize me even so. It never ceases to amaze me."

She looks around in wonder. The grass is green. The oak leaves snap and shine. The sun has come to rest on the blue hill. She can't believe the world is like this. She asks him why he would subject his prophet to such humiliation, or any humiliation at all. What's stopping him from *making* people revere him? Then she gets angrier and enlarges the scope of her critique. What about the suffering of children? What about cities destroyed by volcanoes? What about the indignity of aging? What about the bride who's murdered on her wedding day? What *about* the Holocaust?

But Yahweh smiles mysteriously and says, "What about all the beautiful things in the world? What about the splendor?"

"Exactly. What about it?"

Eva has raised a lot of good questions. Let's take up just one: If Yahweh really does possess the strength of an unicorn, then why can't he have things the way he wants them? How could an omnipotent being be so strictly limited in the exercise of his power?

Some of the early Christian groups, collectively called Gnostics, had a tantalizing answer. They argued that Yahweh was only the demiurge—the creator. They said that he was a monstrously imperfect god, possibly insane, certainly the lowest and worst of the gods, all of whom, in any case, were just facets of the divine fullness from which everything comes. His need to create and then to meddle with a physical world was explained as a symptom of his imperfection, as was his consciousness, or the fact that he was impelled to interact with the material world by means of a consciousness.

And these ideas have their appeal, don't they? Because then it would follow that the higher and nobler gods have nothing to do with matter, nor perhaps with dark matter, if it exists. We are free to imagine that they are creatures of dark energy, woven into the structure of space, which is always expanding, always expanding, and at an ever-increasing rate, no less.

Murphy, for his part, is still wandering around looking for a bathroom. God knows, or he doesn't, what depraved committee approved this floor plan.

Meanwhile, Eva tells Yahweh that she wants a covenant. Nothing big. "Just a simple covenant." She wants his assurance that she and Murphy and any children they have are going to be happy and safe. Can he manage that small thing?

"No."

She closes her eyes and tries to regulate her breathing and slow her heart rate, as Buddhist monks are said to be able to do. If happiness and safety are too much to ask, she says, she will accept safety alone. Could he simply agree not to do anything horrific and terrible to them?

He looks away and says nothing.

"Then just give me some money!"

"Some money?"

"It would make things easier. We could buy Mount Trashmore."

"Why would you want to buy a landfill? Of all the things you could ask your god, you ask for a mountain of garbage?"

"I'm asking for money, not garbage. What I do with it should be my own business. How much would it cost to build a resort on a landfill?"

Yahweh produces a small piece of gum, unwraps it, places it in his mouth, chews rapturously, and says, "Fifty dollars? A billion dollars? It's nothing to me."

"So I can have it?"

"I'll give you seven golden hemorrhoids and seven golden mice."

"Just the money is fine."

"Name your figure."

"A hundred million dollars."

"Fine."

"Fine?"

"Fine."

She's becoming suspicious. She looks around warily. "Why is it fine?"

"I'm pleased that you made the effort in there."

"And you react just like a human. You enjoy a piece of gum. You behave charitably."

"Incorrect. I behave like myself, and you all emulate me, which is how I set it up." He grins. Cars rush by. Fluffy 2 makes a funny mewling noise. "And now let's go over my conditions."

Murphy has at last reached his goal, and in his relief he indulges in a reverie about urinal design. Is it not wonderful that there are people whose job it is to meditate on the shapes and contours of these fixtures? To get such a job, you need years of schooling. It's a fluid-dynamics problem. Then he begins to think of physics more generally, and then, a rarefied topic indeed, of neutrinos. And yet this is reasonable enough when you consider that there are trillions of neutrinos passing through us every second. Even on the quietest days, the quietest mornings, when the trucks have ceased to back up and the leaf blowers are all switched off. What are they? They're uncharged elementary particles produced by radioactive decay, or so the physicists tell us. We have to take their word for it. They say that neutrinos have mass, but not much mass. Again we have to take their word for it. They say that they're a kind of dark matter. They say that all but 5 percent of the universe is dark matter or dark energy. They say that neutrinos come in three flavors. Are they lying to us?

Murphy exits the building in time to see Yahweh pull out of the parking lot and speed away, swerving as he goes in order to knock over some traffic cones. He's driving the Lamborghini again. Eva is sitting on the curb and Fluffy 2 is standing beside her, blinking and sticking his tongue out.

"You did so well!" he says, sitting down next to her and gathering her into a hug. "It'll get easier. The thing about the pot and the city was surprising . . ."

But she doesn't want to talk about that right now. She has to explain the covenant she has just made. Yahweh will give them some money, but he has imposed a surprising condition. He wants her to build a temple on the summit of Mount Trashmore. He has even supplied a magical set of blueprints. The specifications are all there: The threshold of the gateway is one rod wide. From the entrance to the gateway it's ten cubits. From this gate chamber to that one is twenty-five cubits. Here's the chamber where you wash the burnt offering. There are two tables on that side and two on this side, and they're for the burnt offering, the sin offering, and the trespass offering.

"I can sort of go over this myself later on," says Murphy.

"This chamber is for the priests, the sons of Zadok, from the sons of Levi."

"I thought so."

And the walls here will be carved with palm trees and cherubim, she says. And here's the sanctuary. The doorposts are six cubits wide on both sides. The width of the entryway is ten cubits. The chamber is twenty by forty cubits.

"Let's just come back to this another day," says Murphy.

THEY CAMP ON the side of the road in Hoosier National Forest. The morning is cool and blue and primeval, and so far only Murphy is awake. He's trying to enjoy the fragrant woodland air and fluting bird-song, but he is unable to achieve serenity, and not because of Yahweh or Yahweh's temple but because his mind is full of media trash. Bits of language come crackling to the surface and he can't tell the advertising slogans from the NBA memes. "Have you been fouled by your wireless carrier?" "The ability to finish in transition." "Innovation that excites." "You have to come out aggressive." "Power through." "You talk about the high pick-and-roll." "You talk about the ability to finish in transition." "It all starts with a kick." Eva sleeps with Fluffy 2 curled around her head. Murphy watches them. "You talk about coming out aggressive." They are three digestive tubes bathing in neutrinos at the bottom of a gravity well.

. . .

Eva seems refreshed this morning. Only moments after opening her eyes, she reaches back to unzip the tent flap, deposits Fluffy 2 outside, and suggests winsomely that Murphy try to impregnate her. It pleases Murphy to be a figure of such utility. A convenient appendage. A reservoir of genetic material. So now there's another sex scene, a woodland sex scene this time, rapid but not furtive, and afterward they lie together and listen to the wind and the birds. Eva wants to make a joke about how gross sex is—Why would we ever want to do that with the person we love?—but she says nothing. It's so pleasant in here that there's no need for levity.

Alas, they have a job to do, and soon it's time to break camp. Murphy rolls up the tent, stuffs it halfway into its bag, pitches it into the car, and stuffs the sleeping bags in after it. Then they take the road west to Illinois. As Eva drives, Murphy pokes at her phone. First he checks his e-mail. Then he tries to figure out how to buy a landfill, but he doesn't know where to start. Then he checks his e-mail. Then he checks his e-mail. Then he reads an article about the chocolate diet, so-called, which is just what it sounds like and which is based on research that has turned out to be fraudulent. Some filmmakers created a deliberately flawed study in order to expose the relaxed standards of nutritional science and e-journalism. Then he checks his e-mail. Then he longs to not check his e-mail. Then he asks the Internet how he'd go about destroying the Internet, and the Internet has an answer, but it isn't as satisfying as he'd hoped. The Internet is a vast machine, all nodes and wires and server farms, which does mean that it can be destroyed, but it's so diffuse and redundant that destroying it means coordinating an enormous worldwide terrorist operation, and Murphy doesn't have the qualifications for a job like that.

"I don't get it," says Eva. "Do you really want to destroy the Internet? It would be a disaster."

What he wants is a little psychological space. Doesn't she remember the days when you had to wait to look something up? And you had to call people on their house phones, and if they were out somewhere, even if they were just in the yard catching grasshoppers, you couldn't talk to them. Doesn't she remember those days?

"And now everything's out of control," he says, checking his e-mail. "No one's allowed to go out and catch grasshoppers without *sharing* the fact with everyone they know. You can listen to all the songs, but that means that there's no time to listen to any song in particular. And the news! Oh God. It just keeps coming."

He looks wistfully at the country out there beyond the highway. There are some cheerful bluffs, more plowed fields, ornamental clouds, an occasional farmhouse. It's true that Yahweh has turned his phone to wood, but it wouldn't matter if he changed all of our phones to wood. To get back to where we came from, he'd have to change the *memory* of our phones to wood.

Soon the land begins to flatten out. It's just grain elevators and water towers and newly planted cornfields out here, which reminds Eva of a book she read in which a journalist goes to an American cornfield in order to meditate on the effects of a mass extinction. The idea is that a mass extinction doesn't mean fewer total organisms but fewer kinds of organisms. An aseptic modern cornfield provides the analogy. There are only a few species of insect that can survive here, almost no larger animals, and of course very few weeds. It's a poisoned landscape inhabited by corn. This is supposed to be what the world was like after the great Permian-Triassic extinction event, during which up to 96 percent of all marine species and 70 percent of all terrestrial vertebrates disappeared. In the wake of this catastrophe, the ultimate cause of which remains unknown, the earth's various ecoregions were overrun by a handful of opportunistic survivors like Lystrosaurus ("shovel lizard"), which was a sprawling pig-size digging creature thought to have been particularly well adapted to the high-carbon-dioxide, low-oxygen atmosphere that characterized that terrible period.

"Marianne Moore says somewhere that struggle is meat," says Eva.
   "Struggle is meat?"
   "I don't remember the context."
   "I sort of understand. Struggle is meat."
   "It's about predators and prey," she says, peering at the cornfield. "Maybe."

Here's another problem: We can wonder all we like about *why* Yahweh might want to orchestrate disasters like the Permian-Triassic extinction or the biblical flood—assuming, of course, that he's the one responsible—but we also need to ask *how* he orchestrates these disasters. If he can manipulate the weather, for example, by what mechanism does he do so? Does he voluntarily mobilize the same forces that meteorological science describes, or does he exert some other kind of influence, possibly involving neutrinos, or is he himself a kind of force, immanent in all these phenomena but lacking conscious control, such that his relationship to mudslides and hurricanes is something like our relationship to the functions of our gall bladders?

They pass through St. Louis at eleven o'clock. It's here that they cross the mighty Mississippi. It's here that they pick up I-70. It's here that they enter the American West, in a sense, but only in a sense, because at first everything is the same. The trees, the bluffs, the close damp air. It's the old story: You wait for the big moment, and what you get is a gradual transition.

.   .   .

Questions about Yahweh's methods and intentions lead inevitably to the free-will question and its vexing corollary, the self-determination question. We've hinted at this already. If Yahweh is the creator of mankind, a big if, then to what extent should he be held accountable for the bad things humans do? Not just vast crimes like the Holocaust, but smaller crimes too, like a mugging in an Atlanta alleyway. Even if we are permitted some freedom of choice, is our nature not determined and overdetermined by our creator? Is Yahweh therefore responsible for anthropogenic climate change? What about medical conditions that derive from exposure to man-made toxins?

Just west of St. Louis, in Weldon Spring, you can visit an attraction called the Nuclear Waste Adventure Trail. Missouri boasts plenty of other fun destinations as well. The biggest ball of string is in Weston, but the biggest ball of twine, or at least one of the four contenders for the title, is in Branson. In Bonne Terre, you can see the giant fiberglass animal cluster.

"We need the Internet to organize our political resistance," Eva says. "How would we know which legislators to call?"

"It's always the same ones, those fuckers."

Lunch is granola and some tough raw collards from the pots in the back. They enjoy this meal in a park in Columbia, Missouri. Then they visit a food co-op and buy some cacao beans. A mild interest in the chocolate hoax has given way to this: an appetite for chocolate. The hoax doesn't mean that chocolate is necessarily ineffective as a weight-loss aid. It only means that it isn't necessarily effective. Not that either of them need to lose weight. They're interested in cacao beans as a source of protein, fiber, and delicious magical phytochemicals.

As they shuffle up to the checkout line, snatching a few bars of dark chocolate on the way, Murphy wonders about fad diets. Why do Americans love them? It's because Americans like bold and aggressive action. The United States is an Enlightenment nation founded on the idea that problems have solutions. A ridiculous conceit. How many world-weary Englishmen and Englishwomen would make that mistake? But Americans believe it. Americans believe that the solution to the problem of being human is out there, and you just have to find it and buy it by the liter.

The checkout guy says, "Did you know that eating cacao beans will actually help you with color perception? You'll actually see a greater number of colors."

Murphy smirks. More pseudoscience.

"Did *you* know," says Eva, "that the name of the Lord is Yahweh?"

Now they stand out in the sun eating cacao beans, which are so bitter that they must consciously suppress the instinct to spit them out. But they aren't quite as bad if you eat them with a piece of dark chocolate. They're even pretty good. Or are they? At a certain point, because of the incredible purported benefits of chocolate, which do not necessarily not include weight loss, it's impossible to untangle all the inputs. The thought of chocolate is so delicious that it affects the taste.

"But it *is* so colorful out here," says Murphy. "Look at the rich red of that Kia Optima. And the vividness of the no-passing sign. Even the asphalt. Don't you think?"

"The colors are so striking. I was just thinking that."

"What a lovely world."

"It's tempting to think," says Eva, crunching up a cacao bean, "that it isn't the worst of all possible worlds after all."

Unfortunately, this is a short reprieve. An hour later they're at a convenience store in western Missouri and they spot Satan standing by the gas pumps with his hands in his pockets. Like Yahweh, he's immediately recognizable as himself, even if he's not what they expect. He is a stocky and unassuming angel. He has arched, ironic eyebrows. He looks like Salman Rushdie.

"No," says Eva. "No no no. I can't take this."

Satan crosses the parking lot and stands at the entrance to the convenience store, holding the door for a small boy. He bows slightly as the child passes through. The boy's mother gives him a radiant smile.

"If we just pretend he's not here," says Eva.

They've been listing novels that they think their child should be made to read. There are novels you have to read when you're young, they agree, like *Absalom, Absalom!*, *Jane Eyre*, and *One Hundred Years of Solitude*. Their duty as parents will be to expose their child to these things while the window is still open.

"I tried to reread *Blood Meridian* last year," says Murphy, "but I'm too old now. I just kept thinking about how all those murdered people had moms and dads. We're all alive because someone took care of us when we were small."

"I never read *Blood Meridian*."

"You've missed your chance."

Satan is right behind them. He clears his throat. Eva freezes.

"In my darker moments," Satan says, "the only book I can bear to read is *Alice's Adventures in Wonderland*."

They turn around and glare at this shabby fallen angel. But Satan is unhappy as well. He apologizes for intruding. He's here at Yahweh's insistence—Yahweh is busy, or wants them to think he's busy.

"And listen," he says, "I know what you're thinking, but before you say anything, just consider this: You've heard the worst things about me, but who have you heard them from?"

Eva cocks her head.

"It's Yahweh and his acolytes who've been defaming me all this time. Yahweh and his acolytes. Do you understand what I'm saying? And they've been successful."

Eva grins.

"You see my point?" says Satan.

The convenience store is thronged with exhausted travelers. They all have their own problems, but if those problems can be solved by purchasing things, they've come to the right place. There are diet peach "refreshers" available for just $1.19 a bottle. There are Raid Ant Baits, Velveeta Cheesy Bowls, Hot Shot No-Mess! insect fogger, Detour Lean Muscle whey protein bars, Advil, Cutter Backyard Bug Control, Crisco, Laffy Taffy, Meiji Hello Panda choco cream biscuits, Little Trees Black Ice car freshener, and so on, and so on. Chemical afternoon.

"Yahweh has been poisoning everyone against me for so long," Satan says, "that nobody remembers I used to be the angel of the morning."

"Like the song," says Eva.

"Of course."

"Is it secretly about you?"

He shrugs. Lots of songs are secretly about him. It isn't as if being cast as Yahweh's enemy has been bad for brand recognition.

Eva says, "It's a great song. Now we're all going to have it stuck in our heads."

The three of them walk out to the car. The sky is a powdery blue. The new leaves on the honey locust trees are a wild highlighter yellow. A vivid yellow. Satan pays for the gas, bless him. He leans back against the car while the tank fills and mutters a little A. E. Stallings lyric that begins, "Why should the devil get all the good tunes . . ."

Eva says, "There's a Sharon Olds collection called *Satan Says*."

"I've read it," Satan says.

"You've read it?"

"Literature is the element I live in. But could I ask you not to call me Satan?"

He suggests that they call him Lucifer instead. Latin enthusiasts will remember that it means "the bringer of light."

"Did I read somewhere," says Eva, "that it was Milton who first called you Lucifer?"

"I remember Milton. A strange man crying out to be milked. Incredibly, he thought he'd gone blind because of something he ate, and not because it pleased Yahweh to strike him blind. A man who knew so much! He didn't know that."

But now Satan says they need to be going. Tonight's assignment is to antagonize an author whom Yahweh despises. She's reading at a bookstore in Kansas City and they only have an hour to get there. It turns out that Satan—and we can't help but call him Satan, but it's okay because it just means "the adversary"—has been dispatched to guide Eva to the event and to play a special role in the spectacle that will follow. They don't ask him to be more specific, but Murphy does ask why he's beholden to Yahweh in the first place.

"Put it this way," Satan says. "If Yahweh is the light of the light of the light, then I'm the light of the light of the light of the light."

"Oh."

Or, he says, maybe it's just that he's a part of Yahweh's pantheon. No doubt every pantheon has its unique frustrations. For all he knows, another pantheon might be even worse.

· · ·

The bookstore occupies the corner unit in a strip mall somewhere in the city's baggy periphery. There's a pawn shop next door, and some dangerous teens smoking by a Dumpster, and there's a pizza box on the curb with the enigmatic legend "Destinee" written on it in Sharpie. It seems to Eva like a clue. They've got a few minutes to spare, so they feed Fluffy 2 his dinner and watch the wild bloody sunset foaming in the western sky.

"Indifferent as it is," Satan says, presumably meaning the sun, "or indifferent as it *seems* to the works of God and man."

Murphy is examining the dog- and cat-food tins while Fluffy 2 eats. This food is just meat and potatoes and carrots. Somehow the information comes as a great surprise.

"Food is all the same stuff," he says, with an air of revelation. "Dog food, human food, scorpion food. It's all the same components in different forms and combinations."

He elaborates: Wheat is a fruit, like a cherry. And chocolate is a fruit too, but it's the seed part of the fruit, like a pea in a pod. Everything we eat is just cherries and peas. And meat. We prepare these things in different ways, that's all. Bread is like a baked cherry foam with yeast. And yeast is just fungus, like mushrooms. So bread is cherry foam with mushrooms.

"Why are you saying cherries?" says Satan. He turns to Eva. "He keeps repeating the word *cherries*."

The reading is well attended, despite its inauspicious location. Here's a guy in a Star Trek sweatshirt and one of those clear plastic face masks that basketball players wear when they break their noses. He has a CVS bag full of tattered papers and manila folders. There's also a sinewy older man with a rolling suitcase and a portable DVD player. He's sitting in the back watching *Cheers* and eating plantain chips. He has a plastic bottle of cooking brandy in his coat pocket and occasionally he says "That's so funny" in a serene and mellifluous voice. Closer to the front is a respectful group of older women, possibly a book club. Murphy and Eva sit on the left side, near the back. Satan sits by himself a few rows in front of them.

The writer has just published a novel about the 2010 earthquake in Haiti. They have never heard of her before and her writing is undistinguished, but she seems generous and kind and they listen politely, or they pretend to listen. Then the reading is done and the bookstore owner invites questions from the audience. The man in the Star Trek sweatshirt asks if she was in Haiti when it happened. A woman asks if she thinks publishing is dying or just changing. Another woman asks about her daily routine. Then Eva takes a few short breaths, slaps herself in the face, and asks if the writer has heard the name of the Lord, which is Yahweh.

Kansas City is a place where you might expect to encounter modest Christian people who have indeed heard the name of the Lord, whatever it is, and are not unfamiliar with manifestations of religious enthusiasm. That expectation now seems justified. The reading group women incline their heads respectfully, finding fault not with the message, perhaps, but with its abrupt mode of delivery. Yahweh doesn't appear to have hardened their hearts, and Eva's question seems likely to pass without comment.

But no: Satan says that he'd like to take up the issue, if no one objects, and of course no one does. He may not possess the strength of an unicorn, but the audience senses that he's a considerable figure nonetheless. There's a frightening gravity about him as he rises to speak.

"Are we to imagine," he begins, "that the earthquake was somehow 'God's will?' Is that what you're implying? That all of that suffering was inflicted upon these people for some *purpose*?"

He continues in a weary, professorial style, touching with sly eloquence on some different facets of this question and then, more vehemently now, declaring that he doesn't want to live in a world "where there are gods like that." Luckily, as he now insists, there are no gods at all, or angels, and never have been. The injustice is that a person committed to reason must define him- or herself in opposition to so ludicrous a fantasy.

"An *angel*?" he says, laughing bitterly. "A shining little someone with wings?"

The bookstore owner says, "We're getting a little off topic here."

But the audience is mesmerized. There's no stopping him now.

"Why should it be acceptable to construe rules of conduct from an anthology of ancient children's stories? Why those children's stories and not others? *The Lorax* communicates a more wholesome message."

Meanwhile, what about the earthquake in Haiti? Our scientist friends tell us that it was caused by a rupture of the Enriquillo–Plantain Garden fault, which is fine as a description of the mechanism, but no one who has even a passing acquaintance with Yahweh and his deeds will fail to detect the cruel intentionality. Why should such a terrible thing have happened to the poorest country in the Western Hemisphere? A country founded by slaves who freed themselves but who were then forced to make reparations to their former owners, which is to say that the ex-slaves had to compensate the ex-slave-owners for the loss of their slaves, i.e. themselves. Having fought for their freedom, they then had to pay for it. The financial burden crippled the young nation, which was already crippled by economic embargoes.

Satan, meanwhile, presses on. The audience is stricken, wide-eyed, openmouthed.

"We're asked to imagine an insubstantial being who lives in the sky. He knows everything we think, *cares* what we think, and has apparently created the world only to cause devastation and hardship for its occupants, whom he also created."

To accept this premise is also to ask *why*, says Satan. Why would such a being do what he does? Why would he kill people by the thousand, and by the tens of thousands? It's the oldest question, and disagreement about the answer has given rise to centuries of conflict among Christians and Jews and Muslims. But the dispassionate observer can see that there is no program after all. There is no order or plan to anything. If God exists, therefore, then his true desire could only be to produce violent confusion and discord. Persisting in one's religious belief means ascribing to this divine being a nihilist malignancy that boggles the mind. Who wants to live in such a universe?

"And yet," Satan says, "if we remove God from our understanding of the cosmos, we remove agency and thus we remove cruelty."

Speaking of cruelty and agency, here's something else: Hanes, which is of course headquartered in Winston-Salem, makes a lot of its clothing in Haiti, and the company recently fought a determined battle to prevent this benighted country from raising its minimum wage from thirty-one to sixty-one cents an hour. Eventually, the U.S. State Department forced the Haitian government to accept a minimum wage of three dollars per day for textile workers. This perverse miscarriage of justice was moving forward even as the earthquake occurred, and wages have increased only marginally since that time. Maybe the safest hypothesis is that God and man have acted together in their pursuit of Haiti's degradation.

Satan dismisses the audience and everyone stumbles out into the midwestern evening and stands around blinking in the purple light.

"I'm so sorry," he says to Eva. "I'm mortified. I'd have warned you, but I wasn't sure how Yahweh would react."

Eva waves his concern away. He had no choice. She understands.

"I'm playing the Satan role," he says. "Temptation to disbelief and so on."

"Of course. Will he be happy with how it went?"

"It's anybody's guess."

He offers to take Murphy and Eva to dinner, by way of compensation. There's a place he knows on the Kansas side of the city. So now they glide over the wide Missouri, that storied waterway, and come to rest in a surpassingly nondescript postindustrial landscape such as one might find in any American city. But there's more here than empty lots and old warehouses. There's also Kansas City barbecue, the unique contribution of which is the burnt end. What you do is take the brisket out of the smoker, cut off the points, and put them back in until they get that delicious crust. Murphy orders three portions for himself, and fried okra too.

"Or really fried cherries," he says, spearing some okra. "And the cornbread is just more cherry cake."

Satan says, "I still don't understand why he's saying *cherry*."

"It's to illustrate that it's all fruits," Eva says. She looks glum and sounds glum, and who can blame her? The evening has been hard. "He's using *cherry* as a generic word for all fruits. It's a joke. He's trying to cheer me up."

Murphy nods and stuffs some burnt ends into his mouth. The food is so good that he already misses this place. Does that mean he's close to the memory horizon?

He turns to Satan and says, "It seems weird that you need to eat."

"Hush," says Eva.

"No," says Satan, "it's okay. It's a fair point. I actually don't need to eat. I just like it."

He chews heartily for a moment and then stops and appears to lose himself in some glum reflections of his own. Murphy goes on eating and eating. Eva stares at her hands and sighs. There's a country freshness in the air and the restaurant hums with activity. Fluffy 2 is asleep in the car.

"I didn't always look like this," says Satan. "I used to be so pretty. I looked like Ava Gardner."

EVER SINCE THEY began heading west, Murphy and Eva have been monitoring the roadside vegetation for signs of increasing aridity. Things are certainly changing, but it's not going to be the cathartic transformation they hope for. We've said this already. You don't burst through a wall of trees onto the golden grass of the steppe. So where does the West really begin? They've been traveling on I-64 and I-70, right along the boundary between the humid subtropical climate zone (Köppen climate classification *Cfa*) and the humid continental climate zone (Köppen climate classification *Dfa*), a boundary line that extends from east to west and to some extent separates the old slave states from the free states, which is not coincidental, since it loosely describes the boundaries of the cotton-growing region. Moving from east to west, we are indeed moving into an increasingly arid part of the country. We will eventually cross a north-south boundary with a third climate zone, the cold semiarid climate zone (Köppen climate classification *BSk*), which begins in western Kansas. Consider the following annual precipitation averages:

Louisville, Kentucky: 44.91 in.

St. Louis, Missouri: 40.96 in.

Kansas City, Missouri: 38.86 in.

Manhattan, Kansas: 35.69 in.

Salina, Kansas: 30.66 in.

Hays, Kansas: 23.45 in.

The Great American Desert is said to begin at the hundredth meridian, not far beyond Hays, so maybe that's the beginning of the West. Follow I-70 a little farther:

Denver, Colorado: 14.30 in.

Richfield, Utah: 8.34 in.

And if you go southwest:

Las Vegas, Nevada: 4.19 in.

But follow the hundredth meridian up to Canada and you see something interesting. Precipitation totals remain below twenty inches a year, which is often defined as the threshold for aridity, but you start to get forests again. That's because it's colder and the sun is less intense, so there's less evaporation.

Of course, climate change has distorted everything and these figures may already be meaningless. Alas, they're the only figures we have.

Tonight they camp in Paxico, Kansas (pop. 221), on the ninety-sixth meridian, east of Manhattan. Satan has long since bid them farewell. Murphy is beset by aches and pains, Eva is still brooding, and both of them are trying not to think of Yahweh and Yahweh's demands. Such thoughts are not easily set aside, however. After a sorrowful but disconcertingly vigorous sex scene, Eva lies naked and shivering on her sleeping bag and wonders how she can justify bringing children into

Yahweh's depraved and beautiful dream of a world. Murphy places a hand gently on her leg and thinks: If I lose her. If we have a child and something happens. If, if, if.

The next morning, for the first time, something seems different. There are cottonwoods and poplars and an oak on the road near their campsite. There are hills. There's even a kind of stream. There are no tumbleweeds. And yet there is also no birdsong, and even in the tent the air seems dusty and dry. When Murphy pokes his head out and sees their neighbor sleeping at his picnic table in the lavender dawn, he's looking at a tiny man under an endless sky, and he can sense the grassland out there rolling on ahead of them.

Eva is still asleep, so Murphy grabs a few dollars for coffee, slips out of the tent, pulls on his running shoes, and sets off at a leisurely pace. Is he at ease, despite everything? His legs are tight and his hips hurt and his feet feel terrible, but he tells himself that there's less pain than usual. When he gets to the gas station, however, and drinks a little cup of coffee, he is so impressed with himself for running at so reasonable a pace, and also, what's more, for interrupting his run to enjoy this coffee, and he's so impressed by the quiet of the morning, and the pale sky, that he makes the mistake of drinking a second cup of coffee. This is like pouring the liquor of aggravation directly into his soul, and it creates a psychic emergency. Now he has to run farther and more briskly, and soon the pain is almost more than he can bear. It's hard to have a body. The only thing worse is having a mind.

Eva is walking Fluffy 2 when Murphy limps back to camp. He has managed to quiet his nerves a little bit, and it's a good thing, because she's got her Bible out and she's in an unsteady mood.

"How about this," she says. "This is Judges 3:22. Judges is one of the most violent parts. 'And the haft also went in after the blade; and the fat closed upon the blade, so that he could not draw the dagger out of his belly; and the dirt came out.'"

"You shouldn't read that stuff. That stuff is bad for you."

"Then you've got Yahweh and the Israelites at odds with one another: 'And the children of Israel again did evil in the sight of the Lord, when Ehud was dead. And the Lord sold them into the hand of Jabin king of Canaan, that reigned in Hazor.'" She reads quietly for a moment. "Oh sure, well, I might have guessed: 'Then Jael Heber's wife took a nail of the tent, and took an hammer in her hand, and went softly unto him, and smote the nail into his temples, and fastened it into the ground: for he was fast asleep and weary. So he died.'"

"Who died?"

"One of the Canaanite generals. Sisera. He falls asleep from drinking milk."

"There's that *an* again. 'An hammer.'"

"They destroy Jabin at this point. And next comes the War Song of Deborah, which tells the same story again. 'She put her hand to the nail, and her right hand to the workmen's hammer; and with the hammer she smote Sisera, she smote off his head, when she had pierced and stricken through his temples.'"

"Does she fix his head in place by driving the nail through it, so she's able to smite it off more easily, or does she smite it off with the nail?"

"You'd have to ask the rabbis. But guess what happens after Jabin is destroyed?"

"Tell me."

"'And the children of Israel did evil in the sight of the Lord: and the Lord delivered them into the hand of Midian seven years.'"

She's thinking about these verses as they pack the car. A suspicion begins to dawn. What if Yahweh's purpose in sending her out to proselytize is not to make people aware of his name, not at all, but to trick them into contempt and disrespect so that he'll have an excuse to punish them later? Why else harden their hearts and stiffen their necks? Why else dispatch Satan to argue so vehemently against the very idea of religious faith? And there are lots of moments in the Bible when Yahweh seems to yearn for the destruction of mankind. What if that's his real goal, and there's just something about his programming that requires him to create a pretext?

Here's a fun fact about Kansas: An untethered hot-air-balloon ride is considered a form of transportation and isn't subject to the amusement tax. If you ride in the balloon while it's still attached to the earth, however, your ride is taxable.

Here's something else: When the railroads were just beginning to creep west in the second half of the nineteenth century, cowboys had to take their herds north from Texas to the various railheads up here on the High Plains. Townspeople in places like Dodge City and Abilene were afraid of these rambunctious Texans and occasionally hired notorious gunmen like Wild Bill Hickok to protect them, but there were also legal protections. There were strict gun control laws in the Wild West. Cowboys were not permitted to bring firearms of any kind into town.

Eva doesn't say anything this morning, except once when she's alarmed by the shape of a cloud and she says, "What the fuck is that?" and Murphy says, "Just a cloud," and she says, "Right, of course." Signs of increasing aridity are now everywhere to be seen.

.   .   .

In Salina, they leave the highway and drive north to the geographic center of the contiguous United States, which is located outside Lebanon, Kansas, just beyond the ninety-eighth meridian. Here in the heart of the heart of the country, you don't find Matt Damon, and you don't find an extradimensional machine filled with extradimensional shapes. You find a modest plaque, a shed marked "U.S. Center Chapel," and a homemade sign that says "Lebanon Has Souvenirs." The sky is like a dusty eggcup and the grass is already blond after a dry spring. There are cynical observations to be made about all of this emptiness, the rotten heart of the Union, etc., but in fact there is a vast peacefulness out here. If this is what the United States is *at heart*— a place where you can hear the locusts click in the dry grass, a place where you can hear yourself think—then things are better than we imagined.

They eat granola for lunch once again. Murphy calls it cherries and peas. Eva is absorbed by her phone, which bothers him. He tries to tell her something that he learned recently about *On the Road*—another book, dear notional child, that you can only read when you're young, and maybe not even then. It was published in the late fifties, Murphy says, just after the Interstate Highway System was authorized, which means that the world it describes, the two-lane America of the late forties, was already disappearing. It was always about nostalgia.

But Eva isn't interested. She's typing something. Murphy turns away in irritation. It could be a text message!

"Is *On the Road* as misogynistic as it seems?" he says. "For Dean, the end result of treating women so poorly is despair and misery."

Once again Eva says nothing.

"But for my money, *Huckleberry Finn* is the greatest American road novel."

"Or *Moby-Dick*," says Eva, surprising him.

She isn't sending a text message, not that there's anything reprehensible about doing so. What she's doing is looking at her checking account balance. There's a teller transaction dated yesterday—one hundred million dollars have been credited to her account. She keeps counting the zeroes. She logs out and logs in again. A chill passes over her. The dry wind lifts her hair up and sets it down.

The old brick buildings on Main Street in Lebanon are all empty. The windows are broken or boarded up. The Peoples Bank is just a mobile home with a tattered awning. This is how it is all across the plains, from here to Denver. Lebanon is a community of 218 people, according to the 2010 census, and this is down from a twentieth-century high of 822 in 1920—a loss of about 75 percent. All these Kansan towns are emptying out in the same dramatic way, and this phenomenon is called "rural flight." Only 8.4 percent of Lebanon residents are college-educated, for example, and that's because kids who go away to college do not return to their isolated hometown. The place is almost entirely white, although census data indicates that 0.5 percent of the population is Native American and 0.5 percent is Asian, whatever "Asian" means out here. It's disconcerting to think that 0.5 percent of 218 works out to a single lonely person, but it's more disconcerting that the figure given for foreign-born residents is just 0.3 percent—*less* than one person. How have the census people managed to arrive at this figure? Is it a foreigner with a few American-made prostheses? We wouldn't trust an American-made prosthesis. Give us an Asian one any day.

Eva and Murphy are rich. We don't know yet what it means, and Eva has chosen to say nothing. She gazes into the middle distance. She shivers. She's experiencing the exhilarating uncanny out-of-body sensations of the lottery winner.

Unaware of their momentous windfall, Murphy continues to chatter inconsequentially. He says that the Prius is their *Pequod*, and Yahweh must be the White Whale, at least in the sense that he means something and they don't know what. But who's Ahab?

"Fluffy 2 is Ahab," says Eva. "Look at those eyes."

It's the silence that impresses you. And the empty space. And the towering blue sky. Some ecologists have suggested that we give up and surrender the Great Plains to the buffalo. This is part of a larger "rewilding" movement in which we would very much like to believe, except that the famously giant herds of buffalo, so remarkable to the first Euro-American explorers, might have been a recent anomaly caused by the die-off of indigenous Americans or, alternatively, by the disappearance of the buffalo's natural predators and competitors. After all, those same indigenous Americans had hunted most of the large American mammals to extinction ten thousand years before, which is to say that the prehuman plains are gone forever, and although the past is always irrecoverable, it's particularly irrecoverable in this case. We're lucky we even have the buffalo. Euro-Americans came close to exterminating this majestic creature in the nineteenth century. They destroyed the culture of the Plains Indians in the process.

A young man in a Cargill hat stumbles out of the saloon and looks at them with a puzzled expression. Murphy says hello. The man waits a beat and then responds, "Outstanding. How are you?" They gaze at each other across a vast sociocultural divide, and there's nothing whatsoever to say, but they're both trying to think of something. Then the man gestures at Fluffy 2 and asks, "What the hail kind of animal is that?" Murphy says he doesn't know. The man raises his eyebrows. The two of them now squat to examine Fluffy 2. They reach no conclusion, but they part in friendship.

A hundred million dollars. But in the context of the morning's fears, Eva's excitement quickly begins to fade. It's no good pretending that she has won the lottery. The money is a gift from Yahweh, and even if he doesn't intend to destroy mankind, his gift almost certainly means trouble. At the very least, they're now obliged to buy Mount Trashmore and build his ludicrous temple.

And still she says nothing to Murphy, who's now explaining that chocolate is just mashed peas, like peanut butter, which means you're allowed to have a chocolate-and-banana sandwich for lunch.

"Are you going to keep it up with this food classification stuff?" Eva says.

"At first I was joking, but now I think I'm on to something. I should submit a restaurant review using this system. 'Try the cherries with cherry sauce. It's great with a glass of fermented cherry juice.'"

Eva presses her hands together and frowns. She's feeling unwell, and her diet of dry roasted cherries and peas doesn't help.

"I need some acidity," she says. "I need a kiwi or something. I feel like I'm full of free radicals."

They pile into the *Pequod* and continue north to US 36, the road that will take them into the West. A sign says, "Control Disease. Register Your Farm or Ranch." Another says, "Crossroads of Yesteryear." There's a landmark, but it's closed. They listen to the radio as they go. A young black American sings about how much money he has, and the struggle he went through to get his hands on that money, and the resentment that people tend to feel toward him. Eva, who is also rich, listens for clues and tips, but there isn't much overlap with her own experience. The singer reflects that no matter how much money he has, he is always who he is, which could be taken to mean that the money won't change him—Eva, too, plans to remain the same person with the same values—but actually sounds more like a lament. No matter what he accomplishes, he says, he'll always be a black man in America. His extraordinary achievement is a reminder that ordinary, modest achievement is not possible for many of his peers, no matter how hard they work. The system is rigged against them. The attainment of wealth looks like an accidental, undeserved, anomalous event—another of Yahweh's whims. Thus their resentment, and thus his own anguished feelings about success.

They eat chocolate-dipped cones at the Dairy Queen in Norton, Kansas. This relatively prosperous town (pop. 2,928) has a functioning grain elevator and a Jamboree Foods and a yarn store and a Hidden Dragon Chinese restaurant where you can get Beef on a Sticks (8) for $5.55. There's a defunct Conoco with a green peaked roof, but otherwise there aren't many registered trademarks to be seen. Businesses are owned and operated by individual humans: Moffet Drug, J & R Liquor, Walter Motor Company, Boxler Insurance Agency.

"So what's this?" says Eva, holding up her ice cream. "According to your new system."

Easy: The cone is cherries. The chocolate is mashed peas. And the ice cream is made from milk, which is a kind of honey, because honey is the substance that animals make to feed themselves and their young. This is frozen honey foam served in a cherry cup with mashed peas.

Now they visit the Jamboree Foods, where Eva anxiously watches her fellow mortals and feels as never before the weakness of the human position. Here's a Central American teenager eating potato chips at the cash register; here's a big round lady drawing a purple sweater out of her purse like a clown with an endless handkerchief; here's Murphy himself, limping a little and grabbing at his back each time he bends over. Secular humanism teaches that we have a responsibility to take care of one another, and the money, the dangerous God-given money, seems to heighten the importance of that obligation.

"He giveth," Eva mutters. "Sure he does. And then he taketh away."

While Murphy investigates the produce section, she strolls up and down the aisles and asks patrons if they've heard the name of the Lord, which is Yahweh. After a little while she's just saying "Yahweh, Yahweh, Yahweh" in a continuous dreary chant, and a little girl starts following her, also chanting "Yahweh, Yahweh, Yahweh," and this drives her out of her mind with anxiety.

Murphy walks outside and sniffs the dusty air. He wonders what it would be like to settle down here in Norton. They could buy a house for three hundred dollars, eat cold honey foam in the Kansan sun, and spend their time gazing meaningfully down the empty streets. But do they have hospitals and schools in Kansas? He read somewhere that they've all closed.

They drive west into the flat empty country, and a few minutes later they cross the hundredth meridian. The agriculture that's happening out here is dryland agriculture, with the center-pivot irrigation systems that make those perfectly circular green fields so marvelous to the children—tiny humans who have not yet lost their capacity for wonder—who peer down at them from airplanes. They have entered what Wallace Stegner called the "geography of hope," thus distinguishing it from the geography of realistic expectation. The grass is parched and golden, and the sun is hot, and the clouds are small and round and hung with great care at the same height in the big blue sky. It's so quiet that it's possible to appreciate the fact that it's never perfectly quiet. They step out of the car to stand for a moment in the ecstatic loneliness.

Part II

ey now have. Yahweh has allowed her

Murphy, who now seems a little more
ned. "Great fortunes always come from
d anything."

opus should be octopodes, not octopi,
ot a Latin word. But in language there
's only usage, and if we take usage as a
not only octopi but octopuses. Another
st by the way, is that octopodes don't
parents, which is maybe why they can't
ven though they're very smart. There's
igence.

y the care with which the waiters time
t the Palace Arms, they don't surprise
rything is to your liking, nor do they
ur dining companion is still eating.
rtesy, and Eva tests them.
f the Lord?" she says to a busboy. "It's
ng me."

ce such as only the most hard-hearted

Eva, "but couldn't you humor a well-
ead and share the name of the Lord

ittle while to get to that."
h her, and she wonders if this could
t vexes poor mad Saul and so many

RELIGION AND RELIGIOUS devotion are strictly proscribed by secular humanism, but as Murphy and Eva have already established, Yahweh himself, Yahweh the conscious being, is only what he is, and if he exists, then he exists as mountains exist, and neutrinos, and his nature is accessible to rational inquiry. In this sense, he is no threat to a secular humanist worldview. He is simply a wondrous thing to ponder.

We have speculated about his circuitous designs, and we have wondered about the means by which he achieves or fails to achieve those designs, but we have yet to inquire into the nature of his consciousness, in some mysterious crevice of which those designs are presumably born. Thoughtful people have suggested that consciousness is just an epiphenomenon of information processing, which is to say that it emerges organically. Construct a brain, they'll tell you, and a mind will follow. If this is true, and we don't see why it should be, but if it's true, does it mean that consciousness is a phenomenon that always tends to have the same features, whatever the underlying physical structure that produces it? Does Yahweh experience consciousness in the same way that we do, even if he's made of dark matter and we're made of luminous/reflective matter? Or are his thoughts just the skin on a bottomless pudding, hardly implicated at all in his real activities, whatever they are, and does this explain why what he says is so often at odds with what he does? But humans are like that too.

And what about the Internet? Could it become conscious one day? Would its consciousness resemble our own, and would it therefore be murder to destroy it?

A hundred million dollars: It's unsettling and miraculous, but it's something that has happened, a phenomenon, a real event.

"A hundred million?" says Murphy.

He'd like to be the kind of person who takes this in stride, but he needs time to work through it. Somehow the money is more incredible to him than the apparition of God and his angels.

Very slowly, he says, "It's only fair. You're working hard. You're doing a consequential job. There are people in far less important positions who make a lot more. Think of finance people."

It's six o'clock. They're on the street in downtown Denver. Nineteenth-century town houses stand alone in parking lots, surrounded by municipal buildings and glass skyscrapers. The mountains loom in the west. The day has been hot, but the evening is cool, in which respect Denver is like the moon. Even here, in the heart of the city, the air has that aromatic western backcountry smell. It reminds Murphy of childhood vacations in Oregon and California, and it reminds Eva of "Howl."

"Even finance people have moms and dads," Murphy adds.

The streets are thronged with people. There has been a demonstration outside the state capitol. Excited young protestors rush by with their signs.

Murphy says, "We'll love our children even if they go into finance."

money, and money is what th
to trick herself.

"This is how it works," say
comfortable with what's happe
Yahweh. No one ever deserve

The correct plural form of oct
since octopus is a Greek and n
is no correct or incorrect, there
guide, we are forced to accept
interesting thing, and this is ju
live long and never know their
progress, culturally speaking, e
more to intelligence than intell

You can tell a fancy restaurant b
their visits to your table. Here a
you mid-mouthful to ask if eve
whisk your plate away while y
But there are limits to their cou

"Have you heard the name o
Yahweh. Just nod if you're heari

He doesn't nod. He makes a f
of busboys would make.

"I know it's unpleasant," says
meaning stranger and just go ah
on social media?"

He says, "It might take me a l

A spasm of fear passes throug
be the evil spirit of the Lord tha
others.

She says, "He's going to feed you to the birds of the air and the beasts of the field! Just listen to me! Just listen! The days draw near! And the fulfillment of every vision!"

After dinner they take a walk in the cool western air. Fluffy 2 strolls insouciantly before them, swinging his tail, looking left and right. It's a pleasant evening, and soon Eva feels less fretful. But the large plaza in front of the capitol building, so recently the site of inspiring demonstrations, is now full of drunks and suspicious characters, and it's Murphy's turn to be fretful. Never mind that he's a suspicious character in his own right, with his beard and his limp and his darting movements. He suggests that they get out of here and visit the Verizon store.

It may be that he intends to buy a new phone, despite his insistence that phonelessness is his preferred condition. In fact we're almost certain that this is his intention. But first, while Eva is off peering at iPads, he means to have a little joke. Murphy the prankster. He summons a Verizon employee and gives him a coy little smile. Could it be, he asks, that there's something wrong with his current phone? He flourishes this smooth piece of phone-shaped wood and the young man stares at it in disbelief. He isn't in a whimsical mood and he doesn't find Murphy's joke funny, nor does he bother to hide his irritation. This irritates Murphy, who now resolves to make life difficult for him.

"I'm wondering if you can get the data off this thing," Murphy says.

"The data?"

"Sure."

"Like tree-ring data?"

"Pictures and so on. I know it looks like wood, but I think the data is probably still on there somewhere."

"A wooden phone."

"There are some pictures I really care about on there."

The young man is at a loss. Eventually the manager has to intervene, and Murphy guesses that it isn't the first time she's had to mediate between this sullen employee and a dissatisfied customer. The manager apologizes for any confusion and suggests that there may be a misunderstanding here. The root of the problem, she says, holding Murphy's phone in her palm, is that Murphy's phone is made of wood. They actually don't have the ability to service it here at the Verizon store.

"Yeah," says Murphy. "I was worried about that. I thought that might be an issue."

Eva is standing with her hands in her pockets, watching people come and go on the sidewalk outside. Could they settle down here in this vibrant multiethnic city? Could they buy a bungalow in the shade of these extraordinary mountains, plant a peach tree, and eat buffalo? Lines from "Howl" flutter around in her head. Backyard green tree cemetery dawns. Ashcan rantings. Supercommunist pamphlets. Who watched over Denver & brooded & loned in Denver. Waving genitals and manuscripts. Listening to the Terror through the wall.

It's a road-trip poem, after all. But now her reverie is interrupted by loud voices. Murphy, she realizes, is causing trouble. There's no time for this kind of behavior. She walks over there and tells him so.

"This kid has a bad attitude," he says.

"I do," says the Verizon employee. "He's right. I can't stand our customers. The customers are so *offensive* to me."

Eva turns to the manager and explains, "Yahweh turned the phone to wood. Yahweh is the name of the Lord. Tell your friends."

The manager nods politely.

Eva continues, "We're sorry about this. You guys are doing a great job."

"I'm not," says the employee. "But I don't think I behaved all that badly just now, under the circumstances."

The manager says, "Thanks for visiting us. Come back soon."

Tonight they're going to treat themselves to a hotel room. They find a modest place called the Front Range Inn, affirming meanwhile that a modest hotel is perfectly fine. There's no need to stay in a really fancy place. They smuggle Fluffy 2 up in a duffel bag and collapse in exhaustion on the vast blue bedspread. Prompted by additional helpful e-mails, Eva donates a few more hunks of money to humanitarian causes and organizations. It's easy—her payment information is already on file.

After such a day, after the last few days, what can they do but stare vacantly at a movie until exhaustion overcomes them? There are lots of movies available, as always. They pour like neutrinos out of the western sky. Unfortunately, tonight's movie takes up the very subject they're trying to ignore, i.e. our relationship to our putative creator or creators. In this film, the creator figures are alien beings from a distant planet, although it may not be correct to call them aliens. They are genetically indistinguishable from humans. The differences are phenotypic—they lack body hair and they are titanic in stature. In any case, Swedish actress Noomi Rapace and her fellow cast members have determined the location of their creators' world, and they undertake an interstellar expedition in order to learn everything they can. After landing on this remote planet, which at first appears to be uninhabited, the cast makes many unaccountably poor decisions and suffers a sequence of reversals and setbacks, nor does it help that Michael Fassbender, the ship's android, has a secret agenda. Their misfortunes reach a climax when Michael Fassbender discovers a sleeping pod in which one last alien survives. Using techniques familiar to lovers of historical linguistics, he has reconstructed an ancient language in which he thinks it should be possible to communicate with the alien. A conversation with such a being may reveal important information about our origins, although one can only guess what this means to Michael Fassbender, who has been created not by the aliens but by the creatures who were created by the aliens.

Murphy finds a tennis ball under the bed. He lies on his back and tries to toss it straight up in the air, so that it lands in his palm without him having to reach for it.

"Let's turn this off," he says. "Or let's see if there's basketball."

But Eva is absorbed in the story. She reminds Murphy that there are titans all over the Judeo-Greco mythscape. There are titans in the Bible. Yahweh appears to have created them, or else they are the product of miscegenation between humans and angels. Yahweh destroys them in the flood—a genocidal program in which all but a handful of the Earth's humans also perish.

The cast succeeds in reanimating the alien, but no conversation is possible, alas. He is enraged and immediately pulls Michael Fassbender's head off. Then he murders several other actors, powers up his spaceship, and tries to fly away. No doubt he intends to make his way to Earth, there to fulfill a cherished ambition: To destroy all humans. Luckily, the handsome English actor Idris Elba and two of his friends are willing to undertake a kamikaze attack on the alien craft, thus making the ultimate sacrifice and saving humanity, at least for now. But there's another threat, a philosophical threat, because we must ask ourselves why our putative creators should have wanted to destroy us in the first place. Noomi Rapace, who is recovering quickly from an emergency procedure during which yet another variety of alien was removed from her uterus, decides to seek an explanation among the stars. She is assisted by Michael Fassbender's head, which has repented of its earlier betrayals. Its impressive intellectual faculties have not been impaired, thank heavens, by the loss of its body.

Eva turns the television off and stares at the blank screen, thinking of Yahweh and Yahweh's deeds. The correspondences with the film are inexact but suggestive. Her fear, as noted, is that Yahweh, too, is frequently vexed by the suspicion that it might be better to destroy all humans. A troubling thought on this cool night in the West, and she feels a big prophet's love for all those people out there, yacketayakking screaming vomiting, as Ginsberg says, and whispering facts and memories and anecdotes, oh sure, and eyeball kicks and shocks of hospitals and jails and wars.

"The United States," she says, "that coughs all night and won't let us sleep."

But she and Fluffy 2 fall asleep quickly. It's Murphy who lies awake. He's worrying about creation, as so many humans have also worried, millennium after millennium. He knows that it's no problem to make a thing that looks like a person. He has already given his recipe: tube, pincers, kazoo, tent pegs, electrical jelly, sensors. What he's worried about is reproduction, which requires a mechanism of inheritance. If the idea is to make something that can make more of itself, and if you do this by encoding the organism's operating and assembly instructions in a chemical data chain like DNA, then the thing that can make more of itself is not the organism but the DNA. The assembled creature, complete with pincers and kazoo, is just a strutting android that the DNA manufactures in order to facilitate its replication.

The moon is full in the big window. The city is quiet. The mountains march away, north and south. Murphy's thoughts run to distortion and caricature. Eventually he takes a Benadryl and has banal dreams.

YAHWEH GREETS THEM in the quiet chill of the morning. He's in the back seat of the *Pequod*, where he's using a curling iron to press charred ruffles into some of the collard leaves. Meaningless destruction. He has inserted the power cord into his mouth.

"Cut it out," says Eva.

He grins, but he doesn't release the cord, which hangs from his teeth like a noodle.

"I'm serious. Some of us need to eat those."

He tosses the curling iron into the dust and commands them to go south. That's all he came to say. The Southwest is an arid waste, a zone of desolation. Which appeals to him very much.

Eva turns to Murphy and says, "I had a dream that a giant almond was attacking me. Lindsey Graham promised he would help, but he did nothing."

.   .   .

Now begins a period of wearisome activity, and Yahweh comes and goes throughout the next week, checking on their progress. He's with them in Colorado Springs, where he says, "My own people act toward me like a bird of prey. But I am going to feed them wormwood and make them drink a bitter draft."

In Springer, New Mexico, he pulls down a traffic light and causes an accident.

In Roswell, where everything is alien this and alien that, he has a crack-up, just like a human, weeping into Fluffy 2's fur and saying that he's lost Ishtar, that nobody knows his name, that Baal is more popular, that nobody will ever love and respect him as the Israelites once loved and respected him.

"My suffering!" he says. "They drink wrongdoing like water. They worship Baal and they're happy."

Eva wedges a collard leaf into her mouth and chews viciously. "Nobody's happy."

They aren't allowed to plot their own route. In this respect, at the very least, they've lost their power of self-determination. Yahweh is there in person to hustle them to the next town, or else he speaks from the radio, or else his angels come pinging out of mailboxes or trash cans and instruct them to turn around and go back the way they've come. The itinerary that emerges is maddening, circuitous, pointless.

They pass through Indian reservations. The dusty land, the small breeze-block houses, the unfamiliar formatting of the road signs. These are whole nations confined to the most desolate and marginal corners of this desolate and marginal countryside. Yahweh loves to remove people from the land their ancestors have occupied for centuries, he loves dispossession and exile, he loves violence, but so, of course, do human beings, and although it's fashionable to argue that most indigenous Americans died of disease as Euro-Americans overran these continents, that's just an attempt to shift the blame unambiguously to Yahweh. The truth is that Euro-Americans killed as many indigenous Americans as they could, whenever they could, and they did it with glee. Consider the Sand Creek Massacre, which took place in Colorado in 1864. A detachment of U.S. soldiers under John Chivington murdered as many as two-hundred Cheyenne and Arapaho, most of them women and children, in a surprise attack rendered especially surprising by the fact that the victims were living there under the explicit protection of the U.S. Army. Murder, once again, under the white flag of truce. And these things happened again and again. They had been happening for centuries. Francisco Vásquez de Coronado rode through these lands in the sixteenth century and murdered everyone he saw. Why? The course of history is as witless and maddening as Murphy and Eva's route through the high desert.

When they drive through Las Cruces, New Mexico, they learn that the employees of a local distillery have no fingerprints. It's because they have to handle hot metal all the time.

When they visit the Melodrama Grocery in Whites City, they learn that the whole town is being sold at auction.

When they stop to have a look at the White Sands Desert, the world's largest gypsum dunefield, Yahweh is strutting around with a Gatorade and a cockeyed grin, and he's saying, "I've just had a fight with Hephaestus."

Smokey Bear is buried in Capitan, New Mexico.

Murphy peers out the window at the twisted conifers and aromatic desert plants. He doesn't know what mesquite is and doesn't bother to look it up, but he wonders if that's what he's seeing out there. He remembers a plant called "ocotillo" from Cormac McCarthy's acclaimed 1992 novel *All the Pretty Horses*, which, like every western, is about the end of the Old West. There is riotous greenery along the small rivers and creeks, and cactuses of every shape and degree of armament. Sometimes there are Joshua trees—a picturesque type of yucca named for a biblical figure instrumental in the expulsion of the Canaanites from the land their ancestors had occupied for centuries.

They attend a rodeo. This is an American ritual in which impoverished young men are trampled by large animals and then clowns dance around their broken bodies. Eva is horrified, but Murphy can't stop laughing. His laughter comes at the wrong times and is regarded, with perfect justice, as inappropriate and even obscene. The man sitting next to them tells him to shut the fuck up. This fellow has a T-shirt that reads "Beauty is in the Eye of the Beer-Holder."

They're in line at Dairy Queen when Murphy looks up in alarm and says, "What about Jesus?"

"Big problem," Eva agrees.

"He protects us from Yahweh?"

"That's the idea."

"He mediates a little bit."

"It's definitely a comforting idea," Eva says.

"My question is, What is he?"

"That's what I'm saying. Who knows? That's the big problem."

"Is he a god?"

"In Luke, he's only a prophet."

"That's good."

"And there were early Christians who said he was a god," Eva says, "but he was his *own* god. He wasn't associated with Yahweh."

"That's good too."

"It would even be okay if he really were Yahweh's only son."

"Because then," Murphy says, "Yahweh's decision to murder him is bizarre and tragic and just exactly the kind of thing that Yahweh would do."

"The trouble is when you say that Jesus is God."

"Exactly. And that's what everyone says."

"It's a problem because in that case," says Eva, "his death means nothing."

General William Tecumseh Sherman, who was named for an indigenous American and famous for brutality, wrote the following lines at the beginning of the war with the Sioux, shortly after the Sand Creek Massacre: "I will say nothing and do nothing to restrain our troops from doing what they deem proper on the spot, and will allow no more vague general charges of cruelty and inhumanity to tie their hands."

But the Sioux were also riding through the West murdering the peaceable Crow and Mandan. This is just what it is to be human. The strong versus the weak. The terror in the grass. Is it Yahweh's fault? Do erring and causing to err come, as Job alleges, from him? Both Chivington and Coronado claimed to be acting in God's name. Everywhere we turn, it seems, we run into the free-will problem. Satan, whose own existence disproves his thesis, argues that there are no gods and that the universe should seem like a less forbidding place as a result—a system without agency. But if this were true, and we were entirely free to do as we pleased, and Yahweh were only a story we told in order to explain our own vileness, then it would mean that there is no explanation for our vileness. In this respect, it's a comfort to surrender what agency we have and lay the blame at Yahweh's feet. Easier to say that when we cut our enemies from their horses and mutilate their bodies, we do so only at his behest.

.   .   .

Eva tries to set up Yahweh's social media accounts. She posts incomprehensible Bible verses. His followers are mostly robots and white supremacists.

Meanwhile, she speaks his name in every town and hamlet of the American Southwest. She is met almost universally with scorn, and occasionally with derision. Even ostensibly pious people are upset by the spectacle of a young woman shouting the name of the Lord. Their hearts are hard and their necks are stiff.

Sometimes she speaks, as the prophets so often speak, in a kind of ecstasy: "The president has clothed himself in desolation. Now calamity shall follow calamity, and rumor shall follow rumor. And then you'll know that Yahweh is the Lord."

But sometimes she's all too aware of her predicament: "Please, everyone just listen. You don't know him like I know him. He's going to do something terrible to you! Please be alert! Share this warning on your social networks!"

And sometimes confusion overtakes her. She gestures and walks in little circles.

"Hello?" says Murphy. "Yes? Are you there?"

"It was almost time for lunch," she says. "Pain is human. There were roses in the cool café."

In the context of all this confusion and turmoil, it's a relief to discover that they are Mr. and Mrs. Pierce again in Phoenix. Yahweh has instructed them to attend a dinner and presentation at the Orizon Institute, a think tank of some kind, but it's Satan who meets them in the reception area to give them their badges. Unfortunately, he can't stay and chat. He has another errand in Phoenix tonight.

"You have to go so soon?" says Eva. "Right away?"

She looks devastated. Murphy, too, is unhappy. Satan frowns and chews his lip. He doesn't like to leave them like this.

"I'll teach you a trick," he says. "I'll teach you an incantation that will protect against despair. If things are dark, and I'm not around to help, you can repeat it a few times and it'll help. I assume you speak Hebrew?"

Eva shakes her head.

"You don't speak Hebrew?" He seems incredulous. "Are you sure?"

"Sorry."

"No need to apologize. Let's see. The translation would go something like this: 'The world is a narrow bridge, and the most important thing is not to be afraid.'"

Murphy and Eva both repeat this very slowly. Eva says, "That's lovely."

Satan nods. "Just repeat it to yourself when things are bad. You could try different translations too. 'Do not make yourself afraid, the whole world is a narrow bridge.' It would really be better if you knew Hebrew."

Before he goes, he tells them that they can reach him any time by picking up a pay phone. Then he bows deeply. He's singing "Angel of the Morning" as he passes through the revolving doors.

They don't recognize anyone from Winston-Salem, but lots of people recognize them. How nice to relax with people who know who they are! Even if that's not who they are. Murphy has a chummy exchange with a breathless fellow in a broad green vest. He says he's hosting a benefit next month to raise awareness about private jet crashes. He'd be honored if Pierce would attend.

"Did you say jet crashes?" says Murphy.

"After heart disease, that's the number one killer of CEOs."

"The not-so-silent killer."

"My point is that if you consider the degree of public sympathy and awareness, it's pretty silent."

Murphy nods, gracious Murphy. "I'd be happy to come to your party."

Everyone seems to want something from the Pierces. Shadowy people accost Eva and try to win her support for one or another tawdry scheme. Here, for example, is a man in two-tone shoes and a sleek blue suit. He tells her he'd like to get in a room with her husband.

"I've been in a room with him," says Eva. "He's a lovely person, but I don't want to oversell that particular aspect of it."

"There's that Jane Pierce wit. But seriously, I do have an intriguing matter to discuss. I'd just like to get in a room with him for ten minutes."

"A hundred bucks and I'll arrange it. Do you have any preference as far as what he's wearing?"

This fellow will not be distracted. He says, "You're too much, Jane. There's that wit I've heard about. But would you just do me this favor? Would you tell him that Igor Morales wants to talk about aluminum? He'll know what that means."

Murphy looks through the vast window at the eastern end of the reception area. Then he turns around and looks through the window at the western end. Then he turns around again. To Fluffy 2, who has been allowed to join them inside, he says, "There doesn't seem to be any weather out here." And it's true, in a sense. This is the Sonoran Desert (Köppen climate classification BWh—a hot desert), and for much of the year it sits beneath a cap of warm subsiding air, which prevents convective storms from forming. Phoenix receives only 8.03 inches of precipitation per year, the distortions of climate change notwithstanding. This total is far below the threshold at which agriculture is said to be possible, although the sophisticated Hohokam built extensive irrigation systems here, including many miles of canals, before ecological disaster drove them from the region. Thus the name Phoenix—a city that rises from the ashes of these former settlements.

Eva is also thinking about heat, and not just because they're in the desert. She and Murphy heard a strange thing about heat and time on NPR today. She seeks out a mathematician and asks for clarification.

"The idea is that heat doesn't move from hot things to cold things as a rule," says the mathematician. "It's only very probable that it moves from hot things to cold things."

"Because it's just particles in random motion? Random collisions?"

"Right. And heat transfer is the only way you can tell the difference between the past and future, so if heat transfer is probabilistic, then you can argue that time is a probabilistic phenomenon."

Eva frowns. "Time doesn't pass unless it's hot?"

"We're talking about entropy. Think of it in those terms. The most likely thing is that the universe moves from a low-entropy state to a high-entropy state, because the number of possible high-entropy states is much greater than the number of possible low-entropy states. For example, take the atoms in an egg. You can arrange them in lots of different ways, and not so many of those arrangements have the macroscopic appearance of an egg."

"What does that have to do with heat?"

"Put it this way: The Big Bang is a very low-entropy state, and you can tell that time has passed since then because entropy has increased. Entropy is where you get the arrow of time. It's the only way you can tell the difference between the past and future."

"But what about heat transfer?"

"Heat transfer or entropy. Either way."

"You're saying that in the distant future, it's *unlikely* that there are any eggs."

"Exactly."

But if time is only a matter of chance, or, more generally, if it doesn't exist in the way it appears to exist, then there is no cause and effect, and thus no action and intention. The free-will conundrum is soluble after all. In such a world, violence does not happen because Yahweh wills it. Instead, there is no will. There are no decisions. There is only all of it all at once, just as it is. But maybe this can only be true in very cold places.

Now it's time to file into the auditorium for tonight's presentation. The speaker is Dexter Philpot, CEO of Beyond Human, who will talk to us about genetic enhancement. Fluffy 2 and an aggrieved cocker spaniel are left in the care of an animal nanny.

"Did they say 'genetic enhancement'?" Murphy whispers as they take their seats. "Is he going to talk about genetically engineering people?"

"That's what this is all about."

So it's Murphy, not Eva, who gets up during the question period.

"As I'm sure you've observed," he says, in the weary tone of a school-master dressing down his barbarous pupils, "humans are wretched and depraved. Why would you trust such a creature to mess around with its genetic instructions, which are what made it wretched and depraved in the first place?"

Dexter Philpot laughs and says, "I wouldn't put it quite like that, but I do worry, sure. We're being cautious."

Eva says, "And plus, have you heard the name of the Lord, which is Yahweh?"

Quite unexpectedly, Igor Morales says, "You'll be his people, and he'll be your god."

The genial Mr. Philpot doesn't think God bothers very much with this stuff. He argues that DNA is just another aspect of our physical reality. Genetic engineering is therefore no more ungodly than abdominal surgery. Would you refuse an appendectomy on religious grounds? All of this is distinct and separate from the idea of our incorporeal souls, in which he also believes.

Murphy says, "I don't want to be there when you tell Yahweh what he does and doesn't bother with."

Igor Morales says, "Some people *would* refuse an appendectomy on those grounds."

Eva laughs and begins to say something and then, instead of saying what she means to say, says, "The name of the Lord is Yahweh. The name of the Lord is Yahweh." She makes a face and looks around in confusion. "The name of the Lord is Yahweh."

Even if time is real and cause and effect can be depended upon, even if Yahweh himself permits us some freedom of action, there's the danger that we're only androids constructed by our DNA. And yet the situation is even more problematic than it seems. Put this in your pipe and smoke it: Our cells are full of mitochondria, with which we live symbiotically and upon which we are absolutely dependent for the manufacture of ATP, our energy-transport molecule. Mitochondria were once free-living prokaryotic organisms, and even now they have their *own* DNA. They are part of us, they are us, they are not us, without them we are inanimate clay. If free will exists, whose will is it that's free?

MURPHY'S BEARD IS coming in blond and red and black, a reflection of his mixed ethnic background. He tries to keep it pruned. Eva is tying her hair back in a faded blue bandana. They've got their collards in the back and now they've also got callaloo and purslane, although the callaloo isn't well suited to life in a terra-cotta pot. They're shouting Yahweh's name and they've got an animal with them that they can't identify at the species level. You have to concede that they look like wackos, but this is the West, the geography of hope, and they aren't the first wackos to cruise through here.

In an especially empty part of southern Arizona, all blushing mesas and vast tumbled rocky plains, they meet an old signalman who says that he too has known Yahweh face-to-face.

"It was a tough year when God came to supper each night," he says. He spits and shakes his head. He's a little careworn fellow in overalls.

"Ever night he said he wanted peach pie, and ever night my wife baked him one, and ever night he said, 'Where's my apple pie?' Everthing I earned was going for peaches. So one night he says he'd like peach pie and my wife makes him a apple pie and what does he say?"

"Where's my blueberry pie?" says Eva sadly.

He nods and squints off into the distance.

"Another day," James Schuyler writes, "another dolor." Now Yahweh tells Eva to bury her underwear under a rock. She does so. He tells her to dig it up again. She does so. "You will find it ruined," he says. She holds it up and sees that it's torn to shreds. He says, "Just so will I ruin the overweening pride of those who commit adultery with stone and wood."

Meanwhile, the prosaic business of life cranks on. They're rich. They continue to insist that they won't let the money change them, but it works its changes nonetheless. They pay their rent, which in effect makes their Miami apartment a storage unit for their computers and passports. They eat fancy food. Instead of washing their clothes, they buy new ones and donate the others to Goodwill. But somehow their clothes get more and more expensive. One day, as if by accident, Eva buys a pair of leather Dolce & Gabbana leggings for an astonishing $3,400. They're candy-apple red. It's a thrill to spend so much money on something she doesn't need or want, but it also makes her sick. She won't be able to do these things when they have a child. If they have a child. If nothing terrible happens. It will be important to teach this notional child that ostentatious display is crass and unpleasant. For now, though, she tells herself that the purchase is justifiable because these leggings will ultimately pass to a disadvantaged person at Goodwill. To that person, the leggings will seem like a miracle, and in a colloquial sense that will be true, since they proceed indirectly from Yahweh.

Sometimes they rent a lavish hotel suite in order use the shower. They give the name Pierce, although Eva's real name is on her credit card, and they check out after an hour or two. These nice hotels are a lot of fun, but they prefer sleeping in their tent. It gives them a deeper connection with the desert night. Its sounds, its subtle changes. They like their campgrounds, each one a little different and each one the same, and they like brushing their teeth by the spigot outside, and wearing sweatshirts in the clear cool air, and staring up at the appalling multitude of stars. And dawn is beyond description.

One afternoon, without warning, Eva writes a poem. It goes like this:

> I'd like to write a poem for Malcolm X,
> But I know he wouldn't want me to,
> So I won't.

She sets it down on receipt paper and hands it to Murphy without a word. She won't say anything about it, now or later.

There are moments these days when it does seem like they're out beyond the memory horizon. Moments when they seem to glimpse the present as it will appear from the vantage point of the future. A woman in a U-Haul smoking a joint and laughing. A tiny train crossing a red desert basin. The road rising into a green thunderhead. These things are clues, but now they understand that clues are just visions of what will remain in the mind's eye when everything else is forgotten.

Theologian and mystic Thomas Merton says that the desert is the country of madness—"A sterile paradise of emptiness and rage." "Thirst drives man mad," he writes, but even Satan, apparently doomed to wander in dry places, "is mad with a kind of thirst for his own lost excellence." It's hard to credit this assertion, knowing what we know of Satan, but there is indeed something unsettling about the austere beauty of these rocky places. The columns and pillars of red stone, the deep green of the river valleys, the abrupt canyon walls, the sunrise, the sunset, the martian plains. It's terrible to think that this beauty, like Eva's leggings, may proceed from Yahweh.

More clues: An apple on a fencepost. A coyote with a shoebox in its mouth. A sign that says, "Madrean Sky Islands."

All the songs on the radio are about staying up too late or dying too young.

Driving north again, at yet another angel's pointless behest, they stop at a bookstore in Scottsdale and sit wide-eyed as a physicist talks about black holes. The subject seems inevitable and urgent.

Black holes, he says, are punctures in the fabric of space-time, but they are also objects, and like other objects they collide. When this happens, an enormous amount of energy "comes off," more energy than is emitted by all the stars in the universe. Electromagnetic radiation cannot escape a black hole, which is why Matthew McConaughey requires an extradimensional machine to get his data out, so this energy "comes off" in the form of gravitational waves—perturbations in the fabric of space-time. Scientists recently detected gravitational waves from a collision that occurred three billion years ago.

Eva and Murphy sit in stunned silence, saying nothing and thinking nothing.

The physicist now makes a rapid series of claims, like a prizefighter finishing off an opponent who's unconscious on his feet. Chief among them is his assertion that we must now evaluate the theory of loop quantum gravity, which is an attempt to reconcile quantum theory with relativity. Once again black holes will be important. What we're looking for is one that's exploding. That will help us to figure out whether or not space-time is granular. It may be that quanta of space-time appear and disappear just like the elementary particles we so cherish.

"Ultimately," he says, "we'll want to know if black holes are hot."

The next morning, deranged by his exposure to so much science so close to bedtime, Murphy claims that he has "solved the problem" of his legs and feet. The problem is actually his shoes, and the solution is barefoot running. Why has he not considered this before? He explains the principle: Most athletic shoes are profligately cushioned, constricted in the toe box, and made with a significant heel-to-toe drop. The result is an unnatural posture and gait. The Achilles tendon is neutralized. The foot strikes the ground at the wrong angle. The force of each impact "rockets up and down the leg." It's like running in high heels.

"Look at me," he says, affecting a tottering posture. "I've got my hips kind of thrust forward and my upper body is collapsing on itself. It's an effort to hold my head up. As if it weren't hard enough already to hold my head up."

Since real barefoot running is impracticable in a country covered in broken glass and dog waste, he does the next best thing. He locates a cobbler who can make him a pair of minimalist running shoes. He pays the man two thousand dollars to rush the job, and because of the simplicity of the design, it only takes a few hours. The new shoes are like ballet slippers that flare out at the toes.

"You can guess my feelings about this," says Eva, leaning against the *Pequod*.

"But this is different. This is a *solution*."

"Go ahead and test them. See how they feel."

"They don't need testing." He gives her a smirk. "They're absolutely philosophically sound."

"Run around the block, though."

"All the way around the block?"

"Just run around the parking lot if you're afraid."

He runs around the parking lot. Immediately he can feel his feet, knees, hips, and back realigning, or so he imagines. It's a wonderful feeling, and painful, especially in the heels and calves. He will have to get used to it. But the process of getting used to it will in itself entail the working out of a cure. The pain is therefore the signal that soon there will be no pain.

Later, they're in a Home Depot parking lot eating chocolate-and-banana sandwiches—more cherries and peas—when an angel in chef's whites climbs out of a Dumpster and rebukes them for this day of idleness. He, or it, dictates some new driving directions. They are as chaotic and elliptical as always, but ultimately they describe a kind of circle with a radius of about fifty miles. So Murphy and Eva get back into the car and hum away into the desert. It's frustrating to drive and drive and not get anywhere, but today Eva is committed to the idea that a higher logic obtains. They have been traveling in circles for years, she tells herself. They have been wandering in the desert of their indecision. This whole trip is a figurative manifestation of their failure to make clear professional choices and get going in life. It makes perfect sense. She grips the wheel. Everything makes sense. The world is a narrow bridge. Struggle is meat. Never mind that the arrow of time exists only in the context of heat exchange. Never mind that heat exchange is a matter of particles bopping around at random.

Now they endure some long days on the American road. Signs encourage motorists to "Crush Smokes." Someone is offering "Foreclosure Tours." Here you can buy "Guns + Jewelry," and here you get "Free Rodeo Tickets w/ Wrangler Purchase." They listen to NPR and the news is bad. Protests swell across the nation.

One day Fluffy 2 says, "What if I spoke a single articulate sentence, and no one ever mentioned it?"

One day Yahweh corners Eva and says, "You've disrespected me and disobeyed my commands. On every high hill and under every verdant tree, you recline as a whore."

Eva has no idea what he means. He keeps talking about prostitution. She asks for clarification.

"I told you not to eat Oreos," Yahweh says.

"Oreos?"

"You disobeyed me! You defiled my land and made my possession abhorrent!"

"I never ate any, though."

"I forbade it!"

"You never said anything about Oreos!"

"Obedience," he says, leaning close and speaking in a hoarse whisper, with more than a little threat of sexual violence, "is better than the fat of rams."

. . .

The episode is soon forgotten. The next day, the three of them are in Munds Park watching basketball at Pinewoodys Pizza & Grill, which is not to be confused with the Pinewood Bar & Grill on the other side of the highway, or the Pinewood Restaurant. The playoffs are drifting toward their conclusion and the importance of staying aggressive does not need to be emphasized. Alas, Yahweh decides to manipulate the outcome. He gives one player a sneezing fit. He blows out another player's knee.

The commentator says, "You have to treat this game like a game seven."

"I love this," says Yahweh.

The commentator says, "You talk about the high screen-and-roll."

An elfin player hits shot after improbable shot and gestures at the roof in what appears to be a show of gratitude to some benevolent divinity. Yahweh doesn't trust that he is the intended recipient of this gratitude and strikes the player down with an ankle sprain.

"Who set the wild ass free?" he says. "Who begot the dewdrops?"

Murphy runs and runs in his new shoes. Take the weight in the arch, he tells himself. Land with a bent knee. It feels as if the bones in his feet are being ground to pebbles as he goes, and he registers this pain with a kind of satisfaction, believing as he does that every jolt presages a return to orthopedic health. The pain has assumed a progressive character and he jokes that he's heading toward a crisis of well-being.

MURPHY HAS BEEN to Flagstaff before. He was here with some friends in college. In fact, he has been to this very restaurant, which Eva's phone has been so insistent in recommending. He is moments away from realizing this when he sees himself, or rather his younger self, standing under a red awning across the street. Here's an improbable, low-entropy situation if ever there was one.

Murphy is ashamed of his younger self, as we are all ashamed of our younger selves, and he feels a nearly irresistible urge to rush into the street and strike him. Luckily, he is not the impulsive young man he once was—the impulsive young man, that is, who stands there under the awning. He makes a show of concentrating on the menu and he consults Eva's phone in order to discover which items are particularly prized. There's always the one item that you're supposed to get, and if you don't get it you've missed your big chance and you might as well eat a banana peel out of the garbage. Here it's the blueberry buckwheat pancakes, or, to borrow Murphy's language, the griddle-cooked cherry cakes with cherries. Only when they've ordered does Murphy say he needs to step out and retrieve something from the *Pequod*.

Young Murphy is waiting impatiently for his friends to emerge from the thrift store. Murphy walks past him without saying anything, but at the last moment he catches Young Murphy's eye and gestures to the alleyway around the corner of the building. Murphy wants to conceal Young Murphy from Eva, despite the high philosophical interest of the situation, because, what will she think of him if she meets his despicable antecedent? He has been trying to conceal his younger self from her since the day they met.

Now he stares at this familiar face. Young Murphy stares back. What is there to say?

Murphy taps him on the chest. "You just have to be nice to people, okay? That's all I want to tell you. Just quit the act."

"What act?"

"You know what I'm talking about."

Young Murphy looks away. "Did you just come out here to yell at me? I don't see how that's supposed to help anything."

Is this how Matthew McConaughey felt, gazing at his own younger self from within his extradimensional machine? In some ways, present-day Murphy compares favorably with Young Murphy. His face is leaner and more angular, his beard is full, and his hairline, despite recent fears, is intact. He no longer looks like a young man. He is now simply a man. He's also trim and fit and strong, as Young Murphy is not. But there's something off about his coloring. Standing next to this earlier self, he looks faded and worn, like an old couch. And things are different around the eyes. Have his eyes gotten smaller? Young Murphy's eyes are big and bright.

"What you don't seem to understand," says Young Murphy, "is that I'm tired of being who I am. Or maybe you don't remember."

"What?"

"I'm tired of being so nervous all the time. It's exhausting. My head is full of equivocation. I can't say what I mean. I don't even know what I think! I want to break free. I want to be one of those guys who goes straight ahead. You know what I mean? I want to be outgoing and charismatic."

"You should go for a run sometimes. Clear your mind."

"I'm so *hesitant* about everything."

He does look hesitant. He's shifting from one foot to the other and he can't maintain eye contact, although Murphy is having the same difficulty. It's not easy to see oneself clearly.

"But you can understand why it's frustrating for me," says Murphy. "Because you know just what you're doing. That's why you're so culpable, in my view."

Young Murphy smiles a weary smile, and just look at those pretty white teeth.

"You're projecting all this stuff on me," he says, "and I haven't even done anything. I'm not interested in reforming myself because I haven't seen the need for it yet. Do you know what the real problem is?"

"Do you?"

"We've got different values, that's what it is."

This might be true in some way, which is distressing. But does Young Murphy actually know that it might be true?

"I'm not saying what I need to say," says Murphy. "I thought I was prepared for this conversation, but I feel like I can't make myself understood."

. . .

Some things are incomprehensible. But some things make perfect sense. Flagstaff (Köppen climate classification *Dsb/Csb*) receives an average of 21.86 inches of precipitation a year. That's not much, but it's a lot more than Phoenix, which is only two hours away. This is an effect of Flagstaff's elevation. Air masses from the distant Pacific or the Gulf of California run up the mountain slopes, expand, cool, and shed their moisture as snow or rain. This is called orographic precipitation. The same mechanism accounts for the phenomenon we call a rain shadow. When the mountains are sufficiently high, all the moisture is wrung from the air on the windward slopes and the land beyond is especially arid. On a continental scale, this is part of why the West is so dry. The Great Basin sits in the shadow of the Cascades and the Sierra Nevada. The High Plains, Denver included, are further shadowed by the Rocky Mountains.

"What's wrong with your eyes?" says Young Murphy.

"Nothing's wrong with my eyes."

"There's something wrong with them. They don't look right."

"They're fine. Don't look at them if they bother you."

"And your hair isn't really any color at all. Is this what it comes to? You look so tired. Don't you care about things any longer? Look around you! It's the West! Look at those pine trees!"

"They're cedars," says Murphy.

"They're ponderosa pine."

Murphy peers at his younger self in irritation. His essential grievance is and has been that this young man is affected and self-absorbed. This is not, in itself, a damning accusation, and it's one that can be leveled at present-day Murphy as well, but he's aware of this, and in a way that's the point: Young Murphy lacks that self-consciousness, or so Murphy thinks. His affectations are intended to deceive *himself.* Everything he does is part of a program of self-deception.

"Of course I care," Murphy says passionately. "Of course I care about the cedars!"

"The pine trees."

"I see that now."

But if Young Murphy's expressions and gestures are somehow put-on, Murphy is shocked to realize that he has the same mannerisms. Growing up is a process that transforms affectation into habit. Thus Young Murphy is doubly culpable: He has committed these crimes of affectation and he has inflicted those affectations on his future self.

Young Murphy shakes his head. "I don't believe you. Can't you smell the air any longer? Don't you *care* what it smells like?"

"I can smell it," says Murphy, "but it's different for me, because when I smell it I don't just think of the trees and the place and the idea of the West. I think of *you*. I remember *you* smelling it. Do you see?"

The truth is that he can hardly remember anything about this young person's life. Wet flagstones and lyrical rain on the day of an exam. A bottle of rum in a dim room. The smell of Ivory soap, or else not the smell itself but the fact that it had a smell. Life pared away to the essential clues. And did he know they were clues at the time? The yeasty smell of the Bradford pears in the courtyard. A gust of cold air.

"And what's with the shoes?" says Young Murphy, pointing to Murphy's ballet slippers.

There are rain shadows all over the West, but some of the most dramatic ones occur in Hawaii. This tropical island chain, which is said to be part of the United States, is really a submerged mountain range. Thus Hilo (Köppen climate classification *Af* a tropical rain forest climate), on the eastern or windward side of the Big Island (the winds are easterly in the tropics), receives 156.79 inches of rain annually, making it the rainiest city in the United States, at least as long as we accept the proposition that this Polynesian nation is part of the United States, which we do not. The western or leeward side of the island is parched, and there are resorts on that coast that boast annual precipitation totals of around 9 inches per year, hardly more than Phoenix.

The eastern slope of Mount Waialeale, on the island of Kauai, gets something like 450 inches of rain each year, which makes it one of the rainiest places on earth. But the town of Waimea, in the lee of the mountain, gets just 21.70 inches. Slightly less than Flagstaff.

Everything's bigger in Asia. The Tibetan Plateau creates the largest and greatest rain shadow on earth.

"I've got a question," says Young Murphy. "If I cut my ear off, will you suddenly be earless, or am I seeing you from another dimension?"

"I've been thinking about that too."

"Should we give it a try?"

"Should we give what a try?"

"We could cut my ear off. But it could be some other permanent injury if you're squeamish. Let's give me a really bad cut and see if you get a scar. Or just snip the end of my earlobe off."

"Why do you want to mutilate your ear? That's crazy. It would spoil the rest of your trip."

Young Murphy nods. He closes his eyes and listens for a moment. "What I want most of all is to be completely where I am. That's the essence of what I want. Do you know what I mean? I'm trying to concentrate on the weird gray wind and the grasshoppers. I want to breathe in the beautiful idea of this place."

Murphy smiles. "I kind of like you. I can't help it."

There are places in Alaska that get a lot of rain as well. Ketchikan and Yakutat receive about the same amount as Hilo, and the tiny town of Whittier, so small that it hardly counts as an inhabited place, gets

197.8 inches annually. Much of this Alaskan precipitation falls as snow, although the climate of Ketchikan (Köppen climate classification *Cfb*—a temperate oceanic climate) is mild. Alaska is also said to be part of the United States, although this claim, like claims for the statehood of Hawaii, is difficult to credit.

"Just tell me one thing," says Young Murphy. "Just give me a hint."

It's dangerous to tell your younger self things about the future. Without cutting Young Murphy's ear off, they have no idea what effect any of this will have on the inscrutable web of causation, if causation exists.

But Murphy would like to spare this young man some pain. "You're going to develop a peanut allergy," he says. "Just be aware of that. It manifests itself as deep nausea."

Young Murphy is nodding and shifting his weight from one foot to the other. Murphy wants to grab him and tell him to get a grip. But the moodiness is partly an affectation too, since Young Murphy wants to be perceived as a glamorously unpredictable figure. There's no way to untangle it all and figure out what's really going on, and that's because Young Murphy isn't entirely himself yet, just as Murphy isn't entirely himself, just as none of us are entirely ourselves.

"It's possible that you can avoid it if you're circumspect with peanuts at this point," Murphy continues, now in despair.

"That isn't what I want to know."

"But it's also possible that the allergy comes from metabolic changes and not sensitization, in which case you're going to develop it anyway, so you might as well enjoy the peanuts while you can."

"I don't care about that. I want to know if it's all going to be okay. All of it! My life!"

"Eva says I should try to eat . . ."

"Who's Eva?"

"What?"

"You said Eva."

"I didn't. Forget it."

"Who's Eva?" Young Murphy is grinning wildly. "Who is she? Where do I look for her?"

THEY DRIVE AND drive. They shout Yahweh's name. The landscape changes and stays the same. Sometimes the Mobil station is a BP and sometimes it's a Sinclair, and sometimes the McDonald's or the Burger King is a Carl's Jr. or an In-N-Out, but it's always the same place. A fan palm here. A sugar pine there. A Joshua tree if they're lucky.

Murphy doesn't tell Eva about Young Murphy, but he feels funny about keeping it from her, so he says, "I've often had the sense, on this trip, that what we're really looking for is ourselves." She raises an eyebrow and let's this pass.

Thomas Jefferson thought it would take a hundred generations to people the American West. It was already peopled, and then we de-peopled it, but then we re-peopled it, and all in a few short years.

Lord James Bryce, who was appointed British ambassador to the United States in 1907, marveled at this haste: "Why sacrifice the present to the future, fancying that you will be happier when your fields teem with wealth and your cities with people? In Europe we have cities wealthier and more populous than yours, and we are not happy."

They visit the Grand Canyon, where they reflect that the most remarkable feature of this geological formation is that it's not disappointing. This is Murphy's second time at the Grand Canyon and he keeps a sharp lookout for his former self.

And here's the Hoover Dam. And here's Lake Mead.

And here's a message from P. F. Barnum "Barney" Gaines, who must have gotten Eva's phone number in Winston-Salem. He just wants to make sure that they—Mrs. and Mr. Jane Pierce—will be attending his American Ideas Conference in Montana. They promise him they will.

And here's Yahweh again, brooding over some perceived insult. "Oh Christ," he says. And then: "Goddamnit!"

They arrive in Las Vegas just in time for Eva to make a scene during the keynote address at a convention of electrical contractors. Security has to escort her from the auditorium. Now they're out on the crowded Strip, where the wind is hot in their faces and the forbidding date palms rise to an astonishing height. Grinning men stand in doorways and pass out little cards with pictures of prostitutes on them. "2 for $200.

No hidden fees." You can't take a road trip of any duration, it seems, without running across the theme of prostitution again and again.

Eva is agitated and uncomfortable. The casinos and pinging slot machines have stirred up some bad memories. When she was ten, her father's bookie was evicted from his apartment and had to stay with them for a whole week. He was obese and diabetic and she watched in horror as he administered his insulin shots. He screamed at her for not screwing the lid down on a jar of tomato sauce. She was eighteen before she learned that not all fathers had bookies.

She'd like to get out of town as quickly as possible, far from these reminders of her problematic girlhood, but Murphy is in some distress. He's wincing with every step he takes.

"I don't think the ballet slippers are helping," she says.

"They're all that's keeping me from *true* infirmity."

It's hard to tell whether he's joking or not. When he has to turn a corner, he slows down and swings out wide.

"I can't take this any longer," says Eva. "We need to get you to a doctor."

"Are you kidding?" He pretends to look around. "Are we in Canada or Denmark, that we can just go to the doctor?"

"We're rich. We'll bribe them for an appointment."

He insists that it won't work. No one's going to give him an appointment without Nevada insurance. They aren't going to take it on faith that he can pay.

"I *know* these doctors," he says. "This is America. This isn't Norway."

So Eva suggests a concierge medicine service, which is how some rich people do it. Murphy doesn't know anything about concierge medicine, but he knows that you have to join first. It's like a club. And that would mean further delay.

"Then let's go to one of those urgent care places," Eva says.

He dismisses this with a haughty gesture. "Certainly not."

"An emergency room?"

"It's not an *emergency*. The pain has just sort of concentrated itself in my feet. There's the same amount of pain, but it's happening in fewer places."

Eva hands a fifty-dollar bill to a homeless man, who nods and says nothing. Her eyes sting in the hot wind. She's just gotten through telling the electrical contractors that terror will overtake them like a flood, and their food will turn to asp's venom in their bowels, and their affairs will shrivel like mallows and wither like heads of grain. Now she has to contend with this. More lunacy.

Down the street, there's a casino called Paris. And here's one called New York–New York, and another called the Venetian. You can travel to the middle of the desert and visit the whole globalized world.

"This place really is pretty weird," says Eva. "Weirder than I thought it would be."

"There's a kind of truth in it, right? You want to say it's a cheap perversion, but it's also kind of the essence of the whole human experience. The world is a narrow bridge, but it's also a casino."

"I'll tell you one thing. Our own trash mountain resort will be a very different kind of getaway."

"There'll be a temple there," says Murphy.

"But we'll have other stuff too. Educational programming. Pragmatic design. Reclaimed garbage furniture. The motif could be that all the fixtures and everything are scrounged from demolished and condemned buildings. I'm envisioning a sort of anti-resort."

"And we'll be careful," he says, looking distastefully at some young men with gruesome slogans on their T-shirts, "about who's allowed to come."

"I guess."

"No white supremacists. No Christian right. No hate groups of any kind."

"We'll have an ideological test."

"We'll do some extreme vetting on those fuckers. No more tolerance."

But suddenly Eva turns solemn. "Wait, wait. We have to stop talking this way. Don't you get it? This is how *they* talk. We have to find another way."

"You want to have a scone with some KKK terrorist?"

She doesn't respond. She knows he agrees with her, at least in principle. He's indulging himself.

As if there weren't enough to worry about, something's not right with Fluffy 2. He's been lethargic and unresponsive all day. Now Eva sets him down and speaks to him in a high earnest cheerful voice, but he just stands there blinking and sticking his tongue out. Murphy is quick to suggest that they call a vet. Eva isn't so sure. He probably just has a cold. She feels his nose, which is dry, although maybe it's supposed to be dry. Murphy says once again that they should call a vet.

"Veterinarians are no problem," he says.

Eva straightens up and looks at him. He reaches for her phone.

"They've got a different insurance protocol," he says.

What is Las Vegas anyway? Not long ago, there was nothing here at all. The first Euro-American to visit the area was John C. Fremont, who passed through in May of 1844 and left the following description: "After a day's journey of 18 miles, in a northeasterly direction, we encamped in the midst of another very large basin, at a camping ground called *las Vegas*—a term which the Spaniards use to signify fertile or marshy plains, in contradistinction to *llanos*, which they apply to dry and sterile plains. Two narrow streams of clear water, four or five feet deep, gush suddenly with a quick current, from two singularly large springs; these, and other waters of the basin, pass out in a gap to the eastward. The taste of the water is good, but rather too warm to be agreeable; the temperature being 71 in the one, and 73 in the other. They, however, afford a delightful bathing-place."

It sounds very nice. But he was less enthusiastic when describing the surrounding area, which he called "desolate and revolting country."

Luck is with them today. The True Fortune Veterinary Hospital has just had a cancellation. The receptionist tells Murphy she can squeeze him in later this afternoon. Is his pet a dog or a cat?

"I don't know."

"I'm sorry?"

"Let's say cat."

He can hear the woman typing.

"Name?" she says.

"Fluffy 2."

"That's eff ell you eff eff why numeral two?"

"Correct."

"And what's your pet's name?"

On the way over there, he makes one suspicious claim after another. He argues, for example, that "vets are better than human doctors" because they deal with "so many different kinds of mammals." Eva says nothing. "They've seen it all," Murphy explains. Again Eva says nothing. Murphy says that veterinary school admissions are way more competitive than medical school. Eva peers out the window and frowns.

The veterinary hospital is in the real Las Vegas, where people live, or try to live. This is where tennis legend Andre Agassi grew up. There are pink stucco houses and a few garish green lawns, an absurd affectation out here in the desert, but a good many people are turning to xeriscaping. Could Murphy and Eva live here too? Could they plant cacti, enjoy the Vietnamese food, build a tennis court in the backyard, and compel their child to practice and practice, hour after hour, like poor little Andre? We've noted that even under normal circumstances, Las Vegas only receives 4.19 inches of precipitation annually. A frightening thought. On the other hand, it's one of the most water-efficient cities in the country.

They arrive a few minutes early and Murphy steps forward to fill out the necessary paperwork. Eva sits with Fluffy 2 and reads about concierge medicine on her phone. There's one very expensive option called, with who knows what ironic intent, "Universal Health Care." You pay a retainer of sixty-thousand dollars a year and you get a worldwide provider network and a personal health care advocate to help you "navigate the complexities of managing your wellness."

Dogs yowl and cats gaze dispassionately from within the darkened interiors of their cat carriers. Fluffy 2 pays no more attention to the dogs than he does to the cats, and he seems to have recovered from his infirmity. He was probably just hot and uncomfortable.

Now Eva feels the familiar twinge and turns to a lady waiting with her cat. She says, "I don't suppose you've heard the name of the Lord, which is Yahweh?"

"I don't care about that."

"A day comes when it doesn't matter whether you care or not."

"I'll tell you what," says the lady, "I know just what you're talking about and he doesn't have one thing to do with grace."

"What did you say? Say that again."

"You're talking about Yaldabaoth. It happened when the Aeon Sophia began to think. She intended to reveal an image from herself, but she lacked the consent of the invisible spirit. That's how Yaldabaoth came forth. But she cast him away."

"Okay, but what was it you said earlier about grace?"

"You're talking about reality. That's Yaldabaoth. He begot this realm and the seven authorities that rule it, and the other five authorities came from the depths of the abyss. He was ignorant of the fullness, but he perceived his ignorance. It was his longing for the fullness that produced reality."

"The fullness," says Eva. "You've given me something to think about. But I could swear you also said something about grace."

The vet is a small Vietnamese-American woman whose patience is at an end. She takes one look at Murphy and says, "I don't treat humans. I'm not allowed to treat humans."

Murphy explains that they're here for Fluffy 2.

"Under 'Reason for Visit,' you wrote 'pain in the arch of the foot.' You people have to stop coming in here. A guy came in last week and said his bird was getting headaches when it read the newspaper."

"Some birds are really smart," says Eva.

"I know that! I wrote the book on birds!"

"Fluffy 2 was sick," says Murphy. "But now he seems okay. But I'm really having trouble. I need help. It's so hard to see a doctor in America."

"I understand that." She closes her eyes and takes a deep breath. "But you still have to see the human doctor. There's nothing else I can say. I'm a veterinarian. I get this sense that everyone is walking around out there having this revelation where they say to themselves, 'Aha! I'll just go to the vet!'"

"We get it," says Murphy. "We aren't like the others. But just let me ask you this, and let's pretend that this question is about my pet. Isn't it possible that if he's having foot, knee, and hip pain, the problem could be a lifetime of wearing the wrong shoes? And is it really so crazy to think that some additional pain is inevitable when we switch him over to the correct shoes?"

The vet isn't listening. She's looking at Fluffy 2. "What kind of animal is this?"

"You're the expert."

She looks around wildly. "What's going on here? What's happening? Is it a prank?"

But before they go, she gives poor dejected Murphy the following advice: "My basic principle in my *veterinary* practice is that if the treatment is exacerbating the problem, you stop that treatment. Whether that treatment is a drug regime or a pair of shoes."

A JOSHUA TREE stuffed whole into a Dumpster. Headlights rushing toward them in the hot darkness. Toothy mountain peaks rising into a papaya sunset. More clues. More memories from the future. And here's Yahweh, always Yahweh, come to spoil it. He climbs into their tent, pushes a huge wad of chewing gum into his mouth, and says, "It's me, the Lord your God, compassionate and gracious, abounding in loving kindness." Later he's in the back seat of the *Pequod* and he leans out the window and sprays Silly String at the car behind them. His aim is unerring, despite all the complex aerodynamic considerations. He says, "The Glory of Israel does not deceive or change his mind, for he is not human that he should change his mind."

Outside of Baker, California, Eva finally gets around to explaining time.

"You mean that it passes more quickly in hot places?" Murphy says.

"Or it's more likely to pass."

"Don't joke! I really want to know."

The landscape is desolate beyond description, but even more remarkable than the fact that there's so little vegetation is the fact that there is some vegetation. Creosote bushes, cholla cactus, a few Joshua trees. How do these organisms manage? The temperature outside is 109 degrees Fahrenheit, although time doesn't seem to be passing very quickly.

"It's something to do with eggs and entropy," Eva says. "I'm not joking, but I'm not so clear on this either. All I could gather is that there's no time without heat. Or entropy. And they're a matter of chance."

"That's tough to take," says Murphy. "I'm hanging on by a philosophical thread as it is."

"I'm getting it wrong. It's about heat transfer. That's where time comes from. So if you're at thermal equilibrium, it's unlikely that time will pass."

What about the effect of climate change on the passage of time? A warming world is a world out of equilibrium. Is it therefore more likely that time will pass? Are eggs less likely to appear? Will the brief sparkling years begin to slip away even more quickly?

Murphy shakes his head. "If that's truth, give me religion."

Here's another demoralizing feature of the human experience: Murphy and Eva spend a lot of time worrying about what they might be forgetting, but sometimes they have problems when they remember things too *clearly*. On this luminous desert morning, Murphy peers into the trunk of the *Pequod*, where everything is carefully organized in bags and milk crates. He's looking for the raisins, but even though they're within a few inches of his grasping hand, he is unable to see them. Vision happens in the electrical jelly—the eyes just gather the information. He has peered into the trunk so many times in these last weeks that his brain has ceased to refresh the data and he sees only the memory of the trunk. To his credit, he knows that he's experiencing hysterical raisin-blindness. He is thinking of Poe's "The Purloined Letter," that famous story in which the critical letter is hidden in plain sight. Now it occurs to him that he hasn't read that story. Isn't it interesting that he's aware of its themes nonetheless? He probably knows as much about it as he'd know if he really had read it, since he'd have forgotten everything about it anyway. Maybe he has read it and he's forgotten. Anyway, the raisins are right here in this milk crate next to the potted callaloo. Hidden in plain sight.

"Concentrate," Murphy says to himself, staring at them and seeing nothing.

Yahweh is in a fickle mood as they cross the Mojave. When they stop for gas in Boron, so named because it's home to the world's largest borax mine, he tells Eva to go inside and get him some candy, but he won't say what kind. She has to play a guessing game. Does he want a Snickers? Not a Snickers. Does he want a bag of Skittles? Not a bag of Skittles. Does he want Twizzlers? Not Twizzlers. And so on. Eva begins to cry a little bit. All of this is taking its toll. Then he says he wants Necco Wafers, but not to eat. He wants Eva to burn them at his feet while he inhales the smoke. He says, "And I'll requite you for the abominations in your midst. And you will *know* that I am the Lord."

California City is the state's third-largest city by area, although it's home to only around 14,000 people. Houses are thinly scattered on the hard hot ground, and there are blocks on which no one has ever built. Stewart Avenue, Stearns Avenue, Orchid Drive. Empty, empty, empty. The city flickers in and out of existence as you drive through it—a quantum city. Today the temperature has risen to 111 degrees, but here's a man watering his patchy lawn, and here's a woman drinking hot tea on her front porch. To account for such phenomena, we must remember Thomas Merton: A human being would have to be insane to live in California City, but luckily for California City, the desert drives people insane.

In Rosamond, the weary traveler can visit Crazy Otto's, "Home of the Biggest Omelette in the World." Here Eva makes a speech, some of which she later posts on Yahweh's Facebook page:

"We can't know his purposes, but we can guess. He deranges the leaders of the people and makes them wander as if drunk. Is it a joke? Who's laughing? He crushes us for a hair. You need to listen to what I'm telling you. Whatever he tears down cannot be rebuilt. Listen to me! The days pass like reed-boats. City blocks will crumble at a breath from his nostrils. This place will be a den for jackals and an abode of ostriches."

A young man looks up in alarm and says, "There's already an ostrich farm not far from here!"

Her dreams have been so florid and upsetting that she's afraid to go to sleep. There are bags under her eyes. She hasn't been eating much of anything. She sits in silence while Murphy drives, staring straight ahead, sometimes muttering. Backyard green tree cemetery dawns. Another day, another dolor. There were roses in the cool café. There were roses in the cool café.

She thinks of babies. She thinks: Electing to have a child means running the risk of losing that child, and surely there is no greater pain.

"As if pain could be borne," she whispers, quoting something without knowing what. "As if we were sure to find our way."

When an earthquake kills ten thousand people in Nepal, she tries to bite Yahweh in the upper arm. All those people had moms and dads.

All of them were alive because someone had cared for them when they were small.

And yet, and yet, what if there is something like grace, as the Gnostic woman in the vet's office said? What if Yahweh has nothing to do with it? What if Yahweh is really just Yaldabaoth, who is ignorant of the fullness?

They drive through a forest of wind turbines. Wind power is just another kind of solar power, since wind comes from the pressure differentials that arise when the sun heats different parts of the earth's surface at different rates. Never mind about the effect this might have on the passage of time. You could also say that fossil fuels are a form of solar energy, since they consist of photosynthetic products from squished ancient plants. And yet not all energy comes from the sun. Geothermal energy is a nice alternative, but even better is tidal power, which comes from the moon.

Soon they leave the Mojave and cross into coastal Southern California, and it's like arriving in a different country—vast, rich, vibrant, multiethnic. But there's anger on the Golden Coast this summer. In downtown Los Angeles, protesters have staged an enormous demonstration. This dramatic event has a cinematic quality, and not just because it's an important and moving thing but because it's happening in California, where even the most routine activities acquire a hallucinatory shimmer. That's because almost all of our movies are filmed here, even movies ostensibly set in places like Detroit or Louisville. We watch Matt Damon triumph over adversity beneath a powdery blue sky, and this takes place in California. Matthew McConaughey descends into a black hole, there to make the ultimate sacrifice, or so he thinks, and the black hole is in California. A stylish mom buys an Audi, friends buy friends beer, and these things happen in California too. In this way, even if we never visit, we grow up knowing the place in the same deep way that we know the places we lived as children. We understand the character of its light, its flora, its architecture. And then, when *we* buy beer, when we experience longing, when we feel as if we have descended into a black hole, when we imagine that we too might triumph over adversity, we see that low desert light in our mind's eye, the peach blush and the long clear shadows. If our feelings are programmed by the glowing screen, and to some extent they must be, then maybe we can't feel them correctly until we feel them in California.

They drift through the exultant crowd. There is a wild sense that the good guys are winning, that evil is in retreat, that love will triumph. If hatred is ascendant in this troubled time, so is love. It's indifference that's on the wane.

Yahweh will only allow them one night in Los Angeles. They choose to spend it in a suite at the Beverly Wilshire, which costs more than their entire eight-month lease in Miami. They're worried about bringing Fluffy 2 inside, but it turns out that only the shabby hoteliers and moteliers will give you trouble about your pet. In fact, a footman immediately brings Fluffy 2 a bowl of what he calls "hand-sliced" meat. Eva tells him about Yahweh and gives him a hundred-dollar tip. Then they order some hand-sliced meat for themselves. And baked potatoes with nothing on them. Murphy explains that potatoes are just potatoes, but everything else that grows underground is also a potato. Carrots and beets are potatoes. Ginger is a scented potato.

Exhausted after another long hot day, they climb onto the bed and watch a movie. Movies are full of useful information, and today's film is no exception. This is the most famous of all android movies. You know the one. Humans have created an intelligent global security network called Skynet, which is like a weaponized version of the surveillance network that UPS uses to track its drivers. Originally programmed to keep humans safe, Skynet has determined that humans themselves are the greatest threat to humans. This determination leads inescapably to the conclusion that the only way to keep humans safe is to destroy all humans. Skynet has been more or less successful in this campaign, and all that stands between humans and extinction is an underground resistance movement captained by a determined genius. Skynet decides that rather than fight this genius in the present, it would be easier to send an assassin back in time to kill his mother, American actress Linda Hamilton, before she has a chance to give birth to him. For this mission, it selects the android hit man Arnold Schwarzenegger. All of this takes place in California.

By now, the excitement of the day has burned off and dejection settles like the mist from a humidifier. Eva hauls herself off to the luxurious bathroom in order to take a shower, but she gets stuck looking at herself in the mirror. For a moment, just a moment, her mind goes blank and she doesn't have the faintest idea who that person is. Identity is tricky. Arnold Schwarzenegger only *looks* like a person. Underneath his flesh is a metallic endoskeleton and red eyes.

"But that's just me," Eva says aloud, staring at her reflection. "It's me, same as always. I'm from rural Pennsylvania. I went to Johns Hopkins. I'm thirty years old."

"Did you say something?" says Murphy

She steps back into the room and says, "My dad has never used a wallet. He keeps his stuff together with a rubber band."

She looks down at her clothing. What do these garments say about her, and is what they say true? She peels off her clothes and plucks the little gold rings from her ears. She's not satisfied. She'd like to imagine that she stands here now as she really is, her authentic self, free of orna-ment, but it's not true. There are garments that she can't cast off: her posture and bearing, her various facial expressions, her habits of mind, her modes of speech. These things are learned, acquired, affected, who knows. And suddenly they seem false.

"What's wrong?" says Murphy, growing alarmed. "Eva! What's happening here?"

She grips a hank of her hair and contemplates it with distaste.

"Hair is an ornament that can never be removed," she says, "because even its removal is an aesthetic choice."

"I get that, but I don't see why it matters right now. Come over here. Have some potato."

"The fact that we have hair means that we're doomed to give a mis-leading account of ourselves."

"Have some hand-sliced meat. Take a breath."

No surprise, given the level of agitation in this suite, that tonight's sex scene is frenzied and harrowing. At its denouement, Eva pulls a little of her hair out! Then, when the dust has settled, she sits on the floor, dreading her inevitable nightmares, and thinks of Sylvia Plath's living doll: It can sew, it can cook, it can talk, talk, talk.

Early the next morning, an angel in a maid's uniform comes by to tell them that they must leave the city immediately, without eating any breakfast. So now the wearisome traveling begins again. Here are the eucalyptus windbreaks, the oleander in the dusty medians, the distant mountains, the incomparable sky. Here's a rattlesnake dead on the highway, poor thing. And here at last is the broad blue Pacific Ocean, largest and greatest of the earth's oceans, with its relentless foaming waves, its vast beaches and rocky headlands, such a sense of scale, so much space and light, so much possibility. To come all the way west and see it—even God can't spoil the feeling. They park the car and stare out toward Santa Cruz Island. A man with a blue guitar sits on the tailgate of his truck, singing hymns. Eva falls asleep with her forehead on the steering wheel.

The days pass like reed-boats. Their routine is well established. Up at dawn, a walk for Eva and Fluffy 2 and a brief, tentative, almost apologetic run in ballet slippers for Murphy, then a companionable breakfast of roasted cherries and roasted or mashed peas and maybe some fresh cherries, too, if there are any available. Then they get their instructions for the day, and then there's an interval of driving, and then there's some prophesy. There are good days and bad days, like always. Some days just don't work out, and it doesn't have anything to do with Yahweh. This morning, for example, Murphy wakes up in a sour mood, gets tangled in his sleeping bag, and falls through the tent flap. He hasn't been awake more than three minutes, but Eva pokes her head out and says, "Tomorrow's another day."

One afternoon, she tries to explain what the prophetic impulse feels like: "It's like I feel a charge build up. Or a kind of pressure. It isn't painful, but I can't ignore it. To make it go away I have to speak Yahweh's name. That's the best way I can describe it. And it pushes all my other thoughts right out of my head."

"Isn't there anything I can do for you?" Murphy says.

"I don't think so."

He looks glum. "I can't do anything for the woman I love."

"I guess not." She pauses. Then she says, "I have this terrible fear that love comes from God."

"He wants you to think so, but I think it's love *versus* God."

She doesn't respond. Even now she wants to say "Yahweh Yahweh Yahweh."

Murphy shouts: "Eva! Eva! What can I do? Isn't there something I can do?"

"There's nothing. This is just the way it goes."

"There must be something!"

"This is just life. It's just the way it is. It's like Uncle Orson and his chair."

All the televisions in the United States are on, and they get brief muted glimpses of the American pageant, but the news is just reruns. Police murder an unarmed black teen in Florida. The president says that journalists are the most dishonest people in the world. A football player beats up his wife on camera and faces no penalty. Reality begins to look like a cheap contrivance, implausible and garishly lit, like a puppet show in a tanning bed. Murphy and Eva get angry and their anger feels like déjà vu.

Here's one thing he can do for her: He can get her a pair of nonbinding diabetic socks. She isn't diabetic, but she hates when her socks squeeze her calves. He hands them over and she presses them to her bosom and appears genuinely moved.

"They're perfect," she says.

Love versus God. She tips forward onto his chest and remains there, breathing and gripping her new socks, which are made from bamboo fiber. Life is what it is, and either you accept it or you don't. Either you let the current sweep you out to sea or you swim against the current as it sweeps you out to sea.

All of history is a rerun. It's not just the news. History recycles the same elements over and over again. When gold was discovered here in California, prospectors poured in, and what happened then? The same thing that always happens. We can hardly bear to say it. The indigenous Californians, thousands and thousands of them, were enslaved and murdered. When they tried to fight back, retribution was swift. As the *Yreka Mountain Herald* put it in 1853, "Now that general Indian hostilities have commenced, we hope that the Government will render such aid as will enable the citizens . . . to carry on a war of extermination until the last redskin of these tribes has been killed . . . Extermination is no longer a question of time—the time has arrived, the work has been commenced, and let the first man that says treaty or peace be regarded as a traitor."

Only a few years before, the United States had taken California from Mexico in an unprovoked war of conquest.

Tonight, Murphy starts awake and discovers that Eva is in the middle of a speech.

"You know," she's saying, "you know that part. Elijah proves that Baal isn't the real God. Yahweh sends him water and he doesn't send any water to the prophets of Baal. That proves it."

"Proves what?"

"So they *kill* the prophets of Baal and then the soldiers come to get Jezebel and they throw her out the window and there's a dog and all that's left are like her hands and feet, and maybe her nose."

The next afternoon, she pursues an irritated young mother across a playground where they've stopped to stretch their legs and give Fluffy 2 a spin. This hard-hearted and stiff-necked woman, whose children are beating one another senseless not far away, has her own troubles, but that only makes Eva more insistent.

"The name of the Lord is Yahweh," she's saying. "I just have to tell you."

"Get away from me."

"I need to explain this. We're in this together. I was nipped from clay just like you."

"Get away!"

"This town will be a ruinous heap! He's going to *fill his belly* with your dainties."

"My dainties?"

"And stay away from Oreos."

The sky is perfectly cloudless. The eucalyptus leaves have no color. There is no moisture in the ground.

Eva says, "Yahweh will set you down like an empty dish."

"Let him."

"And then he'll rinse you out."

Murphy hopes that the grandeur of Yosemite will have a salutary effect, but their visit is disappointing. It's true that the valley is very beautiful—impossible granite faces, parched air, manzanita, mountain meadows, waterfalls—but it's thronged like Times Square. It's a riotous and frenzied place. There's something in the atmosphere that no one seems able to tolerate. Maybe Yahweh hath mingled a perverse spirit in the midst thereof. Eva feels even crazier than usual and she can't stop shouting his name and making threats. She tells a group of Chinese tourists that this once-lovely place, and every other place too, the whole world, the whole universe, will become a habitation of dragons and a court for owls. They don't understand a word she says.

"The fatness of your flesh shall wax lean!"

Murphy places a hand on her back and says, "Let's move along, why don't we?"

"But I've got to tell them. He's going to make them all sleep an endless sleep."

"Me and Fluffy 2 are pretty hungry. What do you say we break for lunch?"

"I don't know what's happened." She raises a hand to her brow. "I feel so funny. I'm antagonizing these people."

"It's just that Yahweh has hardened their hearts, that's all."

"You think so?"

"Of course."

She nods and says, "Let's try to smile at everyone we see."

"Okay."

"Can we?"

"Of course we can."

"Just that little bit of kindness goes such a long way. It brightens everyone's days."

"I agree."

"We won't smile in a crazy way. We'll just smile a little and say, 'Hey there, friend.'"

They come skidding down out of the mountains, camp in the fertile wasteland of the Sacramento Valley, and the next day they're in Berkeley. Yahweh joins them, disguises himself as a homeless person, and roughs up a college kid who fails to give him a nickel. Eva distributes money to the city's genuine homeless people and donates more money to the ACLU. Then they all stop to rest on a steep hillside near the university. The grass is crisp and golden and prickly. They can see San Francisco across the bay.

Although he knows that no good will come of it, Murphy can't resist pestering Yahweh a little bit.

"Could you just tell me the truth about dark matter?"

"Maybe it's an elementary particle."

"Maybe?"

"I never thought I'd have to explain these things."

Yahweh tosses a ball for Fluffy 2 and then makes the ball disappear at the moment Fluffy 2 tries to pounce on it. Eva is lying with her hands behind her head, blinking into the bright sky, muttering prophet talk or something else, nonsense, poems, who knows. The blue sun in his red cockade walked the United States today. Struggle is meat. First chill, then stupor, then the letting go.

"Humans have really surprised me," Yahweh says, in what almost seems like a charitable admission. But then he says, "It makes me so angry!"

Tonight they're obliged to attend a panel discussion at the university. There are two physicists and two mathematicians, and they're talking about the difference between abstract and applied mathematics. For a while they discuss Alexander Grothendieck, who contributed so much to pure math and then ended his life in monkish solitude in the Pyrenees, eating dandelion soup and worrying that an evil metaphysical force had perverted the harmony of the universe. Murphy and Eva can relate to this bit, but the rest of the discussion is opaque, so it's all the more surprising that when Eva rises to speak the name of the Lord, the panelists nod vigorously and thank her for her comment.

"That's the original Hindu sense of the word *avatar,*" says one of the mathematicians.

"An earthly manifestation of a divine being," says the other.

"Yahweh, Shiva, etc."

They've been discussing what they call "mathematical avatars." The idea, as far as Murphy and Eva can determine, is that each mathematical category, each mathematical entity, maybe even each mathematical theory, is the manifestation of something larger and more abstract. You climb the avatar ladder into a region of greater and greater generality.

The problem is that there are an infinite number of ladders, so there can't ever be a unified theory of pure math.

"And maybe," one of the panelists says, "the whole thing is based on the wrong assumptions."

There's some comfort here. If Yahweh is an avatar in the original Hindu sense, then there must be something beyond Yahweh, a larger and greater divinity, or sequence of divinities. That sounds a little like the Gnostic explanation, and if it's true, then it's likely that violence and hate do not proceed exclusively from man or exclusively from Yahweh. Instead we are all just individual actors doing what we can on this plane of reality, and there are other planes, and competing influences or forces on every plane.

A comfort, maybe, but not comfort enough for poor Eva. Her chest hurts, her stomach hurts, she's crying into her cherries and peas. Murphy keeps saying, "You're okay you're okay you're okay," but she hardly sleeps at all tonight, and in the morning, here in the glorious golden hills of Northern California, she is remote and unresponsive. She can't grasp the content of her own thoughts. Her very essence feels attenuated. Has she been maddened past endurance? Will she decide to shave her head? Murphy grips her knee as she drives and says, "You're okay you're okay you're okay."

Today, Yahweh too is in the grip of some exceptional feeling. They're on the street in Sonoma when they hear the flatulent roar of his Lamborghini, and then the ludicrous orange car comes ripping around the corner and he's bopping the horn and shouting.

"There you are! You avoided out of my sight!"

"Please . . ." she says.

Then she falls down. Murphy tries to help her up and finds that he can't move.

"Mortal!" Yahweh shouts. "Mortal! Did I not pour you out like milk? Did I not congeal you like cheese? Can I not do with you what I like? I'm going to treat this nation like the wood of the grapevine, which I have designated to be fuel for fire."

"Please. I didn't do anything."

"You've multiplied your harlotries!"

"Is it the lecture you're mad about? You *told* us to go to the lecture."

"You played the whore. You spread your legs to every passerby. Even now you're unsated." He fishes around in his pocket and pulls out a slip of receipt paper. "Eat this. Eat what's offered to you."

In a kind of trance, Eva stuffs the paper into her mouth and begins to chew. Murphy is unable to speak or raise his arms.

"Ha!" says Yahweh. Then he hands her some pieces of orange peel. "Now eat this."

She slips them into her mouth and chews mechanically. He seems pacified.

"Let not the strong man glory in his strength, nor the rich man in his riches, but only in this shall one glory: In his earnest devotion to me. For I the Lord act with kindness, justice, and equity in the world. In these I delight."

He tells her to sleep on her left side for ten nights. He tells her to mingle with the uncircumcised of heart and propound riddles and allegories. And then they'll know that he is the Lord.

Privately, Eva feels a deep dejection and interprets the obscene pointlessness of her prophetic enterprise as a harsh analogy for the more comprehensive pointlessness of human life and human civilization. But for an hour or two she manages a little good cheer, so that it appears to Murphy that she has taken Yahweh's rebuke in stride. He is impressed by this show of resilience and speaks rapidly about inconsequential things, trying to keep her distracted.

In the early afternoon, alas, they visit a bookstore and she loses her mind. She yells so loudly that her voice cracks. She thrusts the Staff Picks from their shelves.

"He'll make the sea boil like an ointment pot!" she screams. "*Listen* to me. Listen! They won't speak any longer of Topheth or the Valley of Ben-Hinnom. They'll be talking about the Valley of Slaughter!"

She rushes outside and stands weeping in the sunlight. Murphy limps after her and holds her tightly and gently all at once, like a man carrying an antique chair.

And soon afterward, remembering nothing, she says, "I'd like to stop at a bookstore somewhere and pick up Karen Solie's new collection."

She sleeps for a while as they drive north, but if this nap refreshes her, she doesn't say so. She feels an unnamable feeling. She is unrecognizable to herself. Then she complains of stomach trouble and they pull into a gas station.

Now Murphy is waiting in the parking lot with Fluffy 2, who noses around in the golden grass. The moon is out and suddenly it occurs to him, with the force of a new revelation, that the moon is round. It's a giant rock beyond the sky, and it's round, and it's *up*, and at the same time, if you were walking on the lunar surface, you'd be walking on a flat plane, its surface would be down, and the earth itself would be up. The earth, too, is round and manifestly not round. But the roundness of the moon predates the roundness of the earth, since the earth was flat until we developed the techniques to determine its roundness mathematically. Maybe it only became conclusively round when we took a picture of it from space.

Is there some consolation here? Is it a comfort to say that up and down and round and flat depend on your frame of reference? That they depend on ideas? Maybe so. Last night, one of the physicists claimed that there are quantum-mechanical solutions to cosmological problems that only work when you add a conscious observer. He also speculated that the universe can't exist at all without a consciousness to apprehend its existence. In short, we may not be as inconsiderable as we seem.

Unless, more likely, it's Yahweh's consciousness that sets the thing in motion.

The moon. No wonder people go crazy looking at that thing. Murphy's wits are addled. His face is hot with moonburn. Love versus God. She's okay she's okay she's okay. Do not make yourself afraid.

But is she okay? Here she is in a gas station bathroom, and now, at last, one aspect of her predicament is clarified. The odor is unspeakable and the linoleum is filthy and there's a spider the size of an oven mitt above the door, but these things don't matter to her. The toilet seat is no longer attached to the toilet and there's no toilet paper and there's a mop rotting in a broken bucket and there's a desiccated lizard crushed in a mousetrap and there's enough poison on the homemade shelves to destroy most of the humans and animals in this little town, but none of these things matter to her either. A Guatemalan man bursts in while she's standing before the mirror, apologizes mildly, and pauses a moment to select the appropriate bottle of poison from the shelf, and it doesn't matter because she's looking at the blue + on her First Response Rapid Result pregnancy test and it's the happiest moment of her life.

Stuff this into your Pyrex baking dish and roast it: When physicists tell you that the whole universe was once as small as a Tic Tac, or very much smaller, what they're telling you is that the whole *visible* universe was once as small as a Tic Tac, or very much smaller. That's all we know about because that's all we can see. It could be that the universe, compressed to a smooth hot textureless timeless gravityless paste, was still infinitely large. It could also be that the universe is not a universe at all, but a polyverse or multiverse, and that outside our own local Tic Tac are an infinite number of other Tic Tacs, all expanding just as our own Tic Tac is expanding, a kind of fractal balloon–growth in which the universe, or polyverse, or multiverse, becomes infinitely more infinite at an infinitely rapid rate.

Eva comes bustling across the parking lot and tosses the pregnancy test on the hood of the car.

"Oh my God," Murphy says.

"Interesting that you should put it that way," she says, grinning. "Something has put a baby in me. I hope it was you."

He has often imagined behaving inappropriately in this moment, but now that the moment is here he knows just what to say. He says that he will love this child no matter what, whether it's his own child or a child of God.

Part III

WE DON'T NEED the mathematicians to tell us that Yahweh is the instantiation of a larger principle. When we talk about God, we're also talking about those crucial abstractions: death and chaos, the future, the unknown. But that doesn't make him any less dangerous. Abstractions are dangerous. That's one of the facts of life. We are born into a landscape of metaphor, and we must learn to read it correctly or we'll die or go mad. For any creature that contends with an avatar like Yahweh, literary acumen is an evolutionary adaptation.

And yet what is man, what is woman, that such an avatar is mindful of him, or of her, and he and she of it?

Sometimes it's all too much. Sometimes we have no option but to appeal to a higher power. Outside a defunct supermarket in an unfashionable seaside town, Murphy picks up a pay phone and there's Satan, the adversary, asking how are things.

"Christ," says Murphy, "I'm happy to hear your voice."

He explains the situation. Satan is delighted. "Can you beat that?" he says. He asks Murphy to put Eva on so he can give her his warmest congratulations. The two of them press their heads together and hold the receiver between them, listening to Satan's soothing voice.

"But what do we do now?" says Murphy. "It's overwhelming."

"Doesn't your uncle Ted live around here?" says Eva.

He gives her a blank look.

"You're always talking about Ted's place in the redwoods. Let's go there and rest. I think that would really help."

"Uncle Ted?"

"Concentrate for a second. Uncle Ted's house."

"Okay okay okay," says Satan. "Everybody calm down. How's this. I'll distract Yahweh for a few days. A few days is easy. You two will go to Uncle Ted's house. Rest and reflect. Enjoy the redwoods."

It's good to have a friend like Satan. Murphy calls his uncle, who reminds him that it's never necessary to call—his door is always open, literally and metaphorically—and they get back into the car. It's only an hour and a half. Murphy drives and Eva sits in the passenger seat thinking of the baby. The baby's bright eyes, the baby's smile. Or else the baby's outraged Churchillian face. The baby's anger. After all, the first truth of existence is that none of us start out as willing participants. She wants to apologize to this still-notional baby, and yet, at the same time, she feels very strongly that she wants to meet that baby. This desire is so powerful that it takes her breath away. So powerful that she has chosen to expose the baby—the very creature she is pledged to protect—to all the sorrow of the universe.

· · ·

Uncle Ted lives just a few miles from the beach, but the topography of this rugged coast is such that his house actually sits a few hundred feet above sea level. This means that in the event of a tsunami—an event that is extremely likely and even assured, given the configuration of the Cascadia subduction zone or, if you prefer, Yahweh's lust for catastrophe—he would be safe, relatively speaking. For the last few years he has been living with a woman called Brette, a figure from his shadowy past. Murphy suspects that Brette is not her real name. She claims to be a retired showgirl, a "Las Vegas chanteuse," but no one believes her. Some of Murphy's family believe that she is an ecoterrorist in hiding.

Ted is in the driveway when they arrive. He wears old Levi's and a blue Pendleton shirt rolled to the elbows, and his beard is thick and gray. He's boiling water over a wood fire. The vapor condenses on a curved aluminum hood and runs down into a pie pan.

"Is that seawater?" says Murphy. "Are you desalinizing water?"

"I'm trying to see how much I can recover by this method. Don't think this is how I'd do it under normal circumstances. I'm losing so much!"

He gives them both a hug. He crouches down to greet Fluffy 2. Young redwoods swing and dance in the breeze. Here at the ragged edge of the continent, the air seems thin and full of light.

"My question," Ted explains, "was how good could I do with only the materials in the woodshed?"

Brette greets them as she comes up the driveway from the garden. She has a light fluting voice, not at all the smoky worn-out voice of a Las Vegas chanteuse.

Eva walks down to the lake, strips to her underwear, tumbles into the cold water, and floats there for a long time. Then she climbs out, rolls herself in a towel, and lies shivering on the dock. Is she resting? The expression on her face is fixed somewhere between serenity and alarm. It seems both full of feeling and entirely opaque, like the expression on an Easter Island statue. She looks no crazier than yesterday, and no less crazy.

When Murphy pokes his head over the railing, she says, "How are we going to take care of a baby? What were we thinking?"

Murphy doesn't respond. Now Brette appears and asks if she needs anything.

"What do you even say to the baby at this stage?" Eva says. "In terms of why it's good to be born."

"Raspberries," says Murphy. "And other berries."

"Are you saying you're pregnant?" says Brette. She looks at Murphy, who raises his eyebrows.

Eva says, "I'm so tired. I'm tired all the way to my guts. I'm like a hose that's been out in the sun for too long."

Now Ted comes to the railing as well. All three of them are peering down at Eva.

"The name of the Lord is Yahweh," she says.

Ted and Brette don't blink. She might have said that her favorite ice cream is mint chip or her shoe size is eight and a half. It must be that they're familiar with all kinds of spiritual tics. They're westerners, after all. They inhabit the geography of hope.

"You're not supposed to be talking about that," says Murphy. "Satan said not to talk about that."

Dinner is chicken tacos, which they eat on the deck in the day's last watery light. There's also a little tripe and chicken skin for anyone who's interested. Ted's theory—and already we can detect the same impulses that underpin Murphy's own strategies and tactics—is that the cheapest meats and meat products are the most nutritious. That's because meat is priced according to the amount of connective tissue in each cut. The more connective tissue, the tougher and cheaper the meat, all the way down to the cheapest meat bits, which are all connective tissue and no muscle. But connective tissue, says Ted, is "the most rich and vital foodstuff" because it consists principally of collagen, which is the main ingredient in the human body. The idea appeals to Murphy very much and he's chewing with gusto, although his chompers are giving him some trouble.

As for Eva, she is not allowed to have any of the homemade queso fresco, because of the danger of listeria. A modern pregnancy is all about minimizing risk. She knows that the risk of listeria isn't great, but she also knows that the risk exists, and as long as it exists, however negligible it might be, she must avoid queso fresco and other soft cheeses. We never know when Yahweh will bring the hammer down. Queso fresco isn't even a real cheese, and still she must fear it.

"A baby!" says Ted. "Just think of it. When are you due?"

Eva bops the table with her palm and says, "The name of the Lord is Yahweh." Her voice sounds odd and constricted because she's trying not to shout. "It's Yahweh. Sorry. It's Yahweh. I can't stop saying it. I'm supposed to be resting."

"We could discuss religion," says Ted. "No problem. That's a good topic."

But Eva won't discuss it. The name of the Lord is Yahweh, that's all. There's nothing more to say about it.

"We have to discuss something. Food without discussion has no taste."

"Don't listen to him," says Brette.

"I've got no trouble believing that you can get some utility out of the idea of God," says Ted. "Everybody needs a large idea to structure their days. We used to have these ideas about orgone. We thought it was the anti-entropic force. We'd sit in these orgone accumulators. They were like outhouses. They were supposed to increase the orgone concentration. The idea was that we were fighting against entropy. That's not far from religion."

"It's interesting that you should mention entropy," says Murphy.

Eva says, "No one's listening to me. The only point I want to make is that the name of the Lord is Yahweh."

"She means that it doesn't have anything to do with religion," says Murphy. "It's just that God exists, and he wants you to know it. But everything else stays the same. It isn't really a problem, philosophically."

"The deity paradigm isn't an idea I've had much success with," says Ted, "but for a while I'd try to stare into the sun each morning for ten seconds. And at another time I gave away all my books and devoted myself to chanting. And then there was the phase when I kept a tape recorder by the bed and I'd speak my dreams to it in the night. In the morning they'd turn out to be completely unintelligible."

"You're not listening," says Brette.

"And now I take maybe thirty supplement tablets and capsules over the course of each day."

When they've finished eating, Murphy stands up, gathers a stack of plates, turns toward the screen door, and collapses in a heap, smashing the plates and crying out in pain.

"Good gracious!" says Ted.

It looks as if he has pivoted too enthusiastically and put pressure on his damaged foot. He tries to explain, but then he loses heart and lies back with his eyes closed.

Brette's gaze lingers on poor flushed Eva, but Ted hustles around the table and kneels at Murphy's feet. Does Murphy mind if he has a look? Murphy extends his left foot and twirls it around. Ted takes the foot in his huge brown hands. He says does this hurt, does this hurt, does this hurt, and Murphy says yes, yes, yes. Then Ted switches to the right foot. Then he asks a few questions about the legs. It's clear that the left foot is the trouble area.

"We'll call our own physician in the morning," says Ted. "But in the meantime, I'm a doctor."

"You're a doctor?" says Eva, coming to herself a little bit.

"I have an M.D. It was just another phase. Another paradigm."

If it were anyone else, you'd call him a liar, but Uncle Ted has such a thick dossier of verifiable accomplishments that he doesn't need to invent fake ones.

"I went to medical school when I retired from tennis. I understood I'd never be a top player. But I never did my residency because I was oppressed by the repetition. And anyway, why stick yourself for life with a young man's idea of his future? That's when I took off and had my garlic farm. But you don't have to be that well trained"—and here he applies some pressure to Murphy's left foot, and Murphy shouts—"to know there's a broken bone in here somewhere."

The sun is down and the air is cold and the sky is a pale luminous blue. Before long, no doubt, the moon will spring from the horizon and oppress them with its incommensurable mysteries. Murphy limps inside and lies on the rug in the front room. The rest of them clear the table. Eva is thinking: I'm pregnant I'm pregnant I'm pregnant. Broken bone or no broken bone, Murphy is also thinking: She's pregnant she's pregnant she's pregnant. Ted hauls out his pill organizer, fills a gallon jug with water, and gets to work swallowing vitamins.

Eva says, of the forthcoming baby, "We don't know who it'll be. So at this point it's still everyone. All possible babies."

"It's like that fairy tale," Brette says, "Schrodinger and the Cat."

Eva looks at her for a moment and says, "Have we met somewhere? I've got the funniest feeling." But Brette doesn't seem to hear.

GETTING A DOCTOR'S appointment is not the hardship Murphy anticipates. He has money, which is all that really matters. The next morning, he and Ted leave for town in Ted's old Nissan pickup. While they're gone, Brette is going to take Eva and Fluffy 2 to see the old-growth redwoods on the other side of the ravine.

Eva is pregnant, as we've already established, and even for a person whose nerves are in good trim, pregnancy is a conceptually challeng-ing state of affairs. A nine-month gestation period and then a new phantom emerges from the very body of the adult female. How could this be the way it is? The whole setup seems much less credible and intuitive than the egg strategy, so popular among other members of the animal kingdom, although now that we think about it, the egg strategy is just as magical. How could there be enough nutrition in a bird's egg to sustain the tiny creature through the full term of its gestation?

She thinks of breast pumps and strollers. She thinks of Yahweh. She touches her abdomen and she hopes, but hope is too mild a word, that everything is okay in there.

"How can I forgive him for the world he's made?" she says.

"Who?"

"How can I forgive him for the painfulness of life. The *painfulness* of it. If the world is Yahweh's invention after all."

"But I don't understand," says Brette. "Why do you feel you need to forgive him?"

"It's about making peace with the way things are. Or convincing myself it's not so reckless after all to bring a kid into the world, where Yahweh can get at him. Or her. Why do I want to have a baby anyway?"

"Babies are wonderful."

"I'm worried it's just my programming. I'm a kind of robot."

"Sure," says Brette warmly, "why not? But you'll see how it is. This tiny human comes, and it doesn't speak English, and you have to get up in the night and shake it until it goes back to sleep, and the whole thing is the loveliest thing in the world. It's the very acme of human happiness."

They pick their way across a wooden footbridge, they walk around a steep hill, and suddenly here are the tallest trees on Earth. It's as easy as that. They crowd the road. They are alien and remote. They've out-grown their tree-ness and they brush the next rung on the avatar lad-der. It's like John Muir says: "The clearest way into the Universe is through a forest wilderness." Eva and Brette and Fluffy 2 scramble up the path and experience a kind of diminishment. Their footsteps are no louder than the sound of an ant chewing. The rhododendrons are twenty feet tall and they look like blueberry bushes in a kitchen garden. There is a smell, but who will remember it? The impossible trunks of the impossible trees march away into the hills.

"I can't believe it," Eva says.

"It takes a moment to adjust."

"I *don't* believe it."

Luminous cables of sunlight are threaded through the gloom. The intelligence of the trees hums all around them. Eva's anxiety seems inconsequential in this context and begins to mellow.

"It's just that I've got no control over anything," she says. "I'm like a crash test dummy or something. Just accelerating into the wall."

"I've always wanted a crash test dummy for myself," says Brette. "They have that placid look about them. They know, but they don't say. I'd set it up in the living room, by the Chinese checkers."

"I had a little toy crash test dummy when I was a kid. You pressed a button on its chest and its arms and legs blew off."

Eggs or live birth, the other question is where the animus comes from to begin with. Are we all just loose souls rattling around in the tin can of the universe, moving from vessel to vessel? Could it be that we really are created by God or a god or gods? Or else the animalcule forms when seeds are planted in the menstrual blood. Or we're the fleshy avatars of a more general force or principle. Or we are the light of the light of the aeons of light, and we are God, and God is us. Or we emanate from the imperfect understanding of he who is ignorant of the fullness. These are just stories, and each one is as good as any other.

The secular humanist version of the story goes like this: Two haploid cells derived from two diploid human entities combine to make a new diploid entity, a conceptus, which becomes an infant human by way of a series of implausible, preprogrammed developmental steps.

bians.
ian in
y born
in the
n does
mov-
fathers
rvoirs
can be
ools—
not so
It's all
it, but

Pierce.
it hap-

s away
dwood

it's my
memory
ned yet.

ng. The
nething
among
beyond
verse is

ng this infant human are encoded in that
ady been forced to concede, and this DNA
stensibly distinct human entities that have
ty that the instructions for the new human,
ponents of those instructions, exist before
new human is just a novel combination of
eans that it's not quite new after all, except
nique consciousness, whatever conscious-

t from the avatar theory. DNA encodes
f base pairs, but that sequence is only one
e information, just as writing is one rep-
ge and language itself is a representation
at's why it's possible to represent genetic
You can write it down on paper as a
G's, for example. Or, shocking thought,
of a living breathing creature—a human
we, too, are a manifestation of that infor-
ion made flesh.

vas Baxter. I saw him swallow it whole,
zed and churned in his stomach, because
f and came out separately. Otherwise it
and killed him."

and cure it: Humans lay eggs, in a sense,
ke fish and frogs, and we experience an

aquatic life phase, so it seems okay to say that humans are ampl
Even better, a woman's eggs already exist when she's an amphi
the womb of her own mother, which means that we're halfwa
in the wombs of our grandmothers, who are halfway born
wombs of their own grandmothers, and so on. In that case, wh
life start, and what is an individual? There are mothers out ther
ing around, apparently distinct from their children. There are
too—fathers are useful, as noted, because they function as re
of genetic material, and as long as their instinct for violence
suppressed, they're also good for carrying things and wielding
but the distinction between one human entity and another i
hard and fast. It's an illusion, this traffic of mothers and fathers
just a genetic stew. Maybe it has bits of avatar meat floating ii
it's the same stew.

"In North Carolina, this guy mistook us for a couple named
We went to a party and everything. Murphy gave a toast. Ther
pened again in Phoenix."

Brette raises her eyebrows but says nothing. Fluffy 2 rush
and comes galloping back, his tongue coated with dust and r
needles.

"Sometimes I see something," Eva continues, "and I'm sur
own memory, but not my memory from now. It's like my i
from the future. It's like a kind of déjà vu, but it hasn't happe
It's a clue. Does that make any sense?"

"I know what you're talking about," says Brette. "That feel
light in the orchard. The empty hammock in the breeze. So
means something. It's like the poet says: We're just kangaroo
the beauty. But maybe your pal Yahweh is a kangaroo too. Ant
him there are more kangaroos. I have to believe that the un
busy with cognition."

They're silent for a moment. They brace themselves in the neutrino wind.

"The Pierces are supposed to go to a conference in Montana pretty soon," says Eva. "We still don't know who they are. It would be easy to look them up."

The distinction between humans and other creatures is not so easy to establish either. Accidental genetic novelties accumulate in time, and creatures gradually diverge from their ancestors, just as we do indeed diverge in certain ways from our own parents, but our parents are still our parents, and our ancestors are still our ancestors. It's still the same stew. Follow the family tree back and at a certain point your distant grandmother isn't quite human, although she's still your grandmother, and at another point she isn't quite a mammal, although she's still your grandmother. From Eva to a sea cucumber is not so far to go.

"A big part of the trouble," says Brette, "is time. Time is why it seems like things aren't all happening at once, but then you wonder if time is only the medium we live in. Time is where you find phantoms like us. And maybe there are other media where you'd find other kinds of phantoms."

"Because sometimes," says Eva, "there's that feeling."

"Exactly."

"The communication in the orchard."

"The world's a big bell," says Brette, "and you're just an ear."

Now we've worked ourselves into an agony of confusion and we need to pause and take refuge in the hard facts: We are on the northwest coast, above the inundation zone, on the hundred and twenty fourth meridian, in a town that gets 63.10 inches of precipitation per year. We're west of every American mountain range and there are no rain shadows to contend with. It all makes sense. God scowls in his heaven. The corporations make the products. Through the trees we can see the dark jelly of the lake shining and rippling under a pale blue sky.

But the sky is only blue because this is how the human brain, which is also a kind of jelly, configures the splash of radiation from a distant nuclear explosion. And up and down are up and down only because we feel the tug of gravity, only because we have mass, and the fact that we have mass needs to be explained, as does the mechanism of gravity. And we say "we," but who are we? How is it that we can make these observations and ask questions about them? All of this is awful, by which we mean that it leaves us in awe, in a state of godforsaken wonder, and it takes a kind of faith to accept it.

"I do hope that at some level," Brette says, "there's something that's no longer a something. An eclipse. That must be what people really mean when they say 'God,' because why would they be talking about Yahweh?"

"The real God," says Eva, "is the idea of there being an idea of there being a something that's not something. Right? Or else it's the place where grace comes from. Is it crazy to talk about grace?"

"Call it goodness. Or just that feeling. It has to come from somewhere."

Eva's mood has improved during their stroll. There's no denying that sometimes she feels a certain something. A window bangs in the soul and happiness blows through like a gust of wind.

"Goodness or grace," she says meditatively. "Or something like that. It pours down the cosmic ladder."

. . .

But now Ted and Murphy have returned, and the sound of tires on gravel recalls Eva and Brette to the luminous construct that we call daily life. They start back down the path and cross the footbridge, and when they get closer they can see Murphy swinging across the deck on crutches. He is a phantom, sure, or a hunk of avatar meat in the universal stew, but individuals do assert their prerogatives. They insist on running when everyone knows they should rest. The meat, whatever it is, is the part of the stew that we spend most of our time chewing.

"Were you really a showgirl?" Eva says.

"They called me the Belle of Anaheim."

Eva sighs and places a hand on her abdomen. She hopes the baby is okay in there.

"It's supposed to work," says Brette, guessing her concern. "The whole thing is set up to work. More often than not you could have the baby in your living room."

"But that doesn't help with the worry," says Eva.

"Because the worry is an important part of it. That's how you keep yourself safe. The worry is an evolutionary adaptation."

Murphy has a stress fracture in his left foot. He doesn't have a splint or a cast, but he has to keep weight off the foot for six weeks.

"It doesn't matter," he says miserably. "Let's not even talk about it."

Ted is interested in the asymmetrical nature of the injury, which is evidence of an asymmetrical gait. He speculates that the left leg will weaken while Murphy is on crutches, and the right leg will get stronger, so it's possible that his asymmetrical gait will correct itself that way. The challenge is to discard the crutches at just the right moment, when things are in balance.

Eva says, "The challenge is overcoming the lunacy long enough for the foot to heal."

"I couldn't agree more," Ted says, shaking his head. "Easier said than done."

"I can hardly believe it," says Murphy. "The whole time with those ballet slippers, I was sort of joking. And we both knew it! But now I have to face the consequences anyway."

Eva and Brette cool off in the lake, Ted heads back into town to pick up groceries, and Murphy subsides into gloom. She's pregnant she's pregnant she's pregnant, he thinks. If something should happen. If I should lose her. It would be the. I'd never be able. How could I keep.

He fetches some ibuprofen and makes himself a cup of green tea, which is no simple thing on crutches. Then he tries to distract himself with *Moby-Dick*, but he quickly runs into trouble. The Internet is not yet conscious, or at least not yet capable of manufacturing a real-life Arnold Schwarzenegger, but it exists, and its existence has created a new way of life, a new attitude, an Intertude, such that he cannot sit still and read because he keeps thinking of all the things he needs to look up, like the scientific name of those wild roses that grow in Nantucket, and some figures about the longevity of bowhead whales, and something Hawthorne said about Melville and religion. As he has already observed, it doesn't matter that he has reverted to the phoneless condition of his teenage years. The Internet is all around him. The refrigerator is connected to the Wi-Fi network. Thus his failure to concentrate is a world-historical problem and not a problem of local application. He affirms that the Internet must be destroyed, and soon, before it achieves consciousness and turns good or evil, either of which would be terrible.

. . .

Eva sweeps into the house. The sunlight and the sweet clean air seem to cling to her person. "I don't know anything about babies," she says.

Murphy nods. He doesn't either.

"I try to think of the baby," says Eva, "but I can't think of a little red newborn with a starry glare. You know how they have that starry glare?"

"I don't know anything about newborns."

"They have this glare. I know that much. But I can't think of my baby that way. Instead I think of a little sidekick. He comes with me to do this or that. Or she. Just a tiny person with no impulse control. I imagine the baby drinking a big pint glass of beer."

Murphy nods, but he can't muster a smile.

"A deranged homunculus," says Eva.

Murphy hangs his head.

"What's wrong with you? Are you in pain?"

"I'm embarrassed." He lifts a crutch and thumps it a few times for emphasis. "I feel like an idiot. But that reminds me that you have to go to the hospital too and get your blood removed, so they can test it. That's part of the tradition of being pregnant."

True enough. She probably wouldn't have to go to the doctor at all, she could probably deliver the baby at home, but probably isn't good enough.

What Hawthorne said about Melville was this: "If he were a religious man, he would be one of the most truly religious and reverential."

And Hawthorne had this to say about the birth of his own child: "I find it necessary to come out of my cloud region, and allow myself to be woven into the sombre texture of humanity. There is no escaping it any longer. I have business on earth now, and must look about me for the means of doing it."

209

The afternoon swings by and they hardly get a look at it. Then they eat chicken curry on the deck and watch the cool night coming down. Redwoods rise all around the lake in their abstract swaying singleness, their here-ness, their nowhere-ness. A neighbor plays "Redemption Song" on the flute. They remember it so fondly, this moment. And they remember Savannah so fondly too. And they remember the faded lettering on the old mills in Winston-Salem, and the blue mountains of North Carolina, and the cornfields of the Midwest, and the sun and the locusts and the high towering loneliness of the shortgrass prairie, and Denver stretched out in its rain shadow, and the red deserts and endless freight trains, and the impossible scale of the Grand Canyon, and Los Angeles, and even Yosemite. All these places, longed for as the rosy past is longed for. And meanwhile the neutrinos rain down, or pass up through the earth, and the stars pop and fizz, and the moon raises the hair on their necks. In the morning, they take the road north.

WHETHER YAHWEH IS the worst and lowest of the gods or not, he is the proximate deity, and when he elects to impose his will, there's nothing Murphy and Eva can do about it. He catches up with them in southern Oregon, where they've stopped at an overlook to stare at the ocean, and he sits them down on the guardrail and subjects them to a sermon. Satan can distract him no longer, it seems. Yahweh wishes to reestablish his authority.

"It is not my desire," he says, striding back and forth with his hands behind his back, "that anyone shall die. But if the righteous turn from righteousness, they shall die. Are my ways unjust?"

Does he know that Satan has deceived him? You can never be sure what he knows. Eva and Murphy look at their feet. The wind is blowing hard but Yahweh's hair doesn't even stir. The trees are scraped back against the rocky headland. Eva hopes against hope that he doesn't know about the baby.

"*Your* ways are unjust," he says. "Your ways are unjust! Not my ways. If a man eats at mountain shrines, or defiles his neighbor's wife, or approaches a menstruous woman, or lends at interest, or commits robbery, or requires a pledge for a loan, or looks to the idols, or mistreats the poor, then that man will die, because the wickedness of the wicked will be charged to him."

Murphy mutters, "You don't care about the poor."

Yahweh silences him. "But if that man has a son, and if that son does *not* eat at mountain shrines, or defile his neighbor's wife, or approach menstruous women, or lend at interest, or commit robbery, or require a pledge for a loan, or look to the idols, or mistreat the poor, and if he gives *food* to the poor, and clothing to the naked, then will that man die? He will not! Because the righteousness of the righteous will be credited to him."

This could go on forever, and it does go on for some time longer, but then Yahweh remembers Mount Trashmore. Have they arranged the purchase yet? Have they spoken to any contractors? If not, why not? If not, have they not considered that the vengeance of the Lord is terrible?

He leaves them with this command: They are to attend, as previously discussed, the fifth annual Gaines, Plessy, and Rogerson American Ideas Conference—"summer camp for billionaires"—which will convene in one week at the Peach Valley Club, a private ski and golf community in Peach Valley, Montana. Yahweh is firm about this. It may be that he hopes to turn the power and influence of the conference attendees to his own advantage. In any case, he now departs by leaping from the cliff into the ocean, and Murphy and Eva return to the *Pequod* and continue north up the wild coast. Apparently they're free to pick their own route, so they have lunch in Newport, and afterward they interact with seals. Fluffy 2 shows great interest in these creatures. Could it be that he's a marine mammal who has reverted, by way of an epigenetic miracle, to the terrestrial form of his ancestors?

Eva thinks of an afternoon she spent with an old boyfriend, trimming and packaging marijuana, and she imagines the baby helping her with this project. Tiny fat fingers, little Ziploc bags. The baby enchanted by the boyfriend's neighbor, a big woman with giant breasts. This vision is more real to her than the memory. The baby making pronouncements, like Murphy does, and getting involved in the work; Eva trying to tell the baby this isn't right, something's not right, they aren't going to remember this day with pride.

In Portland, they visit the Rose Garden. They do it mostly for sentiment's sake, because Murphy's father comes from Portland and they used to visit the Rose Garden when Murphy was small. Here, not surprisingly, Murphy sees his much younger self, a child self, clutching an NBA basketball almanac and peering at Mount Hood. He does not trouble this morose little fellow, but he feels a greater kinship with him than he did with the Murphy in Flagstaff. It occurs to him that in some ways, adulthood has meant a return to the habits and inclinations of childhood. The Murphy in Flagstaff was the outlier—a Murphy on a psychological Rumspringa.

Eva may be pregnant, she and Brette may have solved theology, but those things don't stop her from going crazy again here in Portland. She rushes down the paths with an ice cream cone in her hand and screams, "His name is Yahweh, his name is Yahweh, tremble before him, he honors those that honor him but those that *spurn* him will be *dis*honored." Murphy can't catch her on his crutches.

And yet she's quiet and serene by the time they get back into the car. She buckles her seat belt and looks thoughtfully out the window.

"Couldn't we go somewhere else?" she says. "Somewhere good. We have all this money. We could get on a plane. Remember how we said we'd go to Alaska?"

"We can't."

"Why can't we?"

"We have go the American Ideas Conference."

"I want to go to a treeless island in Greece, with blinding rocks."

"I want to go to Oaxaca and learn about all the different peppers."

"We can do it. Maybe Satan can help again. Or who cares? We'll go some other time." She leans back and closes her eyes. "It's the strangest thing, but sometimes I feel this contentment. It seems like everything's okay."

"That's ridiculous."

"It's just a feeling. I can't explain it. Did you read that article about trees?"

"I don't have a phone."

"They have memories. They make choices. It's beautiful. And did you read that article about the guy who writes the blog?"

"The guy who writes the blog," says Murphy.

"Sure, yeah. He writes this blog, and what he does is . . ."

She begins to summarize the article. Murphy has trouble concentrating. He peers apprehensively at the vast northwestern forest. He is not in an exultant frame of mind, and the last thing he wants to worry about is the consciousness of these threatened trees.

They cross the border into Washington and have a nice time on the Olympic Peninsula, where they investigate the wet moss-stuffed Hoh Rain Forest. Thank heavens we have the concept of orographic lift to help us make sense of the geography. The Hoh Rain Forest is on the western or windward slopes of the Olympic Mountains and it gets 142 inches of precipitation per year. Seattle is on the other side of the mountains, in the rain shadow, and despite its reputation for dreariness, it receives only 37.49 inches of precipitation per year, an East Kansan total, far less than the cities of the East Coast.

Very interesting, very interesting, but Murphy's mind is elsewhere. He's thinking about death. As Philip Larkin writes so memorably: "Most things may never happen: this one will." And that's why he decides to compose a letter to his unborn child. He wants to get some simple advice down on paper, in case Yahweh decides to destroy him, which could happen at any time. He tries to exclude his despair from this message, however, and works hard to achieve a balanced and objective tone:

Dear Child, I haven't found a way to get any flavor into a really soft fish, but I can tell you that snorkeling is worth the effort, John Singer Sargent will reward your serious and prolonged consideration, and sauerkraut and other fermented vegetables go well on sandwiches of all kinds, and other foods too. There's no reason to be cautious or parsimonious in that respect. Also, you have to know your jellyfish, because some are harmless, but some are extremely dangerous.

For Murphy, the notional baby is an earnest wide-eyed creature who requires instruction, but for Eva, this creature is imperfectly distinguished from her own self. If the baby is with her now, it seems as if the baby has been with her always. An accomplice in the crimes of her youth. A witness to the quiet sublime moments. The baby with bruised knuckles, emerging from someone's RV and saying, "The clean-house smell of the pines out here only makes me feel oilier." Or

215

sitting there on Christmas morning in Pennsylvania, working through a stack of scratch-off tickets.

They stop to eat blackberry cobbler in Olympia and Yahweh himself is there to take their order. To Murphy he serves a bowl of white sugar with a stone in it. To Eva he says, "You'll eat what is offered to you. You'll eat these napkins." While she chews, he sits down next to them and says, "I'm going to do such a thing that both ears of anyone who hears about it will tingle. This place will be like a scarecrow in a cucumber field. I'll smash them all, one against the other. And *then* they'll know that I am the Lord."

But just as confusing as his indiscriminate abuse is this: his anguish. He comes to them the next day in trembling misery and says "My suffering!" with all the surprise and hurt of a child stung by a bee. He tries to reassure himself. "I'll smelt out their dross. And they'll know that I am the Lord. They'll know." He smiles the saddest smile in the universe, and in a quavering heartbreaking voice, he says, "They will be my people, and I will be their God."

Dear Child, Murphy writes, Do we wish we'd gotten a better god than Yahweh? Of course we do. It's just one of life's many disappointments.

Eva shrugs it all off, at least for now. She rolls down her window and the hot dry air whips her hair around. She and Murphy are both going blond in the summer sun.

She asks, "Did you love me from the day we met?"

"Yes."

...half of the living, that the buffalo would multiply once again, that
...e white people would leave and evil would be rinsed from the
...rth. They believed that everything would be as it had been. They
...elieved that the disaster of the present was a bad dream. Some of
...he dancers wore ghost shirts that were supposed to be impervious
...o the white man's bullets.

...a is pregnant, sick to her stomach, oppressed by the demands of
...e Almighty, but she's in a great frame of mind. She's writing a
...m. She wants to travel. It's Murphy, thinking dark thoughts about
...rica and American history, who requires consolation. There's no
... or justice in these matters. He lies with his head in her lap
...s eyes closed. Eva holds him tight while she reads his letter to
...tional child. Some passages are scrawled in a big looping hand
...e are written with micrographic precision. The sentiments,
...neven. But she knows that he's sensitive to criticism.

...at," she says

... think so?"

...se it is! It's full of good insights."

...g to revise it. It's turned into a list of sorrowful

...you mean, but it's still very good. We might just include
... things, to balance out the mood."

...ks for a long time, and eventually he says, "You can
...top and it'll root down and start to grow."

...ite that down."

...ill produce a pineapple. They're delicate, so you
...he plant never gets cold."

...ierge service Universal Health Care is the only
...d, that's the one Eva chooses. It is among the

"Are you sure?"

"Yes," he says again, this time with a faint note of impatience.

"It was the only time I ever saw you smoke a cigarette."

"I was doing it because you were doing it."

"Why was I doing it? I didn't even smoke."

"It was raining and it was very hot," says Murphy. "Do you remember that I'd just come from the vet school?"

"You were buying meat."

"Unfortunately."

"You were at the vet school buying meat," she says. "There's no way to get around it now. It's part of the story of how we met."

East of the Cascades, in the long rain shadow, there are blushing deserts, creased and rumpled hills, thunderous rocks, wind turbines, balloon rallies, A&W's, wheat fields. Eva makes an insupportable disturbance at a chamber music concert in Kennewick, Washington, and has to be ejected by a pair of ushers, but by now this is almost routine. She turns in the doorway and screams, "I'm filled with the wrath of the Lord. I can't hold it in!" And then Murphy swings after her on his crutches and off they go. The moon is bright enough to read by and the best apples in the world are said to grow not far from here, on a few special hillsides where there's ample groundwater but no precipitation or humidity.

"I guess if they're allowed to sell the meat," Eva says, "there must be all kinds of regulations."

"That was my understanding."

"It wasn't like it was cows they'd experimented on. Or sick cows."

"Of course not. There was all kinds of scrutiny, I think."

"But you never confirmed."

"I was afraid of what I'd learn. It was Florida. Maybe there weren't any regulations after all."

Dear Child, Murphy writes, Remember that capitalist markets are human inventions. There's nothing natural about them. They need to be strictly regulated or they just reinforce existing problems and inequalities. Also remember that cold medicine often makes you feel worse than the illness itself. And if you feel a madness for punctuality, know that I feel this madness too. It can be painful and aggravating, but no one ever missed a flight because they arrived at the airport too early.

They cross back into Oregon and enter the remote Wallowa Valley, the ancestral home of Chief Joseph and the Wallowa Nez Perce. When they leave the valley and head north to Lewiston, Idaho, and then east into the Bitterroot Mountains, they are retracing the steps of Lewis and Clark, but they're also approximating the route that Chief Joseph and his people took when they were forcibly removed from their home and ordered to settle on the Lapwai reservation in Idaho. Murphy looks up the story on Eva's phone. Murphy with his gloomy thoughts. Murphy who is drawn to this ghastly history like a moth to a flame.

"I remember this from eleventh grade," he says, holding the phone up. "I had to write an essay about it."

Joseph's real name was something like Hinmatóowyalahtq'it, or "thunder rolling from the mountains." He had long been committed to peaceful coexistence with the duplicitous Americans, but he could not accept the insulting and unjust resettlement order. His resistance provoked a series of violent clashes that led to the Nez Perce War, so-called, which was not a war at all but a thousand-mile fighting retreat as Joseph and his people, pursued by the U.S. Army but winning every battle, fled to Montana to seek refuge with their Crow allies.

"Oh no," says Murphy. "I remember this part too. From th᾽ Burns series."

When they were betrayed by the Crow, they tried to rea᾽ and claim political asylum, as Sitting Bull had done, bᵛ intercepted a few miles from the border. Here, starving Joseph was forced to surrender, and here, too, he is sᵛ made his famous speech, which concludes: "I will f ever." But the speech might have been written la᾽ nalist, and of course, as we hardly need to say, the ᾽ were not honored, they never are. In this caˢ betrayal goes to none other than William T᾽

Dear Baby, Never make a treaty with ᵃ

Eva listens and tries to concentra᾽ her mind wanders. Baby singiᵑ girl I know." Baby encouragiᵑ in her poetry. Or buying ᵑ driving a stolen golf cart. ᾽ second, she thinks, we'ʳ nut, the next we're cʳ car key to cut the sᶜ

At the end of ᾽ divided Indiᵃ settlers, a ʳ the remᵃ believeᵈ rect ᵖ uniᵛ

most expensive and least universally accessible of concierge medicine services, and she feels guilty about this, but she wants the promised health care advocate. She needs help navigating the complexities of managing her wellness.

So now, easy as anything, she has an appointment in Missoula, Montana, where she is to have her blood removed, as Murphy persists in saying, and subjected to extensive tests. It pays to pay a huge amount for health care. The doctor's office is like a resort hotel, and when she feels light-headed after having her blood drawn, they give her a choice of small pies. Her pregnancy is confirmed, and the tests will shortly reveal that all is well. She is instructed to continue not eating soft cheese.

Murphy, too, gets a kind of going-over at the doctor's office. Meanwhile, he broods over his injury. Maybe it will heal funny and it will never be the same.

"But then again," he says, "it's true every day that we're not what we were yesterday."

He peers out the window. The street ends abruptly in a spray of gravel a hundred yards away, at which point a dramatic treeless butte rises above the city.

"We won't tell the baby that," says Eva. "At least not at first."

The Nez Perce passed through Missoula too. Murphy presses his hands together and frowns. He looks like he might burst into tears.

"I should be the one consoling *you*," he says.

The Ghost Dance was associated with resistance to the Dawes Act, and white officials worried that it would spark violent confrontation. That's why they were so worried when they were told that Sitting Bull intended to support the movement. They sent Lakota policemen to arrest him, and he was killed during the struggle that followed.

· · ·

Everything is just beginning and everything is already over, and it's all happening at the same time. To Matthew McConaughey, time is like a cube that can be entered at any point, and to an entity like Yahweh, time is just the medium in which a certain kind of business must be transacted. To the right kind of physicist, time is a probabilistic phenomenon and the difference between the past and the future exists only in the context of heat exchange, or increasing entropy. But none of that makes history any easier to stomach. None of that makes parenthood any more comprehensible to those who must prepare themselves for it.

"I can't help it," Eva says, lifting her legs and admiring her bamboo socks. "Sometimes I think everything is great. Sometimes I'm happy. I know it's not a defensible position."

THE AMERICAN IDEAS Conference is an annual event at which CEOs and visionaries and writers and artists share their "ideas," if they have any, and discuss the future of the American nation-state, if they believe it has one. The billionaires also do what billionaires do best, which is make deals that will earn them additional billions. Those guests who are not billionaires watch this process with envy.

"It's the biggest test so far," says Murphy. "Be kind to *these* people. Try to respect *their* humanity." He glances around suspiciously.

For context, Peach Valley is on the hundred and thirteenth meridian, receives 13.02 inches of precipitation annually, and has a cold semi-arid climate (Köppen climate classification *BSk*). It's also high up at about 5,200 feet. The Peach Valley Club itself costs something like a million dollars to join. Astonishing figure. It is indeed a lavish retreat, and Murphy and Eva look a little out of place in so rarefied an environment. The *Pequod* is coated with dust, the collards are ragged, Fluffy 2 is stained purple with raspberry juice, and what's more, what's more, there's an ancient Near Eastern god in the back seat, peevishly demanding Gatorade. But they are rich, after all, and in that sense they belong. The shoe Murphy wears on his good foot is a Ferragamo loafer, and Eva is wearing her red Dolce & Gabbana leggings, although she's cut them off at the mid-thigh and she's calling them her "fancy pants." They check in and they are Mrs. and Mr. Jane Pierce, no questions asked.

They're relieved to see old Barney, who embraces them and hopes they had an easy trip. He has a blood pressure cuff velcroed to his left arm.

"Have you heard the name of the Lord," says Eva, "which is Yahweh?"

"I could use his help about now. I think it was when I saw you last that I had the chip in my throat?"

"UPS was tracking you that way," says Murphy.

"The results were not conclusive. There was a biopsy but damn me if it wasn't negative."

"What's the diagnosis?"

"The diagnosis," says Barney, suppressing a belch, "is that there is nothing wrong with me. Do you know what they call my kind of discomfort?"

"Gastritis."

"Gastr*itis*, yes. Gastritis. Which is just Greek for stomach problem."

"Is it Greek?"

"It could be Phoenician for all I know. The outcome is I'm at square one, my friends. I'm no closer to the answer as to what is really wrong with me. I'm only drinking deionized water, to be safe."

. . .

Now it's time to pop off to their suite in order to change and shower and rest. Barney sends up a sterling silver dish of hand-sliced meat for Fluffy 2, who is by now accustomed to luxury accommodations and sniffs disparagingly at this meal. Eva is ravenous and longs to eat some, but the meat is uncooked and pregnant women must not eat raw animal products. Murphy does eat some, which distresses the footman who has delivered it. He soon returns with a fresh portion, presumably to spare Fluffy 2 the indignity of eating from a plate that another guest has touched.

While Eva takes a shower, Murphy turns on the television and lets the electronic colors wash over him. Sporting events are being contested. Celebrities are crashing their cars and making speeches to highway patrolmen. Dams across the nation are close to failure. Here's a commercial for a vehicle that enhances one's sense of individual liberty. Here's a football player boasting that he will be "even more focused on team-based play" this year. Here's the president smirking beneath his unforgivable hair.

Eva is sitting on the edge of the tub thinking about how nice the tub is, and the suite, and everything. She's thinking about all that money in her checking account. It isn't as if she doesn't feel bad about the fancy pants and the Ferragamo loafers and the luxury hotels. To balance things out, metaphysically speaking, she has donated more than six million dollars to the ACLU and a handful of environmental advocacy groups. They've been sending her special updates to tell her what her money's been doing. She wonders idly if these charitable donations count in the great karmic ledger. Are they annulled by the fact that she often donates money after making some extravagant purchase for herself? But maybe this is the wrong way to think about it. Her own soul is of no account. All that matters is that the good guys have the money they need.

Murphy lowers himself gingerly to the floor, sets his crutches aside, and does a few sit-ups and other non-weight-bearing exercises. Then he consults the binder of conference materials. Seminars and panel discussions take place in the mornings, and in the afternoons there are recreational activities. This tapestry of summer fun is checkered with high-quality informal rustic meals.

While examining the schedule, he discovers two things of tremendous interest. The first is that he himself is to discuss his own American Ideas on a panel tomorrow morning, during one of the conference's first sessions. The second is that he, "Pierce," is properly John Ransom Pierce, the heir to a Carolina textile fortune and a senior partner at Byzantium Capital, a firm whose true nature he is unable to grasp, although he grabs Eva's phone and pursues the matter across several websites. The title of his panel will be "New South, Old Problems."

He looks at a few pictures of John Ransom Pierce. He is an aging bon vivant, and he does look plausibly like Murphy.

Eva strolls out of the bathroom and begins to rummage around in her bag. She can't or won't pay attention to what Murphy's telling her.

"John Crowe Ransom?"

"John Ransom Pierce."

She pulls a few items of clothing out and tosses them on the floor. "I've got a present for you," she says. "I wrote you a poem." She pulls out her bag of toiletries and flicks it over her shoulder. She removes a few books and sets them aside. She straightens up and frowns. "It's okay if you don't like it." She pulls a few more things out and then she gives up and dumps everything on the floor. A brochure for a mining museum flutters to the ground. She's written the poem on the back.

"I don't know if it's good or not."

It's not a love poem that rhymes, or a nature poem about standing in a stream, and she hasn't used the words *honeyed* or *riven*. It's a poem about a night out with Baby. Drunk-driving, breaking into that ex-lover's house, playing Big Buck Hunter at Buffalo Wild Wings. If you'll allow us the liberty, it's a poem about the way in which a new baby is incorporated only gradually into a mother's already cluttered and problematic life. A life so full of mistakes and regrets. It ends like this:

> *From the corner of my eye I see him nod,*
> *hold up his glass of beer and take a sip,*
> *as if he's about to tell me everything, right after this—*
> *but he just sits there, staring, slumped on the table,*
> *hot sauce on his belly and lips. I drop the gun*
> *and pick him up. Poor Baby. Something's gone terribly wrong.*

It's not a poem about the baby's innocence, that is. It's about the mother discovering her own innocence, and losing it, or something like that. Who really knows? Poems are poems.

In any case, Murphy is enchanted, but he doesn't have a good and credible way of telling her how much he likes it. This always happens. He'll say he loves it, and she'll never know how deeply he means it.

Unfortunately, there's no time to linger over the mystery of art. Their next task is to outfit themselves for the weekend. Murphy slips the poem into his pocket and they ride back down to the lobby and visit the boutique clothiers.

Murphy's concern is that Pierce has been a figure of fun for too long. He's anxious to project an air of professionalism at his panel tomorrow. The sales associate brings him various shirts and slacks and he selects items of a pronounced and almost offensive modesty. With the exception of the clothing he'll wear tonight, all of this stuff will be modified to his unique specifications by tomorrow morning at the latest. The tailor who takes his measurements isn't fazed by the crutches.

Eva, however, might as well be attending a conference on Mars for all she cares about conventional human clothing. She tries on a pair of $1,400 "floral jacquard culottes." They are wide and garish and billowing and they look deeply strange on her slender frame. No doubt she's working through some self-consciousness vis-à-vis the imminent transformation of her body. Luckily, the person waiting on her says that he cannot "in good conscience" permit her to make this purchase. She nods and asks if he's heard the name of the Lord, which is Yahweh, and he says "Yes, thank you" in a deferential tone.

Tonight's cocktail party and rustic evening meal take place outside among the glowing heat lamps. It is, as promised, an informal gathering. Excessive formality is for the peasants, who are compelled to affirm and reaffirm their significance with empty ceremony. But it's lucky that Murphy and Eva have taken some time with their clothing, because everyone here is in uniform, so to speak. The finance people and the high-class CEOs swan about in slacks and jackets, cable-knit cashmere sweaters, plain black dresses and scarves and flats. The Silicon Valley people wear their iconic hooded sweatshirts, crisp tight jeans, and little slippery shoes. Careful of stress fractures, friends! There's a group we might characterize, unfairly and unpleasantly, as blue-collar CEOs—the manufacturers of pool toys and cat food and so on—and they tend to be dressed more carelessly, with something approaching true informality, like children who have rushed to clothe themselves in their hurry to catch the school bus. The artists are dressed with studied eccentricity. Here's a woman who specializes in outsized LED sculptures, and she's wearing iridescent black tights and a yellow raincoat over a blue bikini top. She looks a little like Eva, who wears a provocatively short black dress, rain boots, and sunglasses. Instead of a shawl or scarf, she's got a child's blanket with sleepy bears on it.

Murphy chats with Dexter Philpot, the wealthy CEO of Beyond Human, whom he accosted in Phoenix. He'd like to know more about genetic engineering, but he's distracted by Philpot's watch.

"It's a Franck Muller Crazy Hours watch," says Philpot.

"The numbers are in the wrong places."

"It's a steal at twenty thousand dollars."

"But can you tell time with it?"

"I use my phone to tell time. But this watch gets me to *think* about time. When I look at it, I realize that time is precious and fleeting."

This sounds just like something Murphy himself would say, but as he stands here on his crutches, his poem in his pocket, his bosom swelling with love and truth, he knows that this watch is a piece of garbage.

Rebecca Hugginson, COO of Whisperer, has a baby on her hip, an accessory that manages to be informal and ostentatious at the same time. She has explained on numerous occasions that her role as a mother is at least as important as her role as an innovator. Alas, she and her husband have recently divorced for what both parties describe as "personal reasons." Both Murphy and Eva sneak frequent glances at the baby. He, or she, isn't drinking beer and doesn't look capable of driving a car.

Mrs. and Mr. Pierce have some friends among the guests. Michael Hock, who made his fortune selling rubber dog toys, greets Murphy warmly and wants to know what's up with the crutches. Murphy says he ran himself over with a golf cart. Hock nods sympathetically. He's having some troubles of his own. He and his CEO pal, timber baron and developer Bill Cruncher, went for a pre-conference hike this morning, but in the mountains they encountered poison ivy or something similar and now their legs are quilted with angry sores. Hock says it doesn't matter. The pain is just another way to experience his strength.

After a kind of respite, Eva is beginning to feel bad again. She can't drink, because of the baby. Nor can she enjoy any soft cheese. Nor will Yahweh let her alone. Again and again, she feels the spirit of the Lord come over her and she speaks in ecstasy among the people.

"His name is Yahweh!" she says to the crowd at the bar. "And can you even contemplate the thunderings from his pavilion? But that's just the mere whisper that we perceive of him. When he holds back the waters, they dry up, and when he lets them loose, they tear up the land."

Some guests are good-natured about it, and others are not. A stern media personality—a woman whom Eva admires tremendously for her outspoken defense of women's reproductive rights—takes her to task.

"Are you saying Yahweh? Am I hearing you correctly?"

"Yahweh Yahweh Yahweh," says Eva, in ecstasy.

"The despotic tyrannical totemic Man God. The Ur-Man. The thing itself."

"I'm sorry. I have to say it. I have no choice. I'm such an admirer of your work."

"I," says the media personality, "believe that we ought to do good in this world because that is the right thing to do. Is it really very hard to say what's good and what's bad? Do we need a demon to tell us? We just need to do things that increase the sum of human happiness and don't add to the sum of misery."

"That's what I believe too!"

"If I wear a tinfoil hat and tell you that the Hubble telescope has instructed me to murder my child, you'll tell me I'm crazy and hopefully you'll call the police. But if I tell you that a Mesopotamian rain god is watching my every move and won't permit me to work on Sundays, custom requires you to treat my claim with respect."

"You sound like Satan. That's exactly what Satan would say."

The woman gives her a doubtful look.

"But I agree!" says Eva. "None of this is my choice. It's not like I *believe* in Yahweh. It's not like I *trust* in him at all. I don't even like him."

Eva explains that when she was young, they made her say her prayers and she thought God was watching her when she got undressed. Then she read books and pulled herself together. Education changed her life. And now Yahweh won't leave her alone. What a joke. But it doesn't mean she's not a secular humanist.

The media personality seems to recognize that something more is going on here. Maybe she sees a young woman deranged by her passage through this cruel man's world. She places a hand on Eva's shoulder and repeats, "Yahweh is a symbol of woman's oppression. It's more important than ever that we understand that. We can give him no quarter."

These ideas are of course central to Murphy and Eva's own secular orthodoxy. But now Eva's tongue won't move. Another of Yahweh's tricks.

Murphy catches sight of her as she crosses the patio, but from a distance she seems more or less in control of herself. Meanwhile, he's hanging around with a group of six Internet people whose cumulative net worth exceeds ten billion United States dollars. He himself possesses a smaller fortune, but he is John Ransom Pierce, a not inconsiderable figure, and he has decided to test the Mount Trashmore idea on them.

"We're locked into about ten feet of sea-level rise. Ten feet at least. That's an optimistic assessment. What nobody understands is that it's a foregone conclusion. This would be true even if the government were still making real policy. The ice is out of equilibrium."

"We understand," says Li Wei, founder and CEO of Klllickt.

"It's certainly doesn't *help* that we identified the worst person in America and made him president. But what nobody gets is that we're committed to this amount of sea-level rise in any case. South Florida is going to be inundated. It's going to happen. It's unavoidable."

"We all know this by now," says Li Wei. "We think about it all the time."

Murphy keeps trying to lift his good leg off the ground and balance on his crutches. He says, "We have to think about this calamity in two ways. First, we in the private sector need to recommit ourselves to climate justice. There's a lot we can do, no matter what's happening in Washington. We've got all the momentum."

"Distributed solar," says Li Wei. "Energy storage on the customer side of the meter."

Guy Pleurisy, CEO of Diddler, says that the new batteries are incredible.

"But the illiberal part of it," Murphy says, "is that we need to be alive to the opportunities that a radically altered climate will provide. Apocalyptic thinking is one thing, but we will need to *live* in the future as well. I'm talking about apocalyptic entrepreneurship. Think about Greenland wheat. And the Northwest Passage. You all are the innovators."

They are; they know it; they nod.

"I do have one project of my own in mind," he says. "I'm involved with some people who are planning to build a lunar-powered resort on a mountain of trash. But forgive me, I don't mean to talk business all night."

Eva is beginning to lose what little composure she's been able to maintain. She is tormented by ecstasy. The spirit of the Lord comes every few minutes, like contractions, and she pursues the CEOs and luminaries across the garden.

"He will destroy your vineyards and make your women barren!" she screams. "Please listen to me! He'll turn your homes into places where the Lilith reposes! He'll requite you for your abominations! And then you'll know that he is the Lord!"

On the other hand, there's a sense in which she doesn't seem any crazier than the more eccentric of the CEOs. Gina Montez, who made her $1.2 billion in frozen empanadas and other ethnic treats, has sent her G550 jet back home to Seattle, where it's to retrieve a bottle of wine from her five-thousand-bottle wine cellar. She has managed to conceive of a desire for the one bottle of wine that the resort itself doesn't possess. And Johnny "Enterprise" Erickson, who earlier described himself to Murphy as "a simple man with simple tastes," has demanded a flavor of Ben & Jerry's ice cream that he calls "Gonzo Malt Madness"— a flavor that does not exist and must be improvised for him by the kitchen staff. Thus his desire for a thing has served to bring that thing into being. It's like George Bernard Shaw says: "The reasonable man adapts himself to the world: the unreasonable one persists in trying to adapt the world to himself. Therefore all progress depends on the unreasonable man."

The media personality is taking Michael Hock to task. "The United States is one of only a handful of countries with no law on the books to guarantee paid family leave," she says. "Depending on what you're talking about, the other countries include Lesotho, Swaziland, and Papua New Guinea." Michael Hock protests that he's entitled to his own opinion, but the media personality corrects him: "You are entitled to *an* opinion as long as that opinion is informed by a responsible consideration of the available data. We seem to have forgotten this in America today. If your opinion is a matter of prejudice or it derives from poor information, it is not an opinion and you are not entitled to it."

Bill Cruncher, by now soggy with booze, attempts to fix a dysfunctional heat lamp and creates a sensation by setting his hair on fire.

"Well," says a famous journalist, accosted by Eva, "what I'd like to ask Yahweh is what was he thinking with the prostate gland? Why make a gland that totally surrounds the vital ureter? If there's any inflammation, it just closes that vital tube right off. Can Yahweh answer that one?"

A candy manufacturer tells Murphy: "What I don't get is how vanilla ever came to be synonymous with plain. Vanilla is an absolutely ambrosial flavor that we derive from the seedpod of a Mesoamerican orchid."

It should be said that many of the billionaires behave well. Surely it's true that people who are pleasant and affable prior to making their first billion generally remain pleasant and affable afterward. But some of them, like Ms. Montez and Johnny Enterprise, suffer from a derangement that sociologists have called Sudden Wealth Syndrome. We understand it like this: Newly minted billionaires know, as we all know, that everything they have will be taken from them by death, or Yahweh, whichever you prefer. There is therefore an enormous imperative to 1) enjoy the new money before the curtain comes down, and 2) use the new money to buy a life that is as free from inconvenience as possible. But since money will not buy any more happiness than each individual is capable of experiencing, and since life is inevitably fraught with inconvenience, a new billionaire is doomed to disappointment, and therefore also to rage, and struggles continuously to come to grips with the ultimate cause of that disappointment and rage, which is death, or Yahweh, with which, or with whom, none of us can come to grips. Thus the demand for Gonzo Malt Madness.

Eva retreats to a quiet corner with Barney, who is too preoccupied with his health problems to mingle freely with his guests. He takes his temperature and records the value in a little notebook.

"I'm sorry I've been so distracted," he says. "You know how it is with illness. It's so difficult to think of anything else. But I'm going to get this thing licked after all."

She thinks: I'm pregnant I'm pregnant I'm pregnant. But pregnancy is not an illness.

"How has your summer been?" he says.

"We went to the Grand Canyon."

"Lovely."

"And we saw the coast redwoods too."

"What a nice time you must have had!"

"I keep telling myself that everything's okay. Despite everything."

"A nice mantra, if you can make it stick."

"Sometimes I think everything *is* okay."

"That makes two of us," he says.

"And also I'm pregnant!"

Barney slaps his forehead and falls back against the wall. It's the best news, he says. He felt his blood pressure go down just like that.

The sense of value judgment in the distinction between old money and new money—between sudden wealth, one might say, and chronic wealth—is distasteful but ancient. Aristotle himself said that the newly rich "have the vices of wealth in a greater degree and more; for, so to say, they have not been educated to the use of wealth. Their unjust acts are not due to malice, but partly to insolence, partly to lack of self-control, which tends to make them commit assault and battery and adultery." But the distinction is meaningless in the United States, where there is no hereditary aristocracy. The great fortunes are made by con men, brigands, ferry captains, computer programmers, and fur traders. Just look at how Murphy and Eva have gotten rich. Just think of John Jacob Astor, who, at one memorable dinner party, is said to have wiped his mouth on his hostess's dress. The whole nation is suffering from Sudden Wealth Syndrome.

By now it's getting late. The sun is down, the night is cold. Some guests are beginning to retire. You don't become a billionaire by sleeping your life away, but you also don't become a billionaire, divine intervention notwithstanding, by burning the candle all the way down on the first night of an exclusive conference. Ms. Montez, her wine safely retrieved, enjoys that wine, or believes she enjoys it, in her hot tub, where time passes more quickly, or is more likely to pass. Johnny Enterprise has his ice cream, but it's a disappointment because the kitchen staff has not had time to work up the garish packaging he envisioned. Michael Hock sleeps on his terrace in the cold, dreaming sweet dreams of his rural boyhood.

"Send me your contact info, will you?" Li Wei says to Murphy. She is genuinely interested in the trash mountain resort. Innovative thinkers are always looking for new ways to use garbage. "Or wait! Let me show you our new app. You'll love this. Give me your phone?"

Murphy produces his phone, which is a smooth dark phone-size piece of wood. He's been carrying it in his pocket this whole time.

"Very beautiful," she says, turning it over in her hand.

"Now let me ask you something. This has been bothering me for a long time. Under what circumstances does destroying an artificial intelligence count as murder?"

"My thinking is that if the artificial intelligence has been designed in such a way as to render it humanlike, which means educated with human educational materials and infused somehow with human values and human instincts, then yes, it's murder to destroy it."

"That's what you believe?"

"It also seems like murder to kill a thing that knows what it is."

"Like trees. Like an octopus."

"Like practically everything."

EIGHT O'CLOCK IN the morning. Murphy and his copanelists sit together in a little sunlit room and prepare to express their thoughts and opinions on the vexed subject of The South. Murphy is wearing some of his new clothes and he has trimmed his beard, but an attempt to subdue his hair has been unsuccessful. He watches Bill Cruncher, copanelist number one, out of the corner of his eye. Cruncher's hair, charred after last night's mishap, has also come unfastened. More significantly, this timber baron is drinking whiskey from an aftershave bottle. With a conspiratorial wink, he tells Murphy that no one knows it's not aftershave. The third panelist is a man whom Cruncher addresses as "Boomer," and apparently he's already known to Pierce, so Murphy has no opportunity to learn his real name, if he has one. Right now he's embroiled in a discussion with a demented drifter who has inexplicably been granted admission to this exclusive event. The man is asking him, "What's gonna happen when you have diarrhea? What's gonna happen when you have diarrhea?" Boomer doesn't possess the strength of will to free himself from this dialogue and acknowledges with sadness that "it could happen any time."

Murphy and Boomer and Cruncher make a dissolute and uninspiring trio, and very few guests have gathered to hear what they have to say, preferring instead to listen to Leon Lemieux, CEO of Future-NOW, who is discussing the colonization of Mars in the main auditorium. That's where Eva is too, at Yahweh's insistence, because Yahweh is anxious about the colonization of Mars. Murphy, an imposter with a broken foot, is in exile out here in this provincial conference room, and despite his earlier resolution to be the best Pierce he can be, he's tired this morning and he's in a bad frame of mind.

With an abrupt flourish, like a superhero stripping off his civilian clothes, the drifter steps up to the lectern and introduces himself as Professor Arnaux Ramirez, moderator of today's discussion. Boomer laughs and shakes his head. "You got me," he says. Ramirez ignores him and addresses the audience, which consists of seven people, none of whom are sitting closer than the fifth row. "I'm sure our guests are sorry to have kept all of you waiting," he says. There's a frosty note in his voice. He pauses to blow his nose into a McDonald's bag and then reads the turgid biographical notes like a judge reading a sentence.

Murphy, alas, fails to listen to the introduction and doesn't hear Boomer's real name or Ramirez's first question. Now Cruncher is speaking, whether in response to that first question or in an extemporaneous manner who can say. There's something comforting in his mad loquaciousness. The audience does not at any point register interest or understanding.

"The economic argument," he says. "The economic reality. You talk about an industrial versus an agrarian economy. Urban versus rural. North versus South. But there's the cultural aspect too. Economic systems are part and parcel of the religious and moral credos that define a people. You have your mode of governance, your manners, your unique food and drink, and all of it composes a way of life that's linked to that economic system."

"I don't know what you're talking about," says Murphy.

"Oh boy," says Boomer. "Isn't that telling?"

"I don't know if you're talking about now or then. Are you talking about slavery?"

Cruncher ignores these interruptions and continues, "When any part of this socioeconomic system experiences a rupture, it throws the rest off-kilter. What you've got then is a way of life that's not matched any longer to the system that's given rise to it, so you have civil strife, you have poverty. It's all interlinked. It's a social ecosystem."

"Drug addiction," Boomer says.

"Hospital closures," says Cruncher.

"Brain drain. Skyrocketing death rates."

"Goodbye to Main Street."

Murphy interrupts: "You're talking about the situation today. You're not talking about slavery."

"*Jobs*," says Cruncher. "Jobs, jobs, jobs."

"But you're right," says Boomer. "It's important to understand the cultural problem. I think of all the talk about coal. The miners sang those songs about how hard it was down in the mines, and now that the mines are closing, they just want to go back underground. That's culture. They've got themselves to where they can't act in their own interest. There are other jobs to do, my friends! Let me talk to you about a diversified local economy!"

.　.　.

Alexis de Tocqueville, that clever Frenchman, was puzzled by the same kinds of contradictions as he traveled through the new American republic. He wondered if democracy itself was responsible. "In the United States," he wrote, "the majority undertakes to supply a multitude of ready-made opinions for the use of individuals, who are thus relieved from the necessity of forming opinions of their own." And elsewhere: "I know of no country in which there is so little true independence of mind and freedom of discussion as in America." And still elsewhere: "I cannot help fearing that men may reach a point where they look on every new theory as a danger, every innovation as a toilsome trouble, every social advance as a first step toward revolution, and that they may absolutely refuse to move at all."

Murphy has his own explanation. "Everything is fucked," he says, "but I think it was fucked from the beginning, because of slavery. This is the one point I'd like to make."

"I'll thank you to watch your language," says Ramirez.

"That's the original contradiction. Liberty and bondage. We live in a former slave society. The deep structures are racist. There's always someone trying to make it illegal for black people to vote."

"The president is getting bad advice," Cruncher allows.

"The president has more in common with Idi Amin than with his American predecessors."

Boomer smiles. "New South, old problems. I've been saying why don't we jettison the Deep South. I'm saying this as a Mississippi man."

"We're not talking about just the South," says Murphy.

"*Jettison* the South?" says Cruncher, himself an Alabama man. "*Jettison* the South?"

"Only the Deep South."

"It's not a North-South thing," says Murphy. "Are you even listening? It's an urban-rural thing. And it's a white versus nonwhite thing. And you can't jettison the South anyway because then the black people down there would be even more fucked than they are now. It's the same reason you can't let the South secede in 1860 and 1861. If you let those states secede, you're abandoning the slaves."

Boomer shakes his head. "That's not what I mean. To me it's an economic issue. If you'd let me explain."

"And to me," says Cruncher, uncapping his aftershave bottle, "it's about the integrity of the Union. I must be an American patriot."

Let's pause and consider a quotation from a letter by Alexander von Humboldt, one of the smartest men of the past millennium, for whom most plants, animals, and geographical features are named. He was writing before Tocqueville, before everything, and yet the problems he saw in the infant United States are problems we have not solved. Who's really free? Who's in charge? What's the point?

"[The] whole there presents to my mind the sad spectacle of liberty reduced to a mere mechanism in the element of utility," he wrote, "exercising little ennobling or elevating influence upon mind and soul, which, after all, should be the aim of political liberty. Hence indifference on the subject of slavery. But the United States are a Cartesian vortex, carrying everything with them, grading everything to the level of monotony."

A painful condemnation! Thank heavens we don't quite know what he's talking about.

Meanwhile, Murphy is discussing patriotism. From a certain perspective, he argues, the "whole point of America" is that our institutions are mutable and our constitution is susceptible to amendment. Unexamined allegiance to anything—to America too—is therefore un-American. The truly patriotic thing is a refusal to be satisfied with the way things are.

"Dissent is patriotic," he says. "*I'm* an American patriot. It's Cruncher who has the Tory mentality."

He makes an analogy with sports fandom. If you always root for the home team, you're declaring an unconditional allegiance to a group with a changing membership. That's a dangerous proposition. Maybe they're nice guys one year and maybe they're "sociopathic cretins" three years later. You have to make a new determination each year. The same goes for one's country.

"Jefferson thought each generation should write its own constitution," he says. "Flag waving leads to murder. Rooting for the home team is un-American and it breeds fascism."

Ramirez is eating a cold Hot Pocket. Boomer is writing something down. Cruncher says, "But by your argument, Lincoln should have let the South secede after all. Southerners were dissatisfied and they wanted change."

"They wanted it all to stay the same. And they made their choice because of slavery, so it doesn't matter anyway. Human rights are more important than politics."

Now he embarks on another sweeping condemnation of the United States. It's a familiar routine by now: mass shootings, the electoral college, etc. From here he moves to a condemnation of human beings—"the cruelest animal"—and their gods—"even crueler than human beings."

"*I'm* the American patriot here," he says again, "because I hate this country. Freedom died at Wounded Knee."

Then he succumbs to despair and falls silent. And no wonder. When you think about slavery, when you think about the Nez Perce, when you think about the president and his hair, it's hard to escape the idea that a sense of hopeful possibility obtains only at this level of abstraction, and only because time, or the illusion of time, or the high probability of heat exchange, prevents us from knowing to a certainty that nothing will change. Unlike Eva, who's been trying to gaze up the avatar ladder toward the fullness or nothingness from which goodness flows, Murphy fears that the struggle between good and evil is a fiction and the worst outcome is assured. If we're avatars, that is, maybe we're the manifestation of injustice, or chaos. Maybe we are the evil in Yahweh. Or maybe Yahweh has nothing to do with it and we bear all the blame. Or maybe, horrible thought, maybe Yahweh is just an avatar of the worst in *us*. And nothing matters anyway because climate change is going to destroy our civilization. How could he and Eva have chosen to bring a baby into such a world?

He slips the poem out of his pocket and rereads it. Baby with hot sauce on his lips and belly. Then he looks out the window at the glowing mountains and the radiant blue sky. Love versus God. There must be another perspective available, even if he doesn't know what it is. The world is a narrow bridge, and the important thing is not to be afraid.

Boomer is describing his own American idea. The Deep South, he reminds them, is by far the poorest region in the United States, and has been since the Civil War. Pick any metric. Access to health care, education, due process, you name it. It's a scandal. And yes, he concedes, this is the legacy of the slave system.

"So what do we do?" he says. "We jettison the Deep South."

It isn't that its institutions can't be reformed. It's that it has no vital institutions. It hasn't ever been part of the modern continental American republic. The sooner we admit it, the better. Take it from him. He's a Mississippi man.

"So I'm talking about a paradigm shift," he says. "I'm actually talking about a great possibility. We could treat the Deep South like what it is—what economists call an 'extractive state.'"

It turns out that his real ambition is to turn the Deep South into a kind of colony. How much would it cost, he asks, to bring Mississippi into the twenty-first century? Too much. But consider the benefits of its programmatic marginalization. If you strip it of its moribund democratic institutions, you might see regrettable consequences in the short term, but ultimately you have a chance to make something new. Its resources can be extracted at little cost and with little restraint. Business will boom. Everyone benefits. Mississippi could be a new Bangladesh.

"I'm thinking factories. Shoes and underwear. Even *microchips*. And all on our own terms."

"Pierce will tell you that you can't abandon the poor," says Cruncher.

"The cost of living in Bangladesh is tiny. You transform Mississippi into Bangladesh and all those poor people will be able to live like kings. It's the unwieldy democratic bureaucracy that makes their lives so expensive now. The welfare state actually makes them poorer."

Cruncher, overtaken by a gust of drunkenness, says, "You're a madman. You're a dangerous lunatic, Boomer. You're crazier than Pierce. This reminds me of the one about the three farmers and a cow, or wait, I know this, a rabbi and a congressman walk into a discount shoe store . . ."

The discussion quickly unravels after this. Cruncher embarks on a textureless drunken monologue. Ramirez eats another cold Hot Pocket. Boomer folds his arms across his chest and, incredibly, falls asleep. It looks like the panel will slide quietly to its conclusion, like a toboggan crumpling neatly against the tree at the bottom of the hill.

But no: There is one more surprise in store. While Cruncher pauses to enjoy a lusty draft from his aftershave bottle, the door opens and in walks John Ransom Pierce, heir to a Carolina textile fortune, senior partner at Byzantium Capital, husband of Jane Pierce, and bosom friend of P. F. Barnum "Barney" Gaines. He too is on crutches.

"I'm so sorry to be late," he says. "I was here last night, but they wouldn't accept my identification and I couldn't raise Barney on the telephone. There's been some kind of mix-up."

IN THE MAIN auditorium, things have taken a different course. Idealism prevails. Human achievement seems boundless. We will send a team to Mars, says Leon Lemieux. They may die—almost certainly they will die—and then we will send another. They too may die. No matter. We will send a third. Lemieux has *faith* in this project. He clicks through his high-resolution images of the Martian surface and talks about habitat modules, water reclamation, nitrogen, soil bacteria. There's something wonderful about the insanity of the project. We will do all of this because we can. We will found an extraterrestrial colony that will never know slavery or its complex legacy. The colonists will die. But so will we all.

Eva is struggling with the spirit of the Lord, and we know very well how these struggles come out. She is flesh; he is the neutrino wind. And so, as Leon Lemieux talks about radiation shielding—Mars, alas, has no magnetosphere—she rises and makes for the stage. No one stops her. Maybe Yahweh casts a spell on the security guards, but maybe not, who knows. There they stand in their distinctive yellow jackets, with their forbidding jowls, and they do nothing.

She walks to the center of the stage and raises a hand in greeting, preparing to speak of ostriches and Liliths. And then, who knows why, the fog lifts and she feels perfectly sane. For the first time in weeks, she knows just who she is. She is a progressive young woman who believes in fermented food and renewable energy and a single-payer health care system. She's going to be a mom. She thinks of her child, a real child and not a hallucinatory poem-child, and her face lights up like an emoji with hearts for eyes.

But she's already up here on stage, so she turns to Lemieux and says, "May I say a few words?"

As long as the security guards do nothing, Lemieux doesn't have much choice. He isn't going to drag her from the stage himself.

"I'm sure you all know that math and Hinduism are the same," she says. A few people nod. "They're just exactly the same. You can prove it with algebra. And it follows that theology and cosmology are the same too. Therefore all disciplines and branches of learning are the same. Therefore everything is the same. Do you see what I mean? The colonization of Mars is the same as a breakfast of peas and cherries. All fruits are cherries. And so on."

"Okay," says Lemieux.

"Put it this way: How do you stay compassionate in a world where God exists? Think of earthquakes and hurricanes and cholera. The *sun* causes cancer. And also, another example, why does Yahweh send us a stress fracture when he knows we're only joking? So much malice. Why should a god like that get to make choices about life and death? How can you accept it and go on living? But I think it's possible that when we talk about him, we're only talking about what he does on this rung of the ladder, and if he has his main existence on a rung above the flow of time, then we can't grasp his purposes because there's no cause and effect in the place where his thoughts happen. There's no direction for logic to flow. That's why we can't connect his actions to his motives. Do you understand? That's the whole thing. You can prove this algebraically."

The audience is silent, stunned or delighted by the turn things have taken. Lemieux appears to be listening closely.

"I can see how this might be confusing if you haven't been with us in the *Pequod*," says Eva. "Think of it like this: Yahweh is just another kangaroo in the cosmic orchard. We can actually be fairly certain of that, based on his behavior. It's kangaroo behavior. Maybe he hears the communication from the higher level, but he lives here with us and he's susceptible to moonsanity just like we are. He can't stand the sound of the apples. Maybe his real name is Yaldabaoth. He doesn't know anything about the fullness, but he longs for it. Like all of us."

"He won't follow us to Mars," says Lemieux.

"The colonization of Mars is the same as nude mud wrestling."

The security guards have come alive. They climb the stage and advance, arms wide, like men trying to calm a shying horse. Eva ignores them.

"A black hole is a puncture in the fabric of space-time, but it's also an object. It's a hole, but it's a fullness. Time moves very slowly when you get close to a thing like that. Unless black holes are really hot. Or doesn't it matter? Heat just makes it more likely that logic exists."

"Are you talking about Boltzmann?" says Lemieux. "Are you talking about entropy?"

"There's another idea that space-time is like granulated sugar and sometimes it's nowhere, so how do you puncture it? I get to this part of my argument and I enter the cosmography of hope. Is the soul the part of the human that exists outside of time? And if that's the part that counts, then is my reason for wanting to have a baby that the baby already exists, and I just want to effect a coincidence that will enable me to hang out with him? Or her. I think my algebra is getting in the way. I've been too logical about this. All summer I've been too logical. Let me put it this way: The Bible is just a record of human experience. All of us are alive because someone took care of us when we were small. The universe seems strange when we learn about it, but it's still the same home we've always had. Backyard green tree cemetery dawns. It's the towns you *don't* see that are the best ones."

One of the security guards puts a hand on Eva's shoulder and says, "Time to go."

"But I wanted to tell you about goodness. That was my whole point. I wanted to say why it's okay to have a baby."

The security guard raises an eyebrow.

"It doesn't make any difference if you shave your head. Matthew McConaughey sees all of time and *he* still cares, so why shouldn't I? I wanted to talk about fusion. I know I'm causing a problem here. Just let me tell you what I really mean. I am the eye of the light. Is there an echo in here? I am the whore and the holy."

She can feel her thoughts unraveling. Is it another of Yahweh's jokes? Is all of this just exactly what he wants her to say?

She follows the security guards off the stage, but before stepping down she turns and addresses the audience one more time: "In the time of Trump there was a prophet named Eva, and this is what she said."

world the way it is, and how can we accept it? We try
ke it intelligible. We say it's raining up there on the
se of orographic lift, and our political geography is an
ry, and the universe is expanding into a fourth spatial
t what point are we just making things worse? Life is
already with the furniture of metaphor, and some-
wood, that baby will be walking and asking why,

arney, and John Ransom Pierce are strolling down
ve Eva from the office where she has voluntarily
rphy has apologized to Barney and Pierce, who
Barney has apologized to Murphy and Pierce,
m; Pierce has apologized to Barney and Mur-
him. Who's guilty here, and of what?

and in Mesopotamia the apes encounter a ra
they call Yahweh. For many years, for thousa
them, murders them, sows discord among
exalts them. And somehow he manages
of the other gods. For the apes it's a night
they turn, there he is, and he's in thei
worry that he's taken away their pow
will they get out of this one?

But their curiosity is insatiable, th
progress is unstoppable, and gradual
conquer some of Yahweh's favorite
genetic instructions, excising or
them susceptible to wretchedr
build a spaceship that carries t
and there in the red dust they
live in peace and harmony.
never any slavery on Mars

When they return to E
that not even neutrinos
nal of miracles. They h
der. They meet Yahw
and they say, "Let's t
Joseph is there. Ma
together. And wh
fishing around fc
Will they do w
has taught the
shove him ou
vail, and cor

WHY IS THE
so hard to ma
mountain beca
artifact of slave
dimension, but
cluttered enough
day soon, knock
why, why.

For now, Murphy,
the corridor to retri
confined herself. Mu
have forgiven him;
who have forgiven h
phy, who have forgive

LET'S IMAGINE THE movie version. In the grasslands of central East Africa there is a community of apes, just tubes really, that's all they are, and they've got pincers and tent pegs and kazoos and sensors and a kind of electrical jelly to coordinate all their activities, and they're like all the other animals, true, but they're smarter. Maybe consciousness is just a symptom of information processing, or maybe it's a kind of miracle, inaccessible to scientific inquiry. In any case, these apes develop techniques and strategies that enable them to outpace biological evolution and survive in every environment on Earth, no matter how inhospitable, and in that sense they are something altogether new, altogether exceptional.

Of course, from another perspective, the apes are just avatars. They are one manifestation of some general rules and principles, and there are other avatars out there, manifestations of other rules and other principles. There are mountains, rivers, stars, gods. The universe is busy with cognition. But some avatars are more problematic than others,

"It's just that I've been trying to take things as they come and do my duty," says Murphy. "I didn't want to disappoint anyone."

"It's really my mistake," says Barney. "I'm damned if I can say how I made it, though."

Pierce shakes his head. "It's the strangest thing. I can't even say how I got here. What I mean is, what have I been doing all summer? Where have I been? I can't remember anything. I remember a box of latex gloves."

The television is on as Murphy and Eva pack their things. A burger appears, followed by the slogan "Eat Thick." Next comes a commercial for a new soft drink. When you remove the cap, the lights go out, loud music begins to play, and beautiful women press themselves against you. Fluffy 2 rushes around the room and yelps, Murphy wonders if Jane Pierce was supposed to be the prophet, and Eva checks to see if Yahweh hath takeneth away all their money, but he hath not. And now here's that Audi commercial.

Resort employees load Eva and Murphy's things into the *Pequod*, which has been washed and vacuumed. Someone has even watered the collards. Barney stands with them in the sun as they prepare to leave. In fact, he insists that there's no reason for them to leave at all. They should feel free to stay the week and enjoy the conference, as compensation for their trouble.

"But Barney," Eva says, putting a hand on his shoulder, "you don't have a clue who we really are."

He shrugs. "The world isn't so chock-full of decent folk that I can afford to let that bother me. Will you come see us in Malibu this winter?"

· · ·

And then they drive away. They have nowhere to go; they can go any-where, at least in principle. They are back where they started and yet not really, because humans are mortal and time is only likely to flow in one direction, especially in the hot summer. They open the win-dows and smell the neutrinos on the breeze. Eva looks at cribs on her phone.

Dear Baby, Around the time of the Big Bang, the universe was in a low-entropy state, but it's been all complexity and confusion since then.

Dear Baby, The Big Bang isn't even the beginning of the universe! It's just the end of our theoretical understanding.

At the entrance to Yellowstone National Park, rangers are passing out leaflets that read, "Many visitors have been gored by buffalo." Inside, a marker informs them that the Nez Perce passed through the park during their astonishing journey. They were nearly trapped here, but they eluded their pursuers in a clever maneuver and fled north up the Clarks Fork Yellowstone River, which was named for William Clark, whose half-Indian son, an old man by then, was a member of Chief Joseph's band.

Here they are, driving and driving, and the country looks pristine and godless. The sky is a clear pale dusty blue. The mountains gallop along out there on the horizon. Black holes are colliding and subatomic par-ticles are winking in and out of existence. Murphy and Eva feel a great lightness of spirit. Suddenly they know that it was all a mistake. A cosmic mix-up. And maybe not even that. Maybe this whole summer is just a dream Eva's been dreaming in Coconut Grove, and in another moment she'll open her eyes and see the jackfruit tree outside the window.

But they're wrong, or else the dream of being a person is simply one from which there's no waking. Outside Gillette, Wyoming, Yahweh leaps in front of the car and waves them to the side of the road. They fear a climactic moment, perhaps even a kind of resolution, but they don't get it. Everything is as it was. Yahweh speaks of his suffering. He stands in the sage and says, "But they will be my people! And I will be their God!"

"No," says Eva. "Please. What about Jane Pierce?"

He slips a Pixy Stick from his pocket and sets it alight with a snap of his fingers. "You're Jane Pierce."

"I'm not! You've got it wrong!"

"You're not Jane Pierce?"

"I'm not Jane Pierce. I'm someone else. This is all a misunderstanding."

He holds the Pixy Stick out for them to examine. The fire burns but doesn't consume it. He draws himself up.

"What I'd like you to do now is visit Tito's Diner in Indianapolis."

Eva is speechless.

"Tito's Diner," Yahweh says again, gazing out over the hot windless plain. "And *there* you will tell them that the name of the Lord is Yahweh."

Dear Baby, In the West, the radio stations begin with K. In the West, the drivers are more reasonable. In the West, it doesn't rain very much. In the West, in the West. The government is the largest landowner. The sage goes on and on.

· · ·

Wyoming was the first state to grant women the right to vote, and Colorado and Utah were next. But Freedom, as Murphy says, died here in South Dakota, at Wounded Knee, when a band of Miniconjou Lakota were massacred by U.S. cavalrymen. They fought back, like always, and managed to kill a number of the soldiers, but the massacre marked the end of armed indigenous resistance in America. The buffalo were gone and the ancestors weren't coming back. The old hunting grounds were full of white settlers. Yahweh was there too. He was chewing his spruce gum and laughing.

Murphy says, "My library books!"

Dear Baby, We don't mean to give you the impression that it's all hopelessness and misery out here. We have plenty of nice things to recommend. Try a little cider vinegar in cold water. Dry some laundry in the sun. Recite Tennyson's "Ulysses" to a pet. Listen to Beethoven's Fifteenth String Quartet on the first snowy day of the year.

And if, Dear Baby, you think you'd like to cut the screen off someone's bedroom window, please don't, please don't.

For a long time there are no trees, and then there are trees. They eat Eastern Carolina barbecue in Rapid City. They visit Wall Drug, famous for being famous. They cross the hundredth meridian and visit Sioux Falls, where the average annual precipitation has climbed to 26.34 inches and there's the tiniest bit of midwestern moisture in the air.

·   ·   ·

"My computer has been on this whole time!" says Murphy.

Sitting Bull's name was Tȟatȟáŋka Íyotake, except it wasn't, because the Sioux had no written language, so he wrote "Sitting Bull" when he gave autographs, and he gave autographs all the time, especially when he was traveling with Buffalo Bill Cody's Wild West show. He didn't save any money because he kept giving it away to homeless people. He made sure his children learned English and were prepared to live in the white man's world, but as for himself, he said, "I would rather die an Indian than live a white man." And when he addressed the hated Dawes Commission, he said, "I want to tell you that if the Great Spirit has chosen anyone to be the chief of this country, it is myself."

This happened yesterday and it's happening today and it will happen tomorrow. Time is some kind of cube, that's what Matthew Mc-Conaughey will tell you, but the big questions have no answers and the big problems can't ever be resolved, and the tragedy of Sitting Bull and the Sioux is only one tragedy among many. How can we explain to you, Dear Baby, that this is the way it works? It doesn't make any sense. We are recent immigrants living on stolen land in a country built by slaves, and we carry on, knowing nothing, saying anything, and feeling inexpressibly privileged to be here frowning in the light of the world.

So Murphy and Eva drive and drive. Maybe they return to the Northeast, where they both grew up, there to live among their former selves, there to be overtaken by their future selves, just as we have overtaken them already, or been overtaken by them.

.   .   .

Dear Baby, We think it was that other Murphy, Beckett's Murphy, or else friends of that Murphy, who said that life is a fever and a dream, and a wandering to find home.

Dear Baby, Happiness comes and goes like weather. Don't count on it, and don't count it out.

There are simply things you can't do anything about. Almost everything, in effect. Maybe that's the lesson. Today Yahweh is jazzed up about the Trash Mountain Temple. He unrolls some new blueprints and says, "And I will enter by this door, and no human shall enter, but if a human shall enter he shall enter by this door, and by the back door I shall enter, but no one may enter after . . ."

They are sitting at a picnic table at a rest stop in Iowa. This is just part of their lives, at least for now. The world is what it is. It's not perfect.

We think of Murphy and Eva on the road that summer, or this summer, or some summer to come. Murphy the heir to a textile fortune and Eva the prophet. We wake up in the darkness and listen to the rain on the roof, and we wonder at the traffic of all those Murphys and Evas in the wet American night. In this world and the next. In this galaxy and the next. In this ballooning Tic Tac of a universe and the next.

Dear Baby, We loved you when you were no more than a thought, and we'll go on loving you.

·   ·   ·

Dear Baby, We think it might have been Emily Dickinson who said that one clover and a bee make a prairie, and you don't even need the bee.

Acknowledgments

I want to express my deep gratitude to the National Endowment for the Arts. May it live forever. Also thanks to: Cynthia Cannell, Audrey Thier, Peter Murphy, Paula Thier, Sam Thier, Zacc Dukowitz, Elizabeth Bevilacqua, Ryan Holiday, Callie Garnett, Sara Mercurio, and everyone else at Bloomsbury. And to Sidney Thier, for all his help. And I want to acknowledge the poets I quote, sometimes without attribution: Weldon Kees, James Schuyler, Frank O'Hara, Marianne Moore, Philip Larkin, Sylvia Plath, Wallace Stevens, Emily Dickinson. But I especially want to thank my beloved real wife, the real poet Sarah Trudgeon, whose real poems I attribute to Eva in this novel. These include "The Mad Pigeon in the Attic," originally published in the *Times Literary Supplement*; bits of "It's a Big-Buck World" and related poems, which appear in *The Plot Against the Baby*; and "Poem for Malcolm X." Thanks to Sarah also for all kinds of help with the manuscript itself.

A Note on the Author

Aaron Thier is the author of the novels *Mr. Eternity*, a finalist for the 2017 Thurber Prize for American Humor, and *The Ghost Apple*, a semifinalist for the 2015 Thurber Prize. A contributor to the *Nation* and a graduate of Yale University and the MFA program at the University of Florida, Thier received a 2016 NEA Fellowship in Creative Writing. He lives in Great Barrington, Massachusetts.